Stay tuned for Book 2

WONDER LENS FRIENDS

Luna Loves Space

Coming Fall 2026

Wagaya wa Kakuriyo no kashihonya san Novel 4
©Shinobumaru (Story)
This edition originally published in Japan in 2020 by
MICRO MAGAZINE, INC., Tokyo.
English translation rights arranged with
MICRO MAGAZINE, INC., Tokyo.

No portion of this book may be reproduced or transmitted in any form without written permission from the copyright holders. This is a work of fiction. Names, characters, places, and incidents are the products of the author's imagination or are used fictitiously. Any resemblance to actual events, locales, or persons, living or dead, is entirely coincidental. Any information or opinions expressed by the creators of this book belong to those individual creators and do not necessarily reflect the views of Seven Seas Entertainment or its employees.

Seven Seas press and purchase enquiries can be sent to Marketing Manager Lianne Sentar at press@gomanga.com. Information regarding the distribution and purchase of digital editions is available from Digital Manager CK Russell at digital@gomanga.com.

Seven Seas and the Seven Seas logo are trademarks of Seven Seas Entertainment. All rights reserved.

Follow Seven Seas Entertainment online at sevenseasentertainment.com.

TRANSLATION: Kevin Ishizaka
COVER DESIGN: Nicky Lim
LOGO DESIGN: George Panella
INTERIOR LAYOUT & DESIGN: Clay Gardner
COPY EDITOR: Jade Gardner
LIGHT NOVEL EDITOR: E.M. Candon
PREPRESS TECHNICIAN: Melanie Ujimori
PRINT MANAGER: Rhiannon Rasmussen-Silverstein
PRODUCTION MANAGER: Lissa Pattillo
EDITOR-IN-CHIEF: Julie Davis
ASSOCIATE PUBLISHER: Adam Arnold
PUBLISHER: Jason DeAngelis

ISBN: 978-1-63858-288-5
Printed in Canada
First Printing: June 2022
10 9 8 7 6 5 4 3 2 1

VOLUME 4
Memories of a Spring Breeze
and the Fox Mask's Wish

WRITTEN BY
Shinobumaru

TRANSLATED BY
Kevin Ishizaka

Seven Seas Entertainment

TABLE OF Contents

PROLOGUE:	Azure Spring	7
CHAPTER 1:	In Spring, the Mountain God Comes Out to Play	15
CHAPTER 2:	What Follows the End at the Northernmost Tip	57
INTERMISSION:	Moments Blending Together	99
SIDE STORY:	Life in a World That Cast Us Aside	103
INTERMISSION:	Life in a World Still Too Small	161
CHAPTER 3:	The Bookstore Ghost	163
CHAPTER 4:	False Memories Imparted on a Flowering Dogwood's Wish	197
EPILOGUE:	A Place for You Alone	247
EXTRA STORY:	Man's Best Friends	255
	Afterword	261

PROLOGUE

Azure Spring

"Hey, come join me for a little excursion, Suimei!"

On a day like any other, Kaori excitedly invited me out.

"Nah, I'm good," I flatly replied. The kudan's prophecy was still on my mind: *The spirit realm's winter will never end.* The prophecy had sparked a chain of incidents, and I had good reason to believe an unknown human exorcist was the mastermind. The exorcist's motives remained a mystery, but it was clear they meant harm. Moreover, I couldn't rule out the possibility that I might be connected to their overarching goal. I'd had plenty of opportunities to earn the ire of other exorcists in the past, so it wasn't completely unreasonable to think one might be trying to get back at me now.

With all that in mind, I refused Kaori's invitation. I couldn't let her get caught up in my problems. Truth be told, though, I was reluctant to refuse. A voice inside my head was yelling *"What are you doing?! Are you seriously throwing away a chance to hang out with Kaori?!"* but I knew I had to make the logical choice over the emotional one. At least, I thought I did.

"What, why? You just said you weren't doing anything!" she pouted, puffing out her cheeks. Her cherry-pink lips curled into a toothy smile far more beautiful than any rose. She leaned in and said, "C'mon, there's something I want to show you. It's not even that far away."

I quickly averted my gaze, my cheeks hot. *Kaori, you dunce. Why are you bringing your face so close?!*

In an instant, my thoughts were in shambles. All the reasons I used to bury my true feelings were swept aside by the fever rising inside of me. Reverted to the young, immature boy I truly was, I chose emotion over logic.

"Jeez," I began with a sigh. "You're not really leaving me a choice here, are you?" I tried to sound as calm as I could while my heart raced a mile a minute. I closed my eyes and mumbled, "Fine."

"All right!" she crowed, grabbing my hands. Her hands were much smaller than mine even though she was slightly taller than me, a fact that I lamented. I felt her body heat warm me through them.

Please... Spare me. The warmth of your hands feels like they'll change the very shape of my soul.

An hour later, we finally reached our destination. It was only a short distance from town.

"Shinonome-san used to take me here to look at the stars when I was little. It's the most beautiful place in the entirety of the spirit realm at this time of year, so I wanted to show it to you."

"Oh really…" I murmured absently, my attention fully taken up by the breathtaking beauty before me. We had reached a small hill in a forest. The surrounding area was completely blanketed in trees save for this hill, which was covered in flowers like one giant flower bed. "These flowers…what are they called?" I asked, struggling to string words together.

Kaori, an incense burner with glimmerfly repellent in her hands, smiled faintly as she told me the name of these flowers that basked in the moonlight. "They're called nemophila. They're a nice blue, don't you think?"

A gentle breeze blew by, filling the air with the rustling of leaves and petals. The breeze slipped through the low-lying nemophila and rose to caress my cheeks as it passed, then disappeared to who knew where. The small flowers were like an ocean as they undulated with the wind, their rustling reminding me of crashing waves. For a brief instant, I found it strange that I couldn't smell the briny breeze.

"Amazing," I sighed, fraught with emotion. The scene before me was so lovely, it felt like a fairy might peek its head out from beneath a flower at any moment. I looked up at the sky and squinted, noticing a color I still wasn't used to seeing. The spirit realm was a world of perpetual night, absent a sun. Its star-studded sky differed in color from that of the human world. Right now, it was pink like the flowers of a cherry blossom tree. Every now and then, hints of aquamarine blue suggestive of spring seemed to be mixed in, accentuating the color of the nemophila.

A glowing butterfly fluttered past me. It was a glimmerfly,

the remnants of a human soul. When a soul fell to despair, and rejected the cycle of reincarnation, they ended up in this form. Ever since I learned of their true nature, I hadn't been able to appreciate their beauty... But today, in this azure land-bound sea that Kaori had brought me to, its luminescence was undeniably lovely.

"C'mon, let's climb to the top of the hill! The whole flower field looks like a carpet from up there!"

I nodded slightly at her words and absentmindedly took her hand. She blushed, looking back at me in shock. I suddenly felt embarrassed as well, realizing what I'd done. But her hand was so warm and comfortable that I didn't want to let go. So instead, I asked, "What's wrong?"

To which she replied, "N-nothing."

I avoided bringing up my mistake, correctly guessing that Kaori wouldn't bring it up either. *I guess even I can play dirty sometimes...* As weird as it was to think, moments like these made me feel gratitude toward the twisted family that raised me. It was thanks to them that my facial muscles were so stunted that I could pull off a poker face like the one I wore in that moment.

If I had to describe the view from atop the hill in a single word, it would be: magnificent. I could think of no better way to express the awe of beholding the uncountable nemophila in full bloom spilling down the gentle slope. I've heard that blue was the color of royalty in some countries. The awe-inspiring and imposing blue field before me made me feel keenly that this must be true.

"I'm glad the weather's good today. We've had nothing but rain lately," Kaori said with relief. Her comment made me wonder: Had she been checking the weather every day, waiting for a good day to show me this place? The thought made me feel warm inside, but I was too embarrassed to ask such a thing directly. Still, knowing her, she very well might have.

"Thanks for, um, you know…bringing me here." Hemming and hawing all the way, I managed to offer my gratitude.

Kaori smiled back at me happily, her expression as endearing as a puppy's. My cheeks grew hot, and I gripped her hand, still in mine, tightly. "You know, I always wind up seeing things I've never seen before when I'm with you," I said. "It makes me glad I came to the spirit realm."

Kaori's eyes opened wide. She blinked a few times, then teared up out of nowhere.

"Wha—h-hey! Why are you crying?" I asked, flustered.

Kaori shook her head and wiped away her tears, blushing with embarrassment. "Sorry, I was just so happy to hear those words that I wound up crying."

"Huh? You cried because you were happy?"

"Yeah. Haven't you ever?"

"No. Then again, I wasn't really allowed to feel emotions until recently."

"Right. Right, of course…" she muttered sadly. She looked at me like she had more to say.

I tensed, my heart starting to race. I had no idea what words were about to follow, and I wasn't sure I was ready to hear them.

Kaori began, "Around the time you first came to the spirit realm, you said you had no home to go back to. Do you remember?"

"Did I say something like that?" I asked.

"You did, back when I said you should return to the human world. You seemed to be brooding about a lot of stuff, and you had this sickly pale look on your face. It was as though you felt you had no place in this world."

Kaori narrowed her eyes as she reminisced and reached a hand toward me. She stroked my head and looked at me with glistening eyes. The deep blue of the nemophila reflected in her pupils was so strikingly vibrant. "Have you found the place you belong? If you have, well…I'd be happy if it were somewhere here in the spirit realm."

The waterworks threatened to come up on me too. "Q-quit treating me like a child," I said, rudely brushing her hand away and pulling my sweatshirt hood up. *Poker face, my ass! I'm such an idiot…*

My heart pounded, and I was clammy all over. I had no doubt that I was making an embarrassing face. Fighting to keep my emotions in check, I peeked out the side of my hood at Kaori. Her shoulders had slumped dejectedly, probably because I'd brushed her away. Perhaps I'd gone too far.

"Kaori."

"Hm?"

Feeling guilty, I reached out a hand and gently brushed her cheek with the back of two fingers. Her cheek was colder than

I'd expected. I gazed into her serene eyes and said, "You can't pat my head. I'm a guy."

"O-oh. Right."

"As long as you understand." I smiled softly. In an instant, she blushed bright red like a tomato. *Heh. What a face.* My chest warmed.

Kaori put her hands to her cheeks and quietly muttered, "Oh, but you can touch my cheek like it's nothing?"

I was about to say something further when I sensed someone approaching. I immediately reached for the talismans in my pouch.

"Relax. It's me."

Approaching without a sound was the black cat Nyaa, Kaori's close friend. She walked with light and silent steps, wearing an arrogant look typical of cats. Her mismatched gold and sky-blue eyes narrowed at us. Once she reached our feet, she spoke in a tone that betrayed no urgency at all: "I've been looking for you. Let's go home. It's not safe to be outside right now."

"What? Why?" Kaori asked.

"A Tsuchigumo child born this winter was kidnapped. There's no telling what the Tsuchigumo will do when they snap, so you should stay inside for a few days."

"What?! But I have my part-time job to think about!"

"Forget it. I don't want to deal with you being attacked while you're out and about."

Kaori continued to grumble, but the black cat didn't budge. I had a bad feeling about this, so—as the black cat let out a great yawn and wagged her three tails—I asked, "Does this have anything to do with other recent events?"

The black cat's whiskers twitched before she turned away with a huff. "Dunno. Nurarihyon seems to be looking into it, but I couldn't care less."

With that, she began walking down the hill. Kaori and I shared a brief look before running after her.

What in the world is going on? My mind was restless. I sighed and took a casual glance toward the dense forest. A chill ran down my spine, bringing my feet to a stop. For a moment, I could have sworn I saw a pale fox mask in the moonlight of the dark, silent forest.

"Suimei?" Kaori's voice brought me back to my senses. I couldn't find the fox mask again, no matter where I looked. "Is something wrong?"

"No... Don't worry about it." Had that fox mask been looking at Kaori? I shook my head and met Kaori's worried gaze. "It'll be fine. I'll protect you."

"Sorry?"

"I finally have a place I belong. I'm not about to lose it."

Kaori seemed deeply flummoxed by my sudden proclamation.

With a new goal in mind, I took in the sight of the nemophila rustling in the wind.

CHAPTER 1

In Spring, the Mountain God Comes Out to Play

SEASONS CAME AND WENT as they pleased. They danced forth with a spring in their step and not a care for anyone's wishes, bringing along whatever fresh winds they so desired.

A lot had happened during the winter that only just passed us by. We'd gone all the way to Hokkaido to collect late fees, visited the spirit realm's Yoshiwara red-light district to borrow books on love, and even had a Christmas party. The most memorable event, however, was hearing of my mother from a friend. It was a painful experience, but also a touching one that had filled an emptiness in my heart. The end my mother met might not have been a happy one, but I was glad nonetheless to learn of all the kindness I'd received from so many, which had led me to where I was today.

Winter met its end. As the cherry blossoms of the human world began to bloom, so too did a warm breeze blow in the world of never-ending night. The spirits who had shut themselves away during the cold winter now took to the streets in droves, catching up with all the old faces they hadn't seen since the season before.

What twists of fate will this gentle breeze bring? My heart was light as I thought about spring.

"I know it's rather sudden, but could I stay here for a bit?"

Out of nowhere, I—Muramoto Kaori—heard a familiar line that brought my thoughts to a standstill.

"...Hwah?" I let out a strange noise and quickly clamped my mouth shut. *No way! Really?!*

I continued to set out tea for everyone on the low dining table while observing the ever-expressionless boy before me, Shirai Suimei. His hair was white like reflected moonlight, his eyes were a light brown that looked almost golden in the glimmerfly light, his skin was pale enough to glow, the bridge of his nose ran straight, and his thin lips had a touch of pink. All in all, he looked like one of those pretty boys you occasionally see on TV. His only drawback was his brusque attitude. I'd also recently learned that the smile he occasionally offered could send me reeling.

"Did something happen?" I asked.

"No, I'm just worried about that exorcist who's been causing trouble lately," Suimei replied. He was referring to the incidents surrounding the kudan's prophecy from last year. The prophecy had foretold that if a pregnant spirit didn't safely give birth, spring would never come to the spirit realm. Of course, spring had managed to arrive, if not without its challenges. Otoyo-san, the Kijo spirit who was our neighbor, had been attacked during childbirth by an Ubume spirit and a Kogakuchou spirit. We had reason to believe an exorcist was involved in these events.

"Shinonome, have you heard about what happened with the Tsuchigumo?" Suimei asked.

"A child was kidnapped, right? You think it has anything to do with the exorcist?"

"I do. They might be trying to use the negative emotions generated from the kidnapping of a child as a medium for something greater. If that's the case, there's a high chance Kaori might be targeted too. She's an ideal target, as while she's liked by many spirits, she's still a powerless human."

So Suimei wanted to stay here for my sake. The realization made my chest grow warm.

"I see…" Shinonome-san began. He stroked his unkempt chin a bit before giving Suimei a distrustful glare. "Do you think I can't protect my own daughter?"

Shinonome-san, my adoptive father, was the Tsukumogami of a hanging scroll depicting a dragon. That scroll had a long history during which powerful people fought for ownership of it. Shinonome-san was also the strongest spirit in town. According to Noname, the power of a Tsukumogami was proportional to their age as well as the value and quality of their main body, making Shinonome-san among the strongest in existence. Every time we got caught up in trouble with spirits, he managed to handily resolve things himself.

"I know full well how strong you are," Suimei said, "but I still want to repay you both for all the help you've given me. Besides, I can't look the other way when an old professional peer causes trouble. Please, allow me to stay at the bookstore for the time being."

Faced with such an earnest request, even Shinonome-san hesitated to refuse. After a brief pause, he groaned and said, "Hmph. I can protect my daughter myself, but...I guess you can stay." He scratched his head messily and frowned. "You seem earnest enough. You better not let me down!"

"I won't! Thank you!" Suimei beamed with a lovely smile. He spun around to look at me and frowned when he saw me sweating buckets. "Uh... What's with you, Kaori?"

"N-nothing..." I looked away and fought to still my racing heart. *H-he's staying here?!*

Full disclosure, Suimei was my crush. What's more, he was my *first ever* crush. Yes, I know—even at this age. I supposed I was something of a late bloomer. I hadn't even realized my feelings for him until recently, to be honest.

So, imagine how I felt when it was decided, out of the blue, that I would be living with my crush? The idea of being with him from dawn to dusk made me sweat. What if I did something stupid? What if he thought I was a loser?! All these what-ifs spun around my head, making me go pale. *Oh boy. How in the world did I manage the last time he stayed here?*

A specific scene from last year surfaced to mind. Rainy season. Suimei had just moved in. I went to wake him up but had forgotten to change out of my tank top and hot pants because I was too busy with my morning duties. At the sight of me, he said, *"Try to conduct yourself like someone your age ought to, got it?"*

"Guh!"

"Kaori?!"

"I-I'm okay! Just remembering something embarrassing I did..."

Aaaaaaaaaaah! I was mortified. It took everything I had to not fall to the ground and roll around in my shame. I deserved to be locked up and the key thrown away. If, by some chance, Suimei were to start thinking I was a loser... *I might wither away on the spot.*

But in the recesses of my mind, a small voice whispered: *But I get to admire Suimei's face whenever I want now... Isn't that awesome?*

"H-hey, Kaori? Are you, uh, really all right?" Suimei asked. I had frozen up and turned bright red at this point.

"I-I'm fine. T-totally fine." Realizing how weird I was acting, I tried my hardest to hold a straight face. My gaze met Shinonome-san's. His eyes were practically out of their sockets. The smoking pipe he had been puffing slipped out of his hands and rolled onto the tatami mat.

Aw, crap. The blood drained from my face. I was too late.

Shinonome-san began to tremble weakly. He glared furiously at Suimei and shook his head. "I-I take it back! You can't stay here! You *absolutely* can't stay here!"

"Wh-what? But you were fine with it last year!" Suimei complained.

"That doesn't matter! I ain't letting no man lodge here when I have a daughter of eligible age!"

Suimei sighed. He reached into his bag and placed something on the low dining table. "Fine. I didn't want to have to do this, but you leave me no choice..." On the table was an envelope full of money—and a thick one too.

Whoa, déjà vu. Again. A similar thing had happened late spring last year.

The assault on the monetary front proved effective against Shinonome-san (money had been tight as of late). He let out an enormous groan and grimaced. "Y-you... You think dirty exorcist money can sway me?!"

"This is money I made working at the apothecary. Please, take it."

"Ngh..." Shinonome-san eyed the manila envelope, his brow covered in sweat. He reached toward it with a quivering hand—before pushing it out of sight. In a pained voice, he managed to say, "D-d-d-do you take me for a fool? Th-this isn't a problem money can solve."

"What if I offered twice the amount?"

"Hngh!" Shinonome-san hesitated. "...N-no! I don't want your money!"

"Good grief. You can be surprisingly willful."

"I don't want to hear that from some brat who uses money to get his way!"

Negotiations broke down, and the two began glaring at each other.

Oh dear...

The door connecting the living space to the bookstore slid open to reveal a starry-eyed raven Tengu boy. "I hope you don't mind me overhearing! Oh, are you two fighting now?"

The young man entered, practically skipping, and took a seat next to Suimei and Shinonome-san. He looked between the two of them with curious golden eyes and an impish smile on his face. "You should let Suimei stay. What could go wrong?"

This raven Tengu boy was Kinme, a childhood friend of mine. I'd discovered him and his twin brother on the ground when they were still normal baby birds. He was something of a freewheeler and never refrained from sticking his nose in other peoples' business when it intrigued him. Like, for instance, now.

"Absolutely not!" Shinonome yelled, glaring at Suimei with bloodshot eyes. "I already have to worry about threats outside my home, I don't want to have to worry about threats inside it too!"

"Pffft, aha ha ha ha! What does that even mean?! Hilarious!" Kinme laughed his head off for a moment, then smacked his fist against his palm. "Oh! I know what we could do!" He stood and made for the door, grinning all the while, then reached through it and pulled out something large, which he dragged in behind him.

"Ginme?!" I exclaimed.

"Kaori..." Ginme sobbed.

It was Kinme's twin, Ginme. The pair looked identical save for their eyes: Kinme's were golden and sleepy, while Ginme's were cheery and silver. I couldn't see Ginme's eyes at present however, as he was covering his face with his hands and sobbing.

"Wh-what's wrong? Why are you crying?" I asked.

"Just the thought of you living with Suimei again brings me to tears..." Ginme sniffed, averted his gaze, and explained no further.

Perplexed by his response, I tilted my head in confusion. Kinme flashed a toothy grin and declared, "Anyway, the two of us are going to live here too for the time being!"

"Wait, *what*?!" exclaimed Shinonome-san, Ginme, Suimei, and I in unison.

Kinme wore a self-assured look as he met everyone's stares and explained, "Think about it! If you can't have one young man and one young woman sharing a roof, just up the numbers! Besides, Ginme and I used to stay over all the time when we were kids, so we're used to it. There's also the fact that we've been too busy with training to play with Kaori lately, so now's a good chance!"

"Good chance, my ass!" Shinonome barked. "Do you even realize how much space you take up? Where are you all going to sleep?!"

"Hmm... I'm sure the three of us could fit in the guest room upstairs if we lined the futons side by side." Kinme glanced my way and grinned. "But I don't mind staying in Kaori's room if I have to. We can chat all night just like the good old days!"

"Absolutely not!" Suimei and Ginme both yelled, loud enough for my ears to ring.

Ginme looked around sheepishly and stammered, "W-well, I guess I could stay. It's not like I can turn a blind eye when Kaori might be in danger. I'll be intruding for a bit then, Shinonome. And Suimei...you don't got a problem sharing a room with us, do ya?"

"O-of course not. I'm sure it'll be a bit cramped, but yeah, whatever."

"Yay, sleepover!" Kinme cheered. "It's settled! Let's go get our things from Mount Kurama, Ginme. Kaori, could you set our futon out for us? Pretty please!"

"Catch you later, Kaori! Oh, I'll bring some meat and mountain veggies back. You know, in lieu of rent money!" Ginme said. He and his twin got up and began to leave in high spirits.

"Hey, don't go deciding things on your own without me! This is my house! Hey! Hey, listen to me!" Shinonome-san complained, but his words fell on deaf ears.

I watched everything unfold in a daze. Kinme beckoned me over as he was about to leave. I drew close, wondering what he could want. He whispered in my ear: "I've set the stage. Now it's all up to you to get closer to Suimei."

"Wh-what?!"

"Good luck!" Kinme patted me on the back with a playful grin and left the room.

"Ngh... Jeez, that Kinme..." My face was hot. I glanced at Suimei and Shinonome-san to see how they were doing. They sighed in unison and shook their heads.

"Sorry, I didn't mean to start all this hassle," Suimei apologized.

"Forget it," Shinonome-san grumbled. "Ugh... Why me?"

I found their sorry state a bit funny and smiled. "Aha ha! Looks like we're in for quite a fun spring."

Suimei frowned. "Do you even realize how serious your situation is, you dimwit?"

Shinonome-san looked up at the ceiling in exhaustion. "This is going to be a long spring..."

Giggling, I made for the closet to prepare futons for the twins. My heart still raced. Spring had only just begun, and a wonderful opportunity had already presented itself. I glanced at Suimei and saw him expressionlessly take a sip of his now lukewarm tea. It took all I had to not break into a grin as I picked up the futons.

Dear Mother in heaven,

Have you been well?

It's been a week since I started living with my crush. I was pretty nervous at first, always worrying he might see me do something weird or not like the food I made, but as time went on, well...I don't know. It's not like there weren't moments with him that made my heart race a bit, but this new routine isn't anything like the bittersweet story of youthful romance that I had envisioned. Here's hoping things change soon.

Yours truly, Kaori.

"How many times have I told you not to go outside alone?"

"I'm sorry..." I slumped my shoulders dejectedly, ambushed by Suimei on my way back from borrowing soy sauce from next door. I peeked up at his face to see it still locked in the same scowl and sadly hung my head again.

Suimei had been staying at our house for a week now, as had Kinme and Ginme. Having so many people around kept things lively, and I liked that, but not all was well...

"I wasn't even out that long," I said.

"It doesn't matter. If something happened to you outside, we'd have no way of knowing."

"I know, but c'mon..."

Lately, Suimei was so overprotective that it was suffocating.

"Please try to understand. I promised Shinonome I'd protect you," he said with a serious look.

"Urk..." I couldn't say anything back to that. Even so, having to get permission to go shopping or hang up the laundry or even sweep around the perimeter of the house was annoying. It was like he thought I was a child.

"Nyaaaa-san!" I called upon my friend, who was currently grooming herself by the storefront, for help. As levelheaded as she was, surely she would take my side.

To my dismay, she turned away with a huff. "Is he wrong? I'm sure you could try a little harder to stay inside."

"Wha—Nyaa-san?! I thought you said you were going to look out for my happiness!"

"Don't be silly. You know I hate doing bothersome things, and trying to keep someone happy is the height of bother."

"Ngh...!" I was frustrated but couldn't find the words to argue further. *Why do you choose* now *of all times to act like a cat?!*

A shadow fell on me from overhead. I looked up to see two starry-eyed Tengu twins looking down at me. They dwarfed me by two full heads; I felt like a child standing next to adults.

"I see, so Suimei's the possessive type!" Kinme said.

"I get how you feel, Suimei, but don't you think you're being a bit too harsh?" Ginme grinned as he put his arm on my head and leaned. "Let us take care of her. We're already going with her to her part-time job, what's a little more?"

Taking into account the fact that even the human world was potentially unsafe for me, Ginme and Kinme had been escorting me to and from my part-time job. Toochika-san, my boss, was kind enough to hire the pair as temporary help.

"Hey, isn't working at that store, like, unexpectedly demanding? The customers are always asking questions about items, and there are so many humans around because it's in the human world. It's honestly pretty draining."

"I feel you, Kinme. But I certainly don't mind getting paid! In fact, I quite love it!"

The twins let out belly laughs. I, on the other hand, felt a bit conflicted, as anyone would in my situation. The general store where I worked was tucked away in a small corner of Kappabashi, Tokyo. It didn't even face the main street. Normally, business was slow. But word of two hot guys working part-time at the shop had spread on social media and now we were flooded with customers. Toochika-san didn't seem to mind the extra traffic though. *Never underestimate the power of good looks, I guess...*

As I was pondering such things, Ginme's weight grew increasingly greater on my head. "Get off me, Ginme! You're heavy!"

He gave me a mischievous grin and leaned on me even further. "Heh heh, c'mon, I'm hardly leaning on you! Man, you're sooo weak. I understand why Suimei is all worried about you now. Maybe you should try training a bit."

"Quit it. I'm normal for a human. It's you guys who are abnormal!"

"Well, we train every day! Look, I even got a six-pack!" Ginme pulled up his shirt to show me his abs.

I reflexively swung a fist up at him and shouted, "Keep your shirt on!"

He stumbled back in a clearly exaggerated fashion, just like how he used to when we were kids. I was still a bit annoyed when suddenly someone hugged me from behind.

"Um…?" Bewildered, I looked behind me to see Suimei there, glaring at Ginme with a displeased look. I hadn't a clue as to why he'd hugged me, but getting embraced by my crush made my body begin to flush. "S-S-Suimei?!"

"Hm? What's up? Something the matter, Suimei?" Ginme asked.

"No," Suimei responded.

Ginme and I both tilted our heads, confused.

Kinme burst into a fit of laughter. "Aha ha ha ha ha! I can't—pfft aha ha ha! This is too much!"

The rest of us were at a complete loss as to what was so funny.

"My! You dears look like you're having fun!" a cheery voice called out to us. It was Noname, the apothecary. She had vibrant green hair that came down to her hips and bull horns protruding from her head, had perhaps once considered herself male, and was the very spirit who had raised me as a mother would. Her thin hips swayed as she strutted toward us in her high heels. Once close, she gave us a look and frowned. "You're laughing too much, Kinme. You've left all your friends quite confused."

"Pfft ha ha ha, b-but, aha ha, they're all so slow on the uptake that I can't help but crack up!"

"Yes, well... They're certainly innocent, I'll say that much." Noname's amber eyes and deep-red lips curled into a smile. "But I think that's fine. It's best they discover their own way forward."

"Whaaaat? No way! Waiting's no fun. We should tell them and enjoy the show!"

"Now that's no good either, dear."

What could they be talking about? I wondered as I watched them happily chat away. Ginme and Suimei looked equally confused.

Suimei understood he was being laughed at, though, and grumpily interrupted. "What do you want, Noname? I didn't hear anything about you coming today."

She gave him a meaningful smile. "I'm here to discuss with Kaori our plans for a particular annual event," she said with great enthusiasm.

"Oh, right!" I exclaimed. I had forgotten, but it was almost that time of year. "It completely slipped my mind. Have you already decided what you're doing this time?"

"Yes. I've already ordered the ingredients; I just need to arrange outfits and choose new books."

"So quick! Thank you!"

"Don't worry about it. I find myself naturally motivated on the day I earn the most."

Suimei, still hugging me, tilted his head curiously. "What are you talking about? Is Kaori going somewhere? That's too dangerous, I can't allow it."

Noname frowned for the first time that day, then walked

over and swept me out of Suimei's arms. With a cold gaze and a threatening tone, she said, "Enough. I respect your decision to protect Kaori, but she is not a doll. Trying to control everything a girl does will inevitably push her away."

"This isn't some time for life lessons!" Suimei protested. "There's a real dan—"

"In that case," Noname interrupted by thrusting a finger toward Suimei, though she giggled before continuing. "You must prove you can protect her without restraining her! Limiting a girl's actions should be off the table from the get-go. If you have the heart of a gentleman, then you should be able to protect her from danger as it comes. That's simply good masculine etiquette."

Suimei's frown was conflicted, frustrated.

Noname grew suddenly jovial again and said to me, "That settles that. Heh heh, I'm putting quite the effort into this year's outfits. Look forward to it!"

"Oooh, really? I always love seeing what you come up with every year!"

The two of us held hands and squealed.

"Oh, is it already that time of year?" Ginme asked. "Hmm... Honestly, I'm not too stoked to hear that."

"Well, I quite like it. It's good fun," Kinme said.

"Seriously? You're something else... I always blank out and it's over before I realize it."

"Nothing wrong with that. That's the good old Ginme way."

Tired of waiting for us to explain what we were talking about,

Suimei interrupted again. "I have no clue what this 'event' you guys are talking about even is. How am I supposed to protect Kaori if you don't tell me?"

Noname and I shared a look and smiled.

I said, "Listen up, Suimei. Spring is the season the bookstore and apothecary rake in the money!"

Noname followed up with, "That's right. Spring is when all those who slept away the winter wake up. That doesn't just include spirits and animals but gods too!"

"After winter, gods are starved for entertainment. That's when we strike!"

Cheeks flushed red, Noname and I let out feverish breaths.

"There are plenty of big spenders among the gods," I explained. "They even order books for their retainers to read, so we can expect massive orders!"

"And all the goddesses are worried about their skin after all that dry winter air. That's why I sell my specially made cosmetics! I'm dying to put my skills to work!" Noname flexed her biceps and smiled. "It's no exaggeration to say our business is dependent on spring sales. And I've been dying for a new pair of heels."

"And I've been dying to order more books! If things go well, I can order all the latest best sellers I want! Ah, I can't wait!"

Suimei seemed a bit taken aback by our enthusiasm. "Pipe down a bit, you two. You haven't explained a single thing. Just what are you planning to do?"

"You mean you haven't figured it out yet?" Noname said.

IN SPRING, THE MOUNTAIN GOD COMES OUT TO PLAY

"We have to put the effort in, if we're to loosen a god's purse strings! And what better way to do that than providing…"

Noname and I put our hands together and smiled, and as one, we said, "Host club service!"

Suimei froze as stiff as ice. Slowly, he opened his mouth and made the most confused noise I'd ever heard come out of him. "What?!"

There existed many different beliefs among the mountain-worshipping faiths. Such beliefs differed among mountain-dwelling and village-dwelling peoples, but among the village dwellers there was a belief in mountain gods. These mountain gods were said to come down from the mountains in spring and transform into harvest gods. Then in autumn, after the harvest, those same gods were said to return to the mountains, whereupon they became mountain gods again. The scarecrows seen in fields often represented these harvest gods. There was even an event known as "Scarecrow Sendoff" in Nagano Prefecture and Niigata Prefecture in which scarecrows were stored away after harvest so that the gods could return to the mountain.

Today was the day that the mountain god of Mie Prefecture became a harvest god. They were an important client of ours and resided in Otogitoge Pass of Iga City, a mountain pass famous for being crossed by Tokugawa Ieyasu right before the historic

Honnoji Incident. This god and Shinonome-san knew each other from way back, ever since the time he first opened the bookstore. Most gods didn't interact with humans and spirits. There existed some that lived near human settlements, but most made a point of not dealing with humans, other than their retainers. This was because gods were so powerful, some able to manipulate the very weather itself, that they could never see people as equals. For that reason, they held no interest in books—which were often based on the lives of people—or cosmetics. Or at least, most of them didn't.

The mountain god of Mie Prefecture was peculiar for a god. They were interested in the lives of people, wanted cosmetics for their skin, kept up with the latest fashions, and spent as much time as they could with man-made entertainment like books. There was a reason for this. The place we were now, Ueno Basin, was also known as Iga Basin. In Japan's Middle Ages (around the Kamakura and Muromachi periods), many people here worked as the now famous Iga Ninjas. This wasn't entirely by choice but because the land—formerly a lakebed—was too rife with clay for rice cultivation. In other words, even when the mountain god descended here to become a harvest god, there wasn't a whole lot of work for them to do. So, they relied on Shinonome-san and Noname to help them kill time until the end of the season.

Nowadays, with all the advancements in land cultivation, there were plenty of rice fields in the Iga Basin. The mountain god of Mie Prefecture didn't have the same free time to kill as before, yet they still continued to rely on us for things. Perhaps not even a god could so easily forget the decadent pleasures of human goods and entertainment.

A few days had passed since the time Suimei froze up out of sheer surprise.

"*Absoluuuuutely* not!"

"Oh, don't be so stubborn, dear." Noname tut-tutted.

"I'm moved, Suimei. To think you'd care about Kaori so much!"

"Hey, what's that supposed to mean, Kinme?" asked Ginme. "I care about Kaori too!"

Suimei flailed against Noname's toned arms, but she didn't let up an inch. The twins cackled at the sight. All in all, nothing out of the ordinary. Just a typical early afternoon.

The five of us were on a mountain in Mie Prefecture, near a vantage point overlooking Otogitoge Pass. The vantage point was in a large clearing and normally offered a clear view of the Iga Basin, but today the whole area was covered in fog, allowing us only a few meters of visibility. Fog was common since the area was a former lakebed. By the side of the clearing was a mossy Buddha figure carved into the side of a rock. Its face occasionally became visible as the fog shifted, adding to the atmosphere.

Currently, we were eagerly waiting for the client we would be entertaining.

"We need to get Kaori home as soon as possible!" Suimei complained, panting so much that his shoulders rose and fell. "Women aren't allowed to be on the mountain on the day the mountain god becomes a harvest god! What if she offends the god?!"

He wasn't wrong. In mountain faiths, today was a day on which women were forbidden from entering mountains. That was because mountain gods were usually women. They were also prone to jealousy and detested human women for what they considered the impurities of human childbirth and menstruation.

Still restraining Suimei with a demure look on her face, Noname said, "It's fine, we do this every year. We left Nyaa-san behind, so as long as nobody sees through Kaori's disguise, we'll be fine." She looked at me and smiled. "Oh, I've outdone myself this year! You look wonderful, my darling!"

"Ehe heh. Thank you." I put on a bashful smile and looked down at myself. I was wearing a white shirt with a checkered vest, black slacks, leather shoes, a black bow tie, leather gloves, and had a fob chain hanging from my vest pocket. My chest was bound by a sarashi wrap, and my hair was styled to look less feminine. All things considered, I looked like a high-school-age boy. Or at least I thought so.

"You don't actually think dressing like a man will work, do you?" Suimei said. "We're dealing with a god here!"

He and everyone else were wearing outfits that matched mine. That included the Tengu twins, of course.

"It'll be fine, it'll be fine," Ginme said. "She's got Noname's special perfume on, so she doesn't smell like a girl. We've ticked every box!"

"Pfft ha ha!" Kinme chortled. "You're such a worrywart, Suimei. It'll be fine!"

"Are you two serious right now? This is dangerous!"

"Mmm...! Nahhh...!" the twins said in harmony.

Suimei looked up at the sky, exhausted. "Damn it! I'm the only one here who's got it together!"

Noname snickered and released Suimei, who finally stopped resisting. She stepped before us. "Before we begin, let's have a little pep talk."

She looked different than usual today. She wore a fancy vest that looked like something a bartender at a high-end bar might wear, her long moss-green hair was done up in a ponytail, and she only wore light makeup. It was a far plainer look than what she usually sported, but some of her natural allure still seeped through. Strands of hair were left untied and hung stylishly, she wore a dazzlingly white wing-collar shirt with a deep-green tie, she had full lips despite not using lipstick, and her light use of eyeliner served to accentuate her long lashes. The vest made her body line more distinct, highlighting her thin figure. The list went on, but I think my point has been made—even now, she looked charming.

Noname's peach-colored lips curled into a confident smile. "I'm counting on you all today! Throw shame to the wind and butter up our client as much as you can! Don't feel bad about encouraging her to spend stacks of money either, because that's exactly what she's here for! If you have any problems, just come to me!"

The twins and I nodded. I tried to calm my racing heart. "I-I'll try my best! I'll lend out tons of books and buy all the new releases I've been wanting!"

"I'll try my best too! Just 'cause it seems fun, ha ha ha," Kinme said.

"I'm starving!" Ginme exclaimed. "Are we starting soon? I wanna see what kind of spread we got this year!"

"I can't believe you guys..." Suimei was incredulous.

At that very moment, the air began to shift. A pressure formed that made my skin tingle. The dense fog around us came alive all at once, filling my vision with white.

"She's here," I murmured. I heard a happy tune reminiscent of a clear, sunny day begin to play.

Dun-dun-dun. The sound of drums. *Fwee-fwee-fwee-ruru.* And the sound of flutes.

I swallowed and gazed into the shifting cloudy-white fog. A large number of figures came into view, all men wearing traditional kariginu garb. Their faces were obscured by veils, hiding their expressions, but I could see some with nonhuman ears, some with furry tails, and even some with long reptilian tails. These were the retainers of the mountain god, and they were naturally all nonhumans. They played drums and flutes, performing a song that reminded me of the songs played at temple festivals.

"We have been awaiting your arrival, Yamakakachi-sama!" Noname spread her arms wide and welcomed our guest of honor.

"Oho ho ho!" A shrill laugh resounded, and I saw an enormous figure move beyond the fog. It was the mountain god.

Cold sweat dripped down my back. I might have done this every year, but I would never get used to the sensation of something vastly larger than me approaching. It terrified me. But I couldn't let my fear show.

A woman's face emerged through the wall of cloudy-white fog. "Has a year passed by already? I dare say you grow more beautiful each time we meet, Noname."

"You flatter me, Yamakakachi-sama."

Rising forth from the fog was the god of the mountain, who took the form of a giant snake. The lower half of her body was that of a snake, with scales as deep green as the forest itself, and her upper half appeared human. She looked somewhat like the half-human, half-snake beast known as a Lamia. The snake half of her body was frightfully long and was coiled in one towering pile. She wore a luxurious junihitoe, a ceremonial kimono that consisted of twelve layers, with a brilliant peony flower pattern on the karaginu outer layer. Normally, such a fancy pattern would look too gaudy, but it felt right juxtaposed with the pattern of her scales. The five brightly colored itsutsuginu layers of her kimono were not only contrasting hues, as was tradition, but also tasteful spring colors. She leaned forward, her long and flowing black hair swaying as she brought her face close to Noname's. "Tell me, what do you think of my kimono? I had it made especially for today."

Yamakakachi giggled, which made Noname break into a big smile. "My! I had a feeling that might've been the case. I absolutely adore the large peony! Modern designs are really something."

"Truly. I commissioned it from Kyoyuzen directly. They said a karaginu of this size would be too heavy, but naturally, that poses no issue for me. I fear none but I could manage such a look this well." She covered her mouth with a cypress fan and smiled, her large pupils narrowing with delight. Noname's compliments satisfied her. Then she noticed the twins and beckoned them closer. "Oh! You two came again this year! Come, come."

"Hello again, Yamakakachi-sama!" Kinme said. "I'm happy you remembered me!"

"Hey, where's the food? I'm starving!" Ginme said.

"The two of you are as adorable as I remember! I'll make sure you get to eat your fill today!" Yamakakachi shifted her gaze toward me and leered. My heart almost jumped out of my chest, but I fought to hide my nervousness and gave a slight bow. She slithered toward me, the ground scraping beneath her as she moved. The sight was most certainly not good for my heart. My hands grew clammy inside my gloves. I thought: *Ah... I'm really not good with enormous nonhuman beings, am I?* I was a bit exasperated with my inability to overcome my fears, no matter how much time passed. I hid my trembling hands behind my back. Gods were capricious; there was no telling what they might take offense to.

Suddenly, somebody grabbed my shaking hands. I turned to see Suimei.

"Are you okay?" he asked. My chest warmed. "I'm right here. Don't worry."

I thanked him with my eyes and steeled myself. I smiled at

the mountain god and said, "I'm glad I could meet you again this year, Yamakakachi-sama!"

"Kaori... Oh, Kaori... I, too, have missed thee!" Her cheeks flushed, she reached out and traced my chin with a finger. She gazed at me with fevered breath and ecstasy in her eyes. "No matter how many years may pass, your gentle features remain unchanging. Your face is so lovely, it could be a woman's. It's irresistible. I do adore the look of the twins, but your face is by far my favorite."

"You're too kind, Yamakakachi-sama." Internally, I was breaking out in a cold sweat.

Yamakakachi stroked the surface of her karaginu and said, "Oh, that reminds me, Kaori. The inspiration for this peony design came from that book you lent me."

"Oh?" I said, not remembering which book she was referring to. A retainer passed me a collection of Japanese folktales compiled and written by Koizumi Yakumo. Koizumi was a Greek-born man, formerly named Lafcadio Hearn. He was the first to compile Japanese folktales and literature and introduce them to the western world, aided by his wife Setsuko. She translated the Japanese he couldn't read for him to transcribe.

"I found myself particularly taken by *Tales of the Peony Lantern*. You're familiar with it, I presume?" the god asked.

"It's a story about human nature written by Sanyutei Encho, the rakugo artist, right? The one where a charming young samurai is visited by a girl every night. When he realizes she's a ghost, he tries to stop her from visiting him but is ultimately killed by her."

"Yes. The girl loved the man in life, enough to haunt him in death. I dare say her tenacity was even greater than that of a snake." Yamakakachi's long forked tongue flickered as she narrowed her eyes. "It was an interesting story, but part of it left me dissatisfied."

"Oh?"

"Indeed. Perhaps you could sympathize, Kaori?" Without warning, Yamakakachi began to coil her large body around me, almost making me shriek. She smiled deeply, her eyes curving crescent. She tightened around me softly, a dim flame of passion visible in the depths of her gaze. "If it were me, I wouldn't fool around and run the risk of love slipping through my fingers. I'd coil my tail around him and his house entire. Perhaps I'd crush his legs so he could never leave me. Or maybe I'd break his spirit and take my time taming him. The possibilities are endless…"

"Urk…"

"It mystifies me to no end how that girl managed to wait so long! The sound of his death throes, the feeling of taking his everything for yourself—ah! It must've been ecstacy! Oh, how I envy her! And it was that very envy that inspired me to have this peony karaginu made!"

"Urgh…!"

I could feel my bones creaking. I'd known Yamakakachi for a long time, and occasionally she lost reason like this. This wasn't something unique to her but a characteristic of all gods, who were said to have temperaments as fickle as the weather. In that moment, Yamakakachi was caught up in her own excitement, and her lower half was constricting around me of its own accord; she meant no harm at all. If she truly wanted me dead, she could squish me flat in a second. *Still, this is getting kind of dangerous...* I grimaced as her tail tightened further.

Yamakakachi continued on, unaware of my plight. "If one desires something, they must seize it with all their might. That's the lesson this story is trying to teach. Don't you agree, Kaori?"

I couldn't answer her question on account of the pain. Feeling ignored, her expression clouded.

Uh-oh.

"That's enough!" Suimei suddenly yelled. Even though it hurt, I did what I could to turn my head and saw Noname holding him back while he tried to charge forward.

Is this it? Have we failed already? I fought the crushing pain and shook my head. Suimei froze, a conflicted look on his face.

"Hm? And who are you?" Yamakakachi asked, her attention diverted. Her grip on me loosened, and the pain faded.

"Kaori, up here!" Kinme acted fast, lifting me up and pulling me away from the mountain god. "Phew! That was a close one. Good grief, how thick-skulled can that hag get? If this weren't a job, I'd have kicked up a fuss a long time ago!"

"Jeez, I thought my heart would stop!" Ginme said. "That creeped me out, man. Why's she gotta touch Kaori like that?"

"Both of you *shhhh*!" I said, covering their mouths with my hands. Anxiously, I looked back at Yamakakachi. To my surprise, it seemed she'd failed to hear the twins' remarks because her attention was completely taken by Suimei, the new face.

"Oh? Oooh. My, my, this is quite something. What a handsome face you have! Look this way now. Oh dear. Bashful, are we?"

Suimei didn't even try to hide his displeasure and recoiled from her. Noname quickly stepped between them. "You have quite the discerning eye! This boy has been staying at my place lately. I thought you might like him, so I brought him by, but..." She looked behind herself and sighed, seeing Suimei with a disgusted look still on his face. "He's a bit shy, as you can see... Please forgive him, I don't think he'll be able to manage a very pleasant conversation with you."

Nice one, Noname! I thought as I did a fist pump. Because of his upbringing, Suimei didn't have great control over his emotions, so it was doubtful whether he would be able to skillfully curry favor with Yamakakachi like the twins and I could. Originally, we planned to have him hide behind the trees, but that plan fell through as soon as Yamakakachi spotted him. The best course of action now was to make an excuse to sideline him. Unfortunately...

"That's quite all right. The challenge of winning over such a feisty boy is amusing in its own right." Unfortunately, Yamakakachi seemed quite taken by Suimei's attitude and picked him up, carrying him under her arm. She disregarded his flailing and carted him off to where all the retainers were gathered. "Let us commence the banquet. Bring the drink! Set out the food! Dance, sing, entertain me!"

She sat on a red felt rug, the seat of honor, and placed Suimei by her side, then leisurely watched her retainers play the flute.

"Wh-what do we do, Noname?!" I asked.

"W-we have to serve her for now! Oh dear, Suimei is making a face. Clear your head and think nothing, boy! Zilch! Kinme, you go make sure Suimei doesn't say anything silly. Kaori, you try to get Suimei out of there, but act natural! Ginme, go liven this whole thing up!"

"Yes, ma'am!"

"Aye aye, captain!"

"Leave it to me! ...But can I eat something first?"

We all set forth on our respective assignments, approaching the mountain god with smiles plastered on. Music echoed throughout the mountain, and our hearts drummed with apprehension—but I would brave anything for the sake of the huge order Yamakakachi might place at the bookstore. Danger was simply a part of the job.

So began the battle between the God of the Mountain and Team Bookstore-plus-Apothecary.

Entertaining the mountain god was no simple task. It required the kind of ingenuity that only a bookstore could provide. For example, all the food we served were dishes found in stories.

"This here is the same curried mutton featured in the Sherlock Holmes story, *The Adventure of the Silver Blaze*. The mutton has been simmered together with curry powder to make a soup. Do you find the smell agreeable?"

"Oooh... I do indeed, Kinme! Heh heh heh, it has such a pungent aroma, I fear it may be strong enough to mask the taste of a narcotic!" Yamakakachi said with great amusement.

Kinme drew close and whispered into her ear. "Never in a million years would I think to drug you unconscious, for I wish for nothing more than to spend as much time with you as I can... Am I wrong to think you might feel the same way?"

She blushed, covering her mouth, and restlessly averted her gaze. "O-oh my..."

"Why do you look away? Would you prefer that I did mix in a little something?" he teased as he nonchalantly reached out to grasp her hand. Yamakakachi began to perspire as he stroked the back of her hand with his thumb, passion burning in his eyes. "Yes... Perhaps I should put you to sleep and hide you away. That way you could be mine and mine alone, forever. But it's not too late, is it? Would you like me to make you mine alone?"

"O-oh, I-I, um..." she stammered, flustered.

Ginme appeared and forced his way between them. In his hand was a dainty little box covered in stars. "Hey, it's not fair if you only talk to Kinme! I've brought you something nice as well: It's the 'goose' from *Night on the Galactic Railroad*!"

"The goose...? Oh, the candy that the birdcatcher gave Giovanni!"

"Yep! In the story, it was described as a piece of goose leg that broke off as easily as chocolate and tasted sweeter than sweets. I didn't know anyone well versed in western candy, so I had to get a confectionery of Japanese sweets who I know to make it instead.

But that got me thinking—in the book, birds rained down from the sky like snow, right? Well, what Japanese sweet *literally* means 'falling geese'? *Rakugan!*"

He opened the starry box to reveal a line of sweets shaped like birds.

Yamakakachi let out an astonished gasp. "Oh my, hardened sugar formed into the shape of a bird. How adorable."

Ginme gingerly picked one up and smiled impishly. "Here, let me feed you one."

"H-huh? N-no, that's quite all right…"

"Don't hold back on me now. Open wide!" He thrust a rakugan into her mouth.

"Ohm?!"

"It's good, right?" he laughed. He opened his mouth wide, gesturing for her to feed him as well.

"G-Ginme, you reckless fool! Such behavior is bad for my heart…" Yamakakachi picked up one of the rakugan with a trembling hand and fed it to him. Ginme broke into a smile that stole her breath away.

Noname, who was doing Yamakakachi's nails, gave an exasperated sigh. "Show some restraint, you two."

"Okaaay," replied the twins.

Yamakakachi gazed longingly at the pair as they parted from her. Noname noticed this and grinned, her full lips curling as she looked at Yamakakachi with her long-lashed amber eyes. She oozed sex appeal and gave Yamakakachi a seductive look that left the goddess gulping for air. "It saddens me that you would flirt so brazenly with others when you have me by your side. Am I no match for the young men?"

"N-not at all!"

"In that case..." Noname brought the back of Yamakakachi's hand to her lips and kissed it. She smiled and furrowed her brows sadly. "I want you to think only of me, even if just for this brief moment we have together."

Assailed by charm beyond description, Yamakakachi arched backward, swooning. The surrounding retainers quickly moved to prop her up.

"Gross..." I muttered under my breath, watching from a distance. A sharp pain ran through my body, and I frowned at the reminder of being crushingly constricted by Yamakakachi's coils. "Ow... This is going to sting for a while." Because of the pain, I couldn't entertain her like a proper host and had to leave it to the other three, relegating myself to behind-the-scenes work. Of course, I wasn't alone. I'd managed to drag Suimei out of the line of fire while the other three had her swooning. Together, we served the food.

"Please line up one by one! There's no need to push, we have more than enough for everyone!" I called out. We were serving the kariginu-wearing retainers and the spirits who lived in Otogitoge Pass. They sat around relaxing as they enjoyed our curried mutton. This, too, was an important part of our job. You never knew when or where an opportunity might crop up, so while entertaining Yamakakachi was a given, one also couldn't neglect the little people.

IN SPRING, THE MOUNTAIN GOD COMES OUT TO PLAY

"What a day..." Suimei, right by my side, let out a tired sigh as he prepared bowls.

I poured the contents of a pot into the bowls and giggled. "At least things are going well. We can expect a good number of orders this year." I looked at Yamakakachi in the distance and saw Noname perched on her lap, applying handmade lotion to the god's face. It was quite a sight—the usually imposing god was rendered a blushing mess, and she looked no different than any ordinary young woman. I watched as she happily ordered a dozen jars of the product. With the way things were going, it seemed Noname had many more sales coming her way.

Suimei looked livid about something. "How can you consider this 'going well'? Do you realize how much danger you were in earlier? Your guts were about to pop through your mouth!"

"That's true. Squeezed out like a tube of toothpaste."

"It's not funny," he said with a sharp look.

I shrugged. "I mean, it's nothing unusual. I'm super fragile compared to everyone else." After spending so much time with spirits, I'd come to the realization that the beliefs and actions of nonhumans shouldn't be measured by human standards. Nonhumans had their own rules that they lived by and didn't let themselves be bound by the rules of others. That was simply their nature. "I got hurt by my own carelessness. I could have navigated the conversation better to avoid trouble entirely. But that happens between humans as well, doesn't it? If anything, spirits and gods are easier to deal with because they're not as sly as humans."

"That's..." Suimei frowned. "You're not wrong."

I let out a small giggle and smiled. "It's good to remember that spirits and gods are something to be feared. They're like a neighbor you don't know all that well. They exist close by, but our lack of familiarity makes us guarded around them. Of course, that doesn't mean we dislike them. In fact, we even wish to grow closer to them, despite knowing the dangers. They don't just invoke fear but curiosity as well."

"Any normal human would run away long before they felt anything other than fear."

"Aha ha ha! You got me there! They're too alien for most humans—not merely in terms of appearance but in terms of beliefs and worldview as well. They're strange and mysterious, but even so, I like them. It's probably because I was raised in their world."

Seeing me giggle again, Suimei frowned slightly. He let out a sigh and shrugged. "I still haven't fully separated myself from the time I hunted spirits, so I can't help but be fearful of them. But there's one thing I've come to understand after coming to the spirit realm." He cast his gaze downward and whispered, "Humans are far more terrifying than any spirit or god."

Worried, I asked, "Are you feeling tired? Do you want to take a break?"

Suimei smiled wryly and gave me a light bonk on the head. "If I seem tired, it's because you're always making me worry with your antics. Ugh, what a day... Even those twins are being more useful than me."

"It's not too late to try again. You can go over to Yamakakachi right now if you want?"

"Ugh... Please, anything but that. I seriously thought I would die earlier..." He trembled, perhaps remembering the experience. I couldn't help but laugh at him and then noticed a spirit standing nearby. It looked similar to a Preta—a hungry ghoul spirit—but was in fact a Hidarugami, a spirit often seen in Otogitoge Pass that ripped travelers' stomachs open and ate the contents. Those who died unnatural deaths in the mountains were said to become Hidarugami; and if you were in the mountains, and felt so hungry you couldn't move, it was said to be the work of a Hidarugami.

The Hidarugami stared at me with its sunken eyes as it staggered forward on uneasy legs. Something felt off, dangerous even.

"Get behind me, Kaori." Suimei seemed to feel the same thing and stepped in front of me without hesitation.

The Hidarugami continued to approach with a blank look on its face. Once it was close, it muttered something in a shrill voice. "Mer..."

"Huh?" I said.

The Hidarugami reached out a thin arm. "Mermaid meat... Do you have mermaid meat?"

"Uh..."

"I heard the rumors. When a spirit is in need, somebody will appear out of thin air and sell them wish-granting mermaid meat. Is it not you two? Do you not have the mermaid meat?" The Hidarugami begged in a raspy voice, grabbing Suimei's clothes. "Give it to me. I need mermaid meat!"

"I'm sorry, but we don't have anything like that," Suimei said flatly.

The Hidarugami began to yell. "D-don't lie to me! You have it, don't you?! Please, I can't bear this hunger any longer! No matter how much I eat, I can never feel satiated! It's a living hell. I just want to feel full. Please, I beg you."

Suimei and I shared a look, both thinking the same thing. We couldn't have any trouble while we were still entertaining Yamakakachi. It was best we deescalate the situation. With that in mind, Suimei said, "Please calm down and tell us what's wrong."

But the Hidarugami's bloodshot eyes went wide. "How am I supposed to be calm, you imbecile?! Why won't you help me?! Why won't you try to understand the pain I feel?! Why? Why?! Ah! It must be because—" The Hidarugami's eyes glared even wider as his tone dropped to a low growl "—you're trying to keep the mermaid meat for yourself!"

"What?"

"I won't let you! That mermaid meat is mine!"

Bewildered by the spirit's nonsensical logic, Suimei took a step back. I took a couple of steps back as well.

"Whoa?!" I tripped backward on a water vessel we had out for dishwashing and fell to the ground, a large volume of water splashing onto me. "Whoops..." I looked down at myself and grimaced. The outfit Noname prepared for me was ruined. I sighed, cursing my luck—when a sudden jolt of fear ran through me. The noise of flutes and drums had abruptly stopped, and a deafening silence took its place. I looked around, fearful of the sudden change, and saw all the retainers who were making merry just moments ago now blankly staring at me.

A bone-chilling voice broke the silence. "I smell a woman." I heard the ground scrape as something slithered toward me.

"Eek!" The Hidarugami fled with a look of utter fear. I couldn't even muster the courage to chase after the spirit who'd caused all this. I heard the scraping sound come closer and swallowed.

Did she find out? But things were going so well. How did she... Oh no. A water droplet trickled down my cheek. I realized what had happened: Noname's perfume had washed off. All of a sudden, the water felt like it was sucking away my body heat. My pulse raced, and my fingertips grew numb. My heart throbbed so loudly I could hear it. I couldn't even cry or scream, could only think desperately of running away.

"Suimei... Noname... Ginme... Kinme..." My voice trembled as I called out my friends' names. I saw something move at the edge of my vision—a pale white hand. It stroked my cheek, my shoulders, my back, my arm. It touched me all over, checking my figure, before eventually coming to a stop.

I heard a woman breathing behind me. "Tell me, why does the stench of a woman taint my banquet on this auspicious day when I become a harvest god?"

My breathing became erratic. Tears clouded my vision. My thoughts were disorderly, and my body froze. The white hand began to move again, tracing my moist cheek. I realized that I couldn't feel any warmth from the hand at all. It wasn't her hand but her *tail*. Her long tail coiled around my body. The memory of the earlier pain flooded my mind. Yamakakachi hadn't meant to hurt me then, but this time would be different. Gods never forgave those who broke their taboos. This time, she would choke the life out of me for sure.

"What is the meaning of this, Kaori?" Yamakakachi peered down at my face, her long red tongue flickering before me. Afraid, I shut my eyes.

I'm dead!

"Oi, Yamakakachi!" A rude voice broke the silence. I whipped my head around, shocked to see Suimei standing there. He looked straight at me and mouthed, *Don't worry. I'll protect you,* before grabbing Yamakakachi's hand with a provoking glare.

Yamakakachi looked back at him, making no effort to hide her displeasure. "What do you want? I'm busy talking to Kaori here. Don't get in my way, or I'll—"

"Shut up. You talk too much, woman," he interrupted. He jerked her closer and brought his shapely face next to hers. With a faint blush, he murmured, "You have some gall to get my hopes up by coming here, only to ignore me and dote on Kaori."

"Huh?" I murmured, not expecting Suimei's words at all.

He cast his gaze down and gave Yamakakachi a melancholic, feverish look through his long lashes. He clumsily caressed her neck and said with confidence, "Don't look at the others. Just look at me and only me. Got it?"

Wh-wh-what?! My mind fell into turmoil. *Suimei, that awkward Suimei, is acting like a gigolo?! And he's actually* good *at it?!* For reasons beyond me, Suimei was smooth-talking, and doing it well. My thoughts raced, wondering where he could have learned such a skill, and more importantly, from whom. *Was it a woman?! I'm definitely grilling you later, Suimei!*

Then I remembered the gravity of the situation and wondered what in the world he was attempting when I was right on death's door. If anything, wouldn't this make Yamakakachi angrier? I cautiously looked toward Yamakakachi and froze, mouth wide open in shock. The mountain god, utterly terrifying moments before, was making a face like a shy maiden in love. Seeing such a mind-boggling sight from up close ground my mind to a halt.

With a daring smile, Suimei whispered into Yamakakachi's ears. "Were you not listening? I asked you a question. Where's my reply?"

"Ah, y-yes..."

"Good girl. Let's head back to the banquet. Come on," he said, offering his hand.

After a moment of hesitation, she meekly took his hand and replied, "Okay..."

Suimei acted with the self-importance and poise of a king, leisurely leading Yamakakachi back to the banquet area as though it were only natural of him to do so. She gazed at him, absolutely smitten, hearts in her eyes.

"I-I'm saved...?" I said, unsure. Yamakakachi's tail unraveled from around me, leaving me to fall to my knees.

The others quickly ran over.

"Kaori! Are you all right? Oh dear, let's get that perfume back on you quick!" Noname said.

"Sheesh! I thought we'd have to fight an actual god!" Ginme said.

"Pfft, ha ha ha ha! Oh gosh, I can't, heh heh! Did you hear Suimei?! 'Just look at me and me alone,' aha ha ha! Ah, my sides hurt!" Kinme was having a riot.

I was, indeed, saved. The flutes and drums had already started playing again, and Yamakakachi was snuggled up against Suimei, having completely forgotten about me. I let out a sigh of relief, but it still didn't feel real. So I pinched my cheek.

The rest of the banquet went off without a hitch. I managed to get twice as many book orders as last year while Noname managed to snag three times as many cosmetics orders. I was happy we were walking away with a tidy profit, but Suimei's earlier behavior still weighed on my mind, so I found time to hound him for answers afterward.

"I used this book I got from Fuguruma-youbi as a reference," he said, holding a teen romance novel called *Falling for My Haughty Prince*. In it, a boy (the titular "haughty prince") tried to make the female protagonist fall for him.

Oh, thank goodness. He wasn't acting from personal experience.

"Women go weak in the knees for these kinds of men. Or at least, that's what Fuguruma-youbi said." Suimei looked a bit unsure himself.

I made as stern a face as I could. "That couldn't be further from the truth! You got lucky that that kind of personality was Yamakakachi's fetish!"

"What's a 'fetish'?"

"Urk. Y-you don't need to know what those are yet! Just don't ever act like that again!"

"Huh? Um, sure, I guess?"

"All right! Good boy, good boy!"

"Don't patronize me, you dork," he huffed.

I let out a sigh of relief, but the emotions swirling inside my chest wouldn't settle. I wanted nothing more than to roll on the ground and vent my frustration. I balled my hands into fists as one thought made itself distinct within the chaos of my mind: *I'm definitely complaining to Fuguruma-youbi later!*

CHAPTER 2

What Follows the End at the Northernmost Tip

WE WERE IN Aomori Prefecture, at Cape Tappi. Called the Northernmost Tip in a famous Showa-era pop song, Cape Tappi faced the Tsugaru Strait and was known for its year-round gales. These gales pushed the clouds up above, urging them to hurry along. Here, only the seagulls and other sea birds could fly unfazed through the harsh elements. As I gave my presentation, the noisy chorus of birds reached my ears while the briny breeze swept past me, disheveling my neat hair and my new spring clothes.

"This book here is *Tsugaru*, by Dazai Osamu. It's an autobiographical novel that came about when Dazai's friend and editor suggested he write about his hometown." As soon as I said these words, a feeling of melancholy swept over me. Dazai was a complicated man. He lived by bottling up the once-pure, since-sullied, ugly emotions that made one human. That was why it was so difficult to explain the author and his work. In my head, I could describe things so simply, but it all felt so wrong once I said it out loud.

Tsugaru was an exploration of Dazai's roots. I imagine it must have been difficult for him to write the book. He was a heavy-hearted man, always searching for some light to brighten his life. It couldn't have been easy to reminisce about his hometown, even if it was for the sake of his work.

The main story of the book begins with the question "Why must you travel?" which was met with the response "Because I cannot bear to stay." His melancholic and introverted nature was evident in his writings, and that was precisely why I loved them. It was unfortunate, however, that I couldn't so easily explain his allure to others. Still, I had to try. The livelihoods of many spirits were tied to this presentation's success.

The copy of *Tsugaru* in my hands seemed to grant me some courage as I continued to speak, trying my best to not let my voice crack from nerves. "This place we are now, Cape Tappi, is in fact featured in this book. Dazai wrote about a lot of different locales that he felt a connection to in his hometown, so in it, you'll find a lot of places you're familiar with yourself! Isn't that great?"

I was giving this presentation to a man the size of a mountain. He had skin that was glossy and dark like the night, a well-built and supple physique, scraggly hair that reached down to his waist, sharp nails, and a pointed black horn growing out of his forehead. He sat in the ocean grasping his knees as he listened to me. He was only visible from the waist up, but even then, he towered as tall as a two-story building. The thought of how tall he must be when he stood up made me dizzy.

He was Kurokami, the legendary god who was said to have created Cape Tappi. He stared at me with round eyes the color of dawn, listening intently.

"That's why I'm proposing a Dazai Osamu *Tsugaru* pilgrimage! You can visit all the places in the book while eating delicious food—though Dazai himself preferred simple foods—drink yourself sick, just like him, and enjoy the beautiful spring scenery of Aomori!" I stated my plan confidently, feeling satisfied afterward. *This plan is perfect! I can imagine nothing better than making rounds with the book in hand and lots of delicious food to be found! Surely Kurokami will be pleased with this!*

"Ouch!" My self-satisfaction was quickly crushed by a chop to the head, however. I looked up, bearing the pain, and saw Suimei giving me an exasperated look.

"Are you an idiot? That's just what *you* want to do," he said.

I blanked. "Wait, what?"

Nyaa-san and Kuro backed Suimei up.

"Kaori... Are you all right? That's that pop-culture tourism thing, right? I know you like Dazai Osamu, but how is someone who hasn't read his books supposed to enjoy your plan?"

"Nyaa's right! Your plan doesn't sound fun in the slightest!"

"O-oh. Well..." The pair didn't hold anything back.

With some exasperation in her voice, Nyaa-san put the final nail in the coffin. "But it's not like I don't understand where you're coming from. Dazai Osamu looks a lot like Shinonome, after all."

"Wh-wha—Nyaa-san?!"

"You *really* like Shinonome, don't you?"

"Stop it, aaaaahh! No more!" I blushed and assumed the fetal position. I liked how Nyaa-san didn't beat around the bush, but sometimes I wished she wouldn't be so direct. I glanced at Kurokami. He was looking at me with his mouth half-open, his fangs in full view. Something told me he wasn't keen on my plan. *What do I do?!*

Perhaps I should explain how I got into this predicament in the first place. It all started a few hours ago...

It was a spring morning, harsh with rain. Glimmerflies took cover under the eaves, dimly illuminating their surroundings with a yellowish glow.

I let out a weary sigh, but it was drowned out by the sound of rain pounding against the roof. I put my hands against my cheeks, tinged red with embarrassment, and looked to my side at the gorgeous young woman who was rolling with laughter. "C'mon. It's not that funny," I grumbled.

"Pfft ha ha ha, but it *is* that funny! Truly! Oh, such a cutie pie you are to complain of such a thing to me!" The woman was Fuguruma-youbi, and she was currently kicking her feet against the ground as she howled with laughter in my living room. Her dazzling, fair-skinned legs, made all the more captivating with the rain as their backdrop, teasingly revealed themselves from underneath the milky-white drape of her long uchikake robe.

"You don't have to laugh so much..."

"How could I not?! I may have lent that boy the book, but I would never have imagined he'd imitate one of its characters to chase a snake away! Pfft, ha ha ha!" Fuguruma-youbi bent forward in a fit of laughter. Each time her shoulders shook, the comb holding her shimada-style updo in place made a shrill sound.

Fuguruma-youbi was the spirit of an unsent love letter. She was also a lover of romance stories, although I wasn't quite sure if that had anything to do with her background. She lived in the spirit realm's version of Yoshiwara and was an expert on romance stories, of which she had an enormous personal library. I'd called her to the bookstore to complain about the book Suimei borrowed from her, explaining the details of what happened with Yamakakachi. To my surprise, my complaints only succeeded in making her double over in laughter.

"But why'd you give him that teen romance novel of all things?" I asked. "There's so many better options for him."

"Perhaps. That boy is still uncorrupted, like a blank canvas waiting to be colored. I'm sure he'll find his own color naturally, but I figured it wouldn't hurt to, say, 'suggest' a color, if you will..."

"Wait... You don't mean what I think you mean, do you?"

"He would be so cute if he grew up to be the haughty playboy type! Ho ho ho, it suited him, did it not?" Fuguruma-youbi flashed a wicked smile.

I shook my head furiously. "It *absolutely* did not! That's your personal preference in men speaking!"

"Oh? Don't tell me you don't know the joy of being pursued by an assertive man? Heh heh heh, or perhaps you're the type who still dreams of a Prince Charming to come sweep you off your feet?"

"O-of course not!"

"Don't lie. I know you prefer the meek and gentle heroes over the so-called 'bad boy' characters in those books you read."

"H-how do you know that?!" I began to break out in a cold sweat.

She gave me a flirtatious sidelong glance. "'Tis a shame you don't know the allure of a bold man. Oh well."

"When did you even manage to give him that book anyway? Last time I checked, he had no interest in romance novels at all."

"Mmm, let's just say something happened that caused his stance toward romance to change. I can't say any more without infringing on his privacy."

"Is that right? But that makes me even more curious!"

"Oho ho ho! I'll tell you once you're capable of speaking of romance yourself! I'm not in the business of spilling secrets to someone who isn't even my friend." Fuguruma-youbi turned away with a huff.

I grumbled. "Whaaat. C'mon. Can't I be your friend already?"

"I'm afraid you are still too green. Perhaps once you've grown up some."

Bah, and here I thought I could make friends with a fellow booklover. Putting that aside, I was curious as to why Suimei was suddenly giving romance novels another shot. He *did* say he was interested in romance when I first introduced him to Fuguruma-youbi... What if he had someone he liked? What if he'd experienced heartbreak before? The thought alone made me want to cry. I was sadly tracing the folds of the tatami mats with my finger when the third party in the room finally spoke up.

"Are you two done talking now? I've been waiting for quite a while."

"Oh my," Fuguruma-youbi said. "You were so quiet, I thought you were a part of the room. You'll have to forgive me. Kaori's all yours."

"I see you're as snide a woman as ever, not that I expected much from you to begin with."

"Why you little…! Ahem. My, my, my. You have *quite* the way with words!"

The woman trading barbed words with Fuguruma-youbi wore peculiar old-fashioned garb. She looked to be in her early twenties, had bewitching long black hair that was tied at the back, and wore a light-purple uchigi kimono over an all-white short-sleeved kosode with a red kakeobi sash draped over her chest, completing what was a common traveler's outfit for women in ancient Japan. Her name was Karaito Gozen, and she was a woman who'd lived in the Kamakura period. Her legend was still told to this day in the town of Fujisaki, in Aomori Prefecture.

She was the lover of fifth regent Hojo Tokiyori. Her unparalleled beauty earned his favor, but she was forced to flee to her hometown in order to escape his wife's harassment. Later, Tokiyori entered the Buddhist priesthood and traveled to Tsugaru to meet Karaito Gozen. At first, she was overjoyed to hear that her beloved would visit, but soon she despaired at how much her beauty had faded over the years of hiding. Distraught, she threw herself into a pond, ending her life.

That same woman now dedicated all her time and effort to preserving beautiful things, working as a conservator for Tsukumogami. Shinonome-san was one such Tsukumogami in her care, as his main body had been damaged in an incident a while back. She'd told us that his repairs would be finished in spring, but she'd been worryingly out of touch for a while, only to now suddenly reappear. Shinonome-san happened to be out of the house, so I'd had her wait in the living room, but she seemed to be getting impatient.

"I'm growing tired of waiting. Can we not talk yet, Kaori?"

"Er, you want to talk to me, not Shinonome-san?" I asked.

"It doesn't matter who it is as long as they bring about the desired results."

What could she want? An exciting possibility came to mind. "Do you want me to give you book recommendations?!"

"Of course not. I have no interest whatsoever in books."

"Aww... That's too bad." I slumped my shoulders dejectedly, my enthusiasm curbed.

Karaito Gozen smiled slightly. "I've come today to make an apology and a request. I apologize for the delay in the restoration of Shinonome's hanging scroll, and I request your assistance in consoling a certain god."

"A god, you say?" The whole recent incident with Yamakakachi came to mind, and I felt exhausted all at once. The marks from where she bound me had lasted for days, and the pain even longer.

WHAT FOLLOWS THE END AT THE NORTHERNMOST TIP

I wasn't too thrilled at the prospect of dealing with another god again, especially so soon, but it seemed my experience with Yamakakachi was exactly why Karaito Gozen made this request of me.

"I initially planned to ask Shinonome for help, but I've heard you're also quite skilled and were even able to lead Yamakakachi around by the nose. Rumor has it she's even been losing sleep over how much she's looking forward to next year's spring."

"Whoa, seriously?" Yamakakachi must have been really taken with Suimei's act. Would he be able to pull it off again next year? I didn't even want to think about what terrible things might happen if he couldn't.

Karaito Gozen smiled softly. "I request you use those skills of yours to appease the unruly god of Cape Tappi."

Allow me to summarize Karaito Gozen's request: There was a lamenting god called Kurokami who lived at Cape Tappi in Aomori Prefecture. To explain who this god was, we need to return to a time when the Hokkaido and Honshu islands were still joined as one. Back then, Kurokami was a god who boasted great physical strength and lived on what was then known as Tappi Peak. One day, he fell in love at first sight with an unbelievably beautiful goddess who lived at Lake Towada. He visited her by dragon every day and demanded that she marry him. However, there existed another god by the name of Akagami who lived on Oga Peninsula in what's now Akita Prefecture. Akagami was a skilled musician, and he also fell in love with the goddess of Lake

Towada. Every day Akagami visited her by deer, played beautiful music on his flute, and kindly asked her to marry him.

But the goddess of Lake Towada fell in love with both the strong Kurokami and the kind Akagami, and couldn't choose between them. Growing impatient, the two gods decided to duel to decide who was a better match for the goddess. Akagami never stood a chance against Kurokami's strength, and the god of Cape Tappi won easily. Akagami returned to Oga Peninsula and hid himself away in a cave while Kurokami let out a triumphant cry and made for Lake Towada in high spirits. But when he arrived, the goddess was nowhere to be found. She had chosen the kindhearted Akagami and left to hide with him in his cave.

Kurokami learned of this and lamented greatly. He returned to his home on Cape Tappi and faced north, letting out a mighty sigh. The powerful winds blown by his sigh ripped the earth apart and formed the Tsugaru Strait. Harsh winds have blown at Cape Tappi ever since.

More than a thousand years had passed, but Kurokami still lamented at Cape Tappi today. With each sigh he made, harsh winds blew, causing trouble for the spirits living there.

"To be frank," Karaito Gozen began, "Kurokami's constant lamenting is nothing new. The problem is that it has been worse as of late."

"Oh, I see... Do you have any idea why that might be?" I asked.

"Not in the slightest, but it happens every so often. I'm truly at my wits' end. With the waters so rough, the materials I need for work can't arrive. I simply can't understand how such an enormous man could constantly cry like a little girl. It's unbelievable."

Uh, is it okay to call a god a little girl...? It seemed Karaito Gozen wasn't one to mince words.

She shuffled closer to me while I was still reeling from her bold remark, then grabbed my hands and looked into my eyes with a fiery gaze. "Please, calm that god for me, like Shinonome did before. You're his daughter, so you can do it, right?"

"Wait, Shinonome-san has calmed Kurokami down before?"

"Yes, he has, and quite wonderfully too. He managed to temper that spoiled brat of a god in no time at all."

Hearing a fact I hadn't known about my father piqued my interest. I immediately imagined him standing off against an enormous god in a torrential windstorm before the waters. He must have looked so cool. *Oooh! I want to know more!*

"No way! How did he do it?!" I shot back, my hands grasping hers.

Karaito Gozen's answer was interrupted by a flat, expressionless voice. "Don't be stupid, Kaori. You *absolutely* cannot accept that request."

I frowned and looked to the source of the voice. "Ugh... *You're* here."

"Rude. Is that any way to talk to someone?" It was Suimei, accompanied by Kuro and Nyaa-san. The three of them all wore different looks on their faces. "Have you forgotten the situation you're in, Kaori? I'm sorry, lady, but you're gonna have to try your luck with someone else."

"Yep, yep! You should really listen to Suimei, Kaori! He always knows best!"

"I don't really care, but could you all leave? You're in the way of my afternoon nap. Especially you, harlot."

"My! Never have I seen such a rude beast," Fuguruma-youbi said. "I was invited by Kaori, unlike that woman over there. Please don't group us together."

"I sympathize with the cat," Karaito Gozen said. "Nobody wants to breathe the same air as some uncouth courtesan."

"Gaaah! I've had it up to here with you!"

The addition of three more people (well, one person and two animals) made the living room a bit cramped. Various conversations sprang up left and right while I pondered. *Aomori, Cape Tappi, Kurokami... What could I do to calm a god?*

I asked, "Hey, Karaito Gozen? What did Shinonome-san do to calm Kurokami down?"

"I don't quite know the particulars, but I believe it involved alcohol."

"Ahh, a classic strategy. No god can withstand a good drink. Maybe he used refined sake...?" I thought out loud as I stood up and stepped on over to my father's room, which adjoined the living room. I searched his bookshelf for a particular book, grinning to myself once I found it.

"What are you doing?" An angry voice behind me said.

"Eek!" I shrieked and cowered. I slowly turned around to see Suimei standing there with his hands on his hips.

"Was I not clear earlier? You are *not* taking that request!"

"But I want to! I wanna console a god and be like Shinonome-san!"

"Don't give me that. Your well-being is far more important than some random god."

"Whoa... You sounded kinda cool just now."

Suimei blushed a bit. "I'm being serious here, Kaori."

I drew closer to him, causing him to bend backward. "Didn't Noname say you need to act like a gentleman and protect me without boxing me in?"

"Th-that's different. Right now you're putting yourself in danger for no reason!"

"Well, I don't see a problem with it." An unfamiliar voice said.

"Eek?!" I shrieked and grabbed on to Suimei.

"I think you should undertake this Kurokami request." Standing beside us was Nurarihyon, the great leader of the spirits. He'd appeared out of nowhere and in a new form, like he always did when I met him. Today he looked like a young man in his mid-twenties with gray hair loosely tied back. He had a white shirt and suspenders holding up black pants, a western style. His face was well proportioned like a doll's but had a cold feel to it that was offset by Nurarihyon's nonchalant air. He looked rather charming.

"Your appearance is really nice today, Nurarihyon," I said.

"Isn't it? I quite like it myself."

"I want to thank the person who invented suspenders just for this look alone."

"What the hell are you two on about?" Suimei said.

"Oho ho ho! I think this Suimei boy is a little jealous that a better-looking man has appeared!" Nurarihyon gave a belly laugh. He smiled like a naughty boy with a new plot. "Truth is, I've also received a number of sincere requests to do something about Kurokami and have been looking for someone to help for a while."

He pulled out a small jellyfish from his pocket and put it into my hand. "Take this in place of a talisman if you're worried about safety. It'll at least do you better than an overprotective guardian would."

"What are you plotting, Nurarihyon?" Suimei asked.

"Nooothing. I just don't want Kaori to be in danger. Although..." Nurarihyon tilted his head and narrowed his silver eyes at Suimei. "I get the impression it might be better for Kaori to distance herself from the spirit realm for a while. You could take this opportunity to do some sightseeing around Aomori, perhaps. What do you think, Suimei?"

Suimei frowned. With a sigh, he nodded. "Fine."

"Great! That settles it!" Nurarihyon's face lit up. He casually turned away and said, "Oh, right. You're probably going to need a vast quantity of liquor. I'll cover the expenses for that. While I'm at it, I suppose I'll give you two some spending money as well. You never know when you might need it! Ha ha, this is getting fun!"

He strolled toward the exit of Shinonome-san's room, then stopped to look over his shoulder with a mischievous smile. "By the way, how much longer are you going to latch on to him?"

We blushed and quickly separated, causing Nurarihyon to grin even wider. "Heh heh heh, I'll keep this a secret from Shinonome. I'm not much for seeing him throw childish fits. Well, I'll be off then. Why, hello there, Karaito Gozen. It appears the girl will be undertaking the Kurokami request after all. I'll be counting on you to help with the preparations!"

Suimei and I slowly met each other's gaze, then immediately looked away.

"Uh, s-sorry for grabbing on to you," I said. "C-can I count on your help with Kurokami?"

"F-fine, I guess. I-I mean, I'm supposed to protect you anyway."

"Thank you."

"Don't worry about it."

We stood in silence. I tried to distract myself by thinking of the challenge to come, worried that my pounding heart must be loud enough for Suimei to hear.

Afterward, we were urged along by Nurarihyon and made our way to Aomori. There was sunny weather when we arrived in the prefecture, but the clouds grew thicker as we approached Cape Tappi. The winds seemed to howl, making the task ahead feel all the more foreboding.

"Another god, huh? Think we'll be all right?" I asked. "Remembering what happened with Yamakakachi makes me shiver…"

Suimei frowned and shook his head. "You should've refused if you were scared. Well, at least this god isn't the type to hurt people; according to Nurarihyon, that is."

"Kicking up winds every time he gets moody is harmful enough if you ask me!" Kuro said.

"Suimei means that Kurokami's not a god who holds a grudge against humans. But you're right, that doesn't mean this god isn't a hassle. If he were to throw a fit, he might wipe the area clean with a few strong gusts," Nyaa-san said.

"Wha—Nyaa-san, don't say that!" I exclaimed. "What if you jinx us and it really happens?!"

Karaito Gozen, walking behind us, warned, "I'll have you all pay compensation for the damage if that happens. Please take care that it doesn't."

"Eek! U-um, are we under any damage insurance?" I asked.

"As if the spirit realm would provide such a thing, dummy," Suimei chided.

"Urk... I'm kind of having second thoughts now," I said, feeling the color drain from my face. Someone's hand plopped onto my head, and I looked up to see Suimei, as expressionless as always.

"We've come this far, we might as well see it through. Don't worry, I'll be supporting you as best I can."

"Y-you're right. We can't turn back now!" I couldn't let anxiety hold me back, especially when the repairs for Shinonome-san's main body were on the line!

"Heh heh. I have high hopes for you." Karaito Gozen smiled warmly before walking away. The veil of her straw hat fluttered behind her. Suimei and I shared a brief look before following after her. Our destination: the tempestuous Cape Tappi.

Kurokami was located next to Obi Island, just past Tappi Fishing Pier. Obi Island was an uninhabited island named after the legend in which Minamoto no Yoshitsune unfastened an obi belt to reach Hokkaido. The sight of the giant god leaning up against the island invoked fear in me, but I neared him nonetheless, determined, and gave him the presentation recounted earlier.

Our plan to console Kurokami was simple: We wanted to get him moving and doing anything other than soaking in the cold northern ocean under this drab, cloudy weather. In other words, we were hoping a change of pace would lighten his spirits. That meant helping him make some fun, new memories and enjoying some delicious food. I thought I had the perfect plan for such a thing, but...well, we all know how that went.

I stood stock-still before the violent waves of the gray sea. "What do we do?!" I yelled. "I don't have a backup plan! I was so sure my *Tsugaru* plan would be enough!"

"How can you be so careless?" Suimei chided.

"Ehe heh. I got a bit carried away once I thought about being able to visit all the places in *Tsugaru*. It didn't even cross my mind that the plan could fail."

"I don't think I've ever met anyone as airheaded as you."

"I was too excited imagining situations like giving a plump sea bream to the inn I was staying at and begging them to grill it whole, only to get it back sliced!"

"I...what? That reference is way too niche for me to follow."

I doubled over in laughter at Suimei's retorts, but soon enough my shoulders slumped in dejection.

"Oh dear. Maybe my hopes were misplaced?" Karaito Gozen said.

Ack. It kind of hurts to hear that. I could manage nothing, despite the ease with which Shinonome-san supposedly consoled this god. Even now, tears flowed from Kurokami's eyes, and his strong gales blew forth.

How did Shinonome-san pull it off? Things would be easy if I could have asked Shinonome-san directly, but he still hadn't returned by the time we left. To make matters worse, neither of us had phones or the like to get in touch.

"I didn't think Kaori would be so poor at planning..." Karaito Gozen said.

"Hey, why don't we wait for Kurokami to cry himself to sleep?" Kuro suggested.

"This isn't some little brat we're dealing with, it's a god," Karaito Gozen scoffed. "You're not much of a thinker, are you, Inugami?"

Nyaa-san shot Kuro a look and said, "She's calling you stupid in a roundabout way, Kuro."

"Wait, really? I couldn't tell at all! You're so smart!" Kuro replied.

"Are you all right in the head? You realize you're supposed to get mad at her, right?" Nyaa-san sighed. "I guess a mutt will never be anything more than a mutt."

I ignored everyone behind me and gazed up at Kurokami. He stared blankly at us, not saying a word. *Strange. His eyes look a lot softer than I thought they would. Wasn't he supposed to be a super physically powerful god?* His eyes were tranquil, like the coastline just before sunset. I thought I could hear waves quietly brushing the coast as I fell deeper and deeper into his entrancing gaze.

The god broke his silence. "Might you be Shinonome's daughter?"

I managed a nod through my surprise.

"I see," he said. I drew closer to his large face. He let out an impressed sigh, and a lukewarm, briny breeze flowed past me. His lips curled into a smile, revealing sharp teeth. "You're just as he described. Adorable."

"Ador—*what?!*"

"His own words. Said you were the apple of his eye, he did."

"How old does that coot think I am?" I groaned. I was a grown woman for crying out loud.

"Well, this was more than ten years ago. You were probably even cuter than now."

What kind of nonsense was my father talking to a god about?!

Seeing me tremble from sheer embarrassment, Kurokami laughed. He said, "Don't tell me, are you here to console me like Shinonome did back then? I suppose I have been rather down as of late. Forgive me, I must be causing many people trouble. But I can't help myself." He looked down at me apologetically.

Puzzled, I asked, "You're Kurokami, right? Not Akagami?"

The way Kurokami spoke was so gentle, much like how the gentle-hearted Akagami from the legend might speak.

"K-Kaori?!" Suimei worriedly said. I returned to my senses and realized how rude I'd been. I thought back to the what-if Nyaa-san had mentioned earlier and paled.

But Kurokami showed no sign that he minded, only gave a shrug and said, "I am indeed Kurokami. People would laugh at me if I called myself Akagami despite having pitch-black skin." He was right of course, since *aka* meant red in Japanese, while *kuro* meant black. He squinted sadly, a glittering tear running down his cheek. As it did, a cold wind howled by, dispelling any doubt as to whether Kurokami was the one bringing the winds to Cape Tappi.

Thank goodness. I feel like words could get through to this god, unlike with Yamakakachi. I steeled myself and said, "Pardon my mistake, Kurokami. As you say, I am here to calm your unruly heart."

He fixed his eyes on me, gave a light sniffle, and wiped his tears away. He smiled and nodded. "First the father and now the daughter. How nostalgic. I still remember that time Shinonome invited me to drink with him when I was moping."

So, it was true that Shinonome-san had used alcohol to calm the god. "How exactly did my father help you?" I asked.

"He pulled me away from here. Ha ha ha, took me all the way to Hokkaido, he did. We ate, drank our fill, and talked about a lot of things. That's when I heard about you."

"I see…" My plan wasn't too far off the mark then, it just had the unnecessary element of Dazai Osamu's *Tsugaru*. Thinking about it calmly now, there was no way anyone unfamiliar with the book would be interested in going to all the locations featured in it, plus I doubted a god had much interest in human culture to begin with. *I'm utterly floored by how book crazy I can get... Perhaps it would be best to withdraw and make a new plan?*

While I agonized over how to revise my plan, a black finger as thick as a log suddenly entered my field of view. It was Kurokami's. He looked at me with a slightly embarrassed blush and said, "All right. I've decided. I'll try out that proposal of yours."

"...Huh?"

"I don't know who this Dazai Osamu author you mentioned is, but your proposal sounds interesting. Show me around. While we're at it, it would be nice to hear more about that Dazai fellow as well. I could use the distraction for my aching heart."

He...liked the plan? I was stupefied. "Kurokami, have any other gods ever told you you're a bit strange?"

"Hm? Sorry, what did you say?"

"*Ack*—n-n-nothing! Nothing at all! I'm looking forward to guiding you around!"

Woo-hoo! That's the first step of the plan done! I grabbed Kurokami's bulky finger with both of my hands. He gave me a satisfied nod and looked off into the distance, surprising me with his sorrowful look.

"How fun," he began. "While we're at it, can I ask you take this opportunity to learn about me? Not the me from legend but who I truly am?" A strong gust of wind blew as a large tear fell from one of his huge, dawn-colored eyes.

"Hm? Yes, of course."

"Good. Good, good…"

Hm? What was up with that? This god really is a bit strange, I thought, mystified by his request. There was a tiny, tiny bit of unease inside me, like a puzzle piece that wouldn't fit into its slot.

"I'd like to promptly begin preparations if the plan's been decided. There's a lot we need to cover," Karaito Gozen said.

"O-of course!"

But I wasn't given time to figure out the source of my unease. With a faint, lingering feeling that something was off, I joined my friends to work on the preparations.

※

Two days later, we completed our preparations and were ready to begin our *Tsugaru* pilgrimage.

Dazai Osamu journeyed to Tsugaru on May 12th, 1944 (Showa 19). He took the night train from Ueno to Aomori and visited his acquaintances one after another.

"This is about the same time of year that Dazai made his journey to Tsugaru," I said.

"Is that right? Well, he chose a good time to visit. Now's when the flowers bloom."

Cherry blossoms, plum blossoms, apple blossoms—a wide variety of flowers chose May to bloom, making it the Tsugaru Peninsula's most beautiful season. The blooming period also happened to overlap with the Golden Week holidays, so people often held flower-viewing parties, the most famous of them being Hirosaki Park's cherry blossom festival. Seeing the park's flowers in full bloom was wonderful, but nothing could compare to the sight of Hirosaki Castle's moat filled to the brim with fresh-fallen cherry blossom petals.

"When Dazai first arrived in Aomori, he commented on how cold the northwest was. It's a bit warm for us right now, so it's kind of hard to relate."

"You're right. If anything, it's almost clammy."

Kurokami and I conversed as we made our way southward across the coastline of the Tsugaru Peninsula. Of course, we couldn't feasibly walk side by side, what with his size, so the whole group hitched a ride on his head, sitting on his soft hair and holding on to his black horn. He was dizzyingly tall when he stood, but he walked with care, so we didn't shake too much. Of course, normal humans couldn't see us. They just went about their lives below, unaware of our existence.

"Whoa, look how much hair he has! You could practically swim in this!" Kuro was having a blast, laughing as he rolled around in Kurokami's hair.

Nyaa-san flashed her claws, annoyed by the dog's behavior. "Be quiet, mutt. You're not a puppy, so simmer down a bit!"

"Hey, don't fight, you two!" Suimei stepped in out of worry they might accidentally hurt Kurokami and incur his wrath.

Far from it however, Kurokami laughed, tickled by their antics.

"You're different than I expected," I said to him.

"How so?" Kurokami asked.

"Well, I studied a bunch of your legends in preparation for this day, even the ones from Akita Prefecture, but they all portrayed you as a short-tempered sort of god."

At times, folktales and legends had different settings or events depending on where they were passed down, yet Kurokami was always painted as a vulgar, quick-tempered god who solved all his problems through force. It was possible all that had been added to highlight the difference between the powerful Kurokami and the artistic Akagami.

"That's why I'm surprised you're actually really kind and easy to talk to," I said.

His shoulders shook as he gave a jovial laugh. "Yes, I certainly was a wild one in legend. You must have been pretty worried thinking you'd have to deal with such a god. Not that most gods aren't selfish and unpleasant to begin with." He sounded as though it didn't concern him at all as he stepped over the national highway, carefully making sure not to squash any cars. Out of the blue, he asked, "So, what kind of person is this Dazai Osamu author to you?"

"Hm? As in specifically to me?"

"Yes. Oh, don't tell me, is he someone you know?"

"No, no. He's an author who passed away a long time ago." I carefully considered my words. "I've never met him, and he's not *exactly* famous, but, well... From the anecdotes surrounding him and through his stories, I have an image of what he was like. But it's hard for me to express that image, since I never actually met him, and it'll never be anything more than my personal belief of what he was like, not the whole truth. Only the gods know that."

Such was the case with any author, but particularly so with Dazai Osamu. He wrote many evocative works, but *No Longer Human* stood out as one of his most prominent and impactful.

The main character of *No Longer Human* was born into a well-to-do family in Aomori. Despite his high birth, he led a life full of tragedy that got worse as the story continued. The conflicts and internal dilemmas portrayed in the book were raw and gripping and drew the reader in without fail. Finishing the book left you with an indescribable sinking sense of guilt, like you had glimpsed something you weren't meant to see, and at the same time, a frisson of excitement. Dazai was that powerful of a writer; his words always found their way into the readers' hearts, intoxicating them.

It was thought that Dazai based a good portion of *No Longer Human* on his own experiences. While not everyone agreed, some believed *No Longer Human* fell under a Japanese literary genre known as I-Novels. I-Novels, called such because they were told in the first-person, were a common style of writing in that time period that made use of the author's own personal experiences. It was clear, however, that *No Longer Human* had fictional elements worked in as well, so it couldn't be considered a true I-Novel. Be that as it may, the fictional and real elements of *No Longer Human* were so wonderfully woven together, readers couldn't help but reach one particular conclusion: Dazai Osamu himself was no longer human.

"Those without more than a passing interest in Dazai might think of him as a terrible person. Perhaps they're right. He tried to drown himself many times, he was addicted to painkillers, and he had many lovers. Putting his writings aside, as a person, he wasn't a respectable man."

Kurokami suddenly stopped walking. "Lovers? You mean this author slept with women other than his betrothed?"

"Ack." A bead of sweat ran down my back. I had completely forgotten, but the goddess Kurokami loved had been taken away by another god. His heart had been broken, and there was no telling how aggravated he might get at the idea of a man being repeatedly unfaithful to his wife. I hemmed and hawed, "Th-that's, um, well, uh…"

To my surprise, however, Kurokami showed little interest in the topic. "How foolish. But perhaps all human men are like that? Please, continue."

What was that all about? I wondered.

"Is something the matter?" he asked when I remained silent.

"Oh… No, not at all. Let's see, where was I? Oh, right. There's no denying that Dazai lived a life many would consider shameful, and I completely understand why some might criticize him for that. Even so, I really like the Dazai portrayed in *Tsugaru*."

Unlike *No Longer Human*, *Tsugaru* was easily classified as an I-Novel. It was, after all, written through his very real experiences of visiting Aomori and the places of his past. Only scant bits of fiction were included. Readers even thought it was a travelogue when it was first published, although later research identified the book to be more of an I-Novel. As it should. Anybody who read the novel would understand the "I" in the book was based on Dazai himself.

Tsugaru was released to wartime Japan. At that time, the food reserves in Tokyo and various other areas were dwindling, causing many to beg those in the countryside for food. Dazai mocked such people. He wrote, "I didn't journey to Tsugaru to scrounge for food. I may look like a beggar in purple, but I come not to beg for white rice but for truth and love!" Although he also called the act of taking pride in hunger, "foolishly comical while also somewhat endearing." He had a good sense of humor but was a little prone to showing off, and a bit self-contradictory. That ignoble part of him seeped through his writing, and I loved it with all my heart.

"The protagonist of *Tsugaru* is quite the character, to say the least," I began. "In each place he visits, he always finds an excuse to drink. He's very cynical, in stark contrast to the simple people of Tsugaru, and he has the snobbery of a city-dweller but maintains the humble roots of a country-born man. In the book, there's this one scene where he reunites, for the first time in thirty years, with the person he thought of as a mother. That part really hit home for me; I even teared up the first time I read it. I believe this protagonist was Dazai himself, without any embellishments."

Remembering the book warmed my heart. I continued with a smile. "One couldn't travel freely during the time when the book was written, but that only makes the lengths he went to provide an entertaining story more apparent. In my mind, Dazai is an outstanding author."

Having finished what I wanted to say, I let out a tired sigh. I felt some worry. As I had mentioned before, it was difficult for me to explain Dazai and his work. There were still a lot of feelings pooled in my heart that remained beyond expression. I hoped I'd conveyed some of what I'd wanted to.

I glanced at Kurokami's face, trying to gauge his reaction. To no one in particular, he muttered, "I see... So, the Dazai you see and the Dazai the masses see are different men." He began to laugh, causing his body to shake. I hung on to his horn for dear life. He smiled and said, "Sorry about that, ha ha. This Dazai fellow is very interesting. Please, tell me more about him."

"Really? Of course!" I grinned as my heart raced happily, elated to share an author I liked with another. This was but one of the many joys of being a reader. I felt my eyes welling up from the sheer joy. *What should I talk about next?*

A small hill came into view. Around its peak were a number of stone slabs, as well as Karaito Gozen, who had gone ahead to prepare. This was Kanran Hill, only a short distance away from Japan Rail's Kanita Station. It was the place Dazai went to for a flower-viewing party in *Tsugaru*. Sadly, there weren't many cherry blossoms left in bloom, making the pine trees all the more conspicuous instead. From atop the hill, there was a clear view of Mutsu Bay, and on clear days one could even make out the Shimokita Peninsula in the distance. A strong, briny breeze rolled in toward the mount where a monument to Dazai stood. It read, "He was a man who loved nothing more than to bring joy to others!" an excerpt from Dazai's novel *Justice and Smiles*. It had been erected by one of Dazai's closest friends.

"Let's move over there, Kurokami!" I said. "We prepared some Aomori sake and recreated the bento lunch Dazai ate here for you. The helmet crab should taste wonderful at this time of year!"

"Oooh. I'm looking forward to that."

"Of course, I have plenty more stories about Dazai to share. There's this part in the book where he sings Kanita's praises, then says, 'Now that I've praised Kanita a bit, surely no one can blame me for airing my grievances about this place as well?' And then he proceeds to do just that. There's also this part where he absentmindedly insults a more senior author, making the gathering they were at really awkward for everyone."

"What an eccentric man!"

"Heh heh. I have enough anecdotes about him to share for days!"

"Well, don't hold back on my account."

Kurokami and I laughed as we walked to Kanran Hill. I waved to Karaito Gozen, hoping that all this would truly console the god.

The sky was so clear it made the windstorms that buffeted me at Cape Tappi seem a world away. Violet crept closer on the horizon, slowly eating away at the rose-red sky. A cool wind that gently brushed my cheeks told me night was near.

"Wow, wow, wow! Dazai *really* liked Akutagawa Ryunosuke, huh?" Kuro said.

"Understatement of the century there," I replied. "People have found sketches Dazai drew of Akutagawa's likeness as well as pages he wrote with literally just Akutagawa's name written over and over."

"I guess becoming famous means all your embarrassing secrets eventually come to light. Kind of scary to think about," Suimei said.

After Kanran Hill, we made our way to all the other Dazai-related places, ending up at the last one—Shayokan, located in the town of Kanagi which itself was farther within Goshogawara City. Shayokan was the home where Dazai was born, since made into a museum. It was named after another one of his books, *The Setting Sun*, or *Shayo*. It had a blend of Japanese- and Western-style architecture with a classic East Asian hip-and-gable red-tiled roof. The whole estate, including the rice granary, was built from Aomori hiba cypress wood. The place had a profound air but a modern make, lending an impression indicative of the Meiji era.

Given Kurokami's size, we couldn't go inside the building. So instead, we had Kurokami cast a spell that prevented us from being seen by other people, and we all sat on the roof of Shayokan, talking about Dazai as we watched the evening sun.

"Dazai really respected Akutagawa Ryunosuke, so it comes as no surprise that he wanted to win the Akutagawa Prize." I was a bit emotional about this. The Akutagawa Prize was a biannual Japanese literary award that many authors aspired to win.

The others nodded understandingly at my explanation. Along the way here, they all seemed to have developed an interest in Dazai from hearing me talk to Kurokami. Kuro, of all people, was even planning on reading a book I recommended to him as soon as he got home, something that astonished Karaito Gozen. She maintained her total non-interest in books.

"Aaah... Today was fun! I feel like my spirits are really uplifted," Kurokami said with satisfaction. The earlier gloom on his face was gone without a trace.

"I'm glad to hear it," I said.

"Woo-hoo! You did it, Kaori!" Kuro exclaimed.

"Well done," Karaito Gozen said. "Look at how clear the sky is now; it's proof that Kurokami's turbulent heart has been calmed. It seems I was right to expect great things from the daughter of Shinonome."

"Ehe heh, you're too kind." I gazed out at the evening sun, so brilliantly red that it stung, and smiled. But I couldn't hold the smile. While I was relieved at accomplishing my goal, something clouded the happiness I should have felt.

"Kaori? Is something wrong?" Suimei immediately noticed something off with me, which I'd admit made me pretty happy.

I timidly looked up at Kurokami. He said, "Is there something you want to ask? We're strangers no more after today. Go ahead and ask whatever you like without any reservations."

"C-can I? Um, well..." I hesitated. There was a good chance what I wanted to ask would offend him. After getting to know Kurokami for a whole half-day, I had come to feel there was something about him that didn't add up. I even had an idea of *what* it was. The only problem was that it contradicted a major premise of his legend. I could be wrong. Even worse, this might not even be business I had any right sticking my nose in. But I had this gut feeling that if I didn't ask him here and now, Kurokami would revert to his same old lamenting self, once again causing the storms to return. That didn't sit right with me. He was kind enough to listen to me prattle on about an author he'd never heard of before. I wanted to help him. I wanted to let him overcome his worries.

I pushed my apprehensions aside and asked, "Um, let me apologize for what I'm about to ask first. I know full well how rude it is." I swallowed. My hands were clammy. My heart pounded. But I had made up my mind. Meeting his eyes, I asked, "Kurokami... Are you perhaps already over the goddess of Lake Towada?"

That very instant, a cold breeze brushed my cheeks. A shiver jolted down my spine as the wind picked up even further. Even so, I didn't look away from Kurokami's round, dawn-colored eyes. "If one is to speak of Dazai's life, they must surely touch on his relationships. There's Tanabe Shimeko, who tried to drown with him in Kamakura; his first wife, Oyama Hatsuyo; his second wife, Ishihara Michiko; his lover Ota Shizuko; and finally, Yamazaki Tomie, who he ultimately committed suicide with. Today I felt like I was walking on thin ice when mentioning Dazai's relationships—because of what happened with you and your goddess, but..."

Kurokami's hair fluttered in the air, the wind scattering it wildly. His eyes betrayed no emotion, but the wind continued to build.

"It was as though you didn't think anything of it at all," I continued. Back when I accidentally brought up the topic of Dazai's adultery, I wasn't sure how Kurokami would respond. I thought he might even blow a fuse, and all our work would have been for naught. But he had merely let it slide, saying, *"How foolish. But perhaps all human men are like that? Please, continue."* It made no sense for him to care so little if he were still a god with a broken heart.

The clear evening sky started to cloud over. Wind swirled, and we were at its center as the red glow turned to dark gray and our surroundings dimmed.

I kept on speaking to him, even so. "That led me to think maybe you weren't crying because of the goddess of Lake Towada anymore. If I'm right, and there's another reason you still cry, then please, let me help you."

Thunder clapped in the distance. The clouds around us swelled faster than I thought possible and hung low. I tried my best to hold down my tousled hair but made sure not to break eye contact with Kurokami for a single moment. "Tell me what's wrong," I said. "Let me return the favor you've done by listening to me gush about an author for a whole day."

The wind began to howl. The windows of the Shayokan rattled as though they might shatter any moment. The building itself trembled slightly, reminding me how terrifyingly high up we were. It wouldn't end prettily if I were to fall, but I wasn't about to run away.

Kurokami finally spoke. "Hmph. Allow me one question. In your eyes, what kind of god am I?"

I was caught off guard. I blinked, taking some time to think, and answered, "You are a very kind god. That was my first impression of you, and it is my impression of you still. Your kindness reminds me of the still ocean, and your eyes remind me of the morning sun. Your presence is comfortable, so much so that I want to talk with you even more."

It was the truth, but I felt a pang of fear because it hugely contradicted the image he had in legend. I worried he might shout, *"What do you know about me?!"* But he didn't.

A warm, briny breeze brushed my cheeks. I thought it strange as Kanagi was near the center of the Tsugaru Peninsula—far from the ocean—but my attention was soon stolen by the sudden ray of light that shone down from the sky. I looked up and saw a hole in the clouds above us, as though we were at the eye of the storm. From it, rose-red light poured through.

"Ha... Ha ha ha." I let my gaze drop and saw Kurokami trying his hardest to hold in his laughter. He wiped a tear from his eye, then reached out and brushed my cheek softly, like he was touching something frail. He said, "So that's how you see me. Not bad. Not bad indeed. You were able to see me for who I truly am, not my legend." He flashed me a grin before continuing. "It's as you say. I have long since moved on from that goddess. To be perfectly honest, I can't even remember her face anymore."

"Then why are you always crying?"

"Why...? Yes, why indeed... I'm not too sure how I could ever explain to you this jumble of emotions inside me." He gazed forlornly at the sinking sun on the horizon. "But I think it's because I am Kurokami. I *exist* to lament at Cape Tappi forever."

He began to speak of the time that followed his rejection; of the days full of nothing but tears, grief, and loneliness.

"I raged for some hundreds of years after the goddess rejected me. I resented her for stringing me along for so long, only to choose a god I'd defeated in a duel. Of course, I resented Akagami as well." He stopped to shrug before continuing. "But it didn't take long for all that resentment to run dry. It's as they say: Love born at first sight is fleeting; it comes as fast as it goes. Before I knew it, I was over her. The pent-up grudge I held against both of them soon faded, and I was left with nothing but my own self-hate. Full of regret, I kept asking myself: What could I have done to make her choose me? What was it that was so wrong about me?"

Kurokami ruminated on those questions for many years. Eventually, he came up with an answer: It was wrong to think that strength alone could win someone's heart.

"From that day forward, I set about changing myself. I started lending my ear to the cries of the birds and tried to understand the beauty of the sunset on the horizon. I began watching the schools of fish dance in the waters and practiced softening my tone to sound more intellectual, like Akagami."

Oh... So that's why I mistook him for Akagami when we first met, I thought.

"Thanks to that, I've become who I am now. I no longer use violence to get my way and have come to love the world and its nature. I am surrounded by things dear to me and am satisfied by that alone. I'm no longer a god who laments over his heartbreak, so my sadness should fade in time... Or so I thought." A strong gust of wind blew past. Large, crystal ball-sized tears fell from his dawn-colored eyes. "No matter how many years passed, my tears wouldn't stop. The winds at Cape Tappi kept storming almost year-round."

His large tears scattered into the wind the moment they fell. I watched, spellbound, as they glistened in the evening sunlight before fading to mist.

"That's when I finally realized," he said. "No matter how much I change, I will always lament for as long as I am Kurokami. It doesn't matter how I feel. It is my role to summon the winds of Cape Tappi continually, for I am the god who grieves his heartbreak forever, as is told in legend."

As long as a god had a legend, they could not change from it. No cruel god could miraculously change into a kind one. How they were perceived in their legend bound them to who they were. Those perceptions were also nearly impossible to change, for people have passed down the same legends for generations on end. Even Kurokami himself wasn't free from holding on to such perceptions, as he had called other gods selfish and unpleasant, an impression that was widely shared by the world, myself included. Of course, this also meant the gods who were considered wild and unruly were, in fact, only acting in accordance with the popular perceptions of them. Take Yamakakachi for example: as a mountain god, she *had* to detest women, as per her legend.

"No matter how much I myself change, I will always be the god of Cape Tappi whose sighs formed the Tsugaru Strait and whose weeping makes the winds blow. My legend is set in stone." He smiled, defeated, tears still falling from his eyes. "Occasionally, I lose control of myself and cause the winds to storm more than usual. Continually crying even when you're not sad does a number on the mind, you see. Aha ha. I'm sorry that I've caused everyone so much trouble. But then again, perhaps that's just what gods do."

Kurokami struggled with the disparity between his true self and his self in legend, as well as the fact that he was a god. Looking back on his words over the course of our day together, I could see some of that struggle reflected here and there.

"While we're at it, can I ask you take this opportunity to learn about me? Not the me from legend but who I truly am?"

"I see... So, the Dazai you see and the Dazai the masses see are different."

I wanted to help him somehow, but was there anything I could do? I thought for a moment. "Can I ask you something? Why have you continued to stay at Cape Tappi? You visited many different places with us today, so it's not like you're bound to the place. Why not go, when it clearly hurts you to stay?"

Kurokami's eyes swelled with tears again. His lips trembled slightly. "I stay for the birds."

"The birds?"

"The birds. They need my wind to cross the sea."

Cape Tappi was known among birdwatchers as an excellent place to observe migratory birds as they crossed from Honshu to Hokkaido and back the other way around. Such was especially true now, since birds migrated in the spring. Many birds of prey visited the area to hunt during these periods, and the skies of Cape Tappi bustled with activity.

"I didn't realize it at first," Kurokami began to explain. "After all, the wind was a byproduct of my raging emotions. I never would have thought it could be used by anything or anyone."

Before he knew it, the wind he inadvertently blew became the lift those small creatures needed to sail across the waters. Admirers even gathered to watch them.

"What's more, you humans have even put up wind turbines. I couldn't believe it, ha ha... My wind was being used for so many different things. Life will always find a way, I suppose. But it's because of all this that I've decided, no matter how much I despair over my fate, I'll remain at Cape Tappi as long as my wind is needed."

You really are kind, Kurokami... My chest and eyes warmed. Like a puzzle piece had finally slid into place, an idea came to mind, one that might just free Kurokami from the legend that bound him. My heart raced as I stood up, spread my arms wide, and yelled, "Kurokami!"

He gave me a look of surprise, tears still pouring from his eyes.

"Can you bring your face a little closer?" I asked.

"Huh? Why?"

"Don't worry about it, just come closer! Before I fall off the roof!"

"Huh?" He gave me a quizzical look but obliged regardless.

I flashed a toothy grin and hugged his large nose as hard as I could, causing him to blink with confusion. "You've done your best, Kurokami!"

"Huh?" I'd bewildered him even further. He froze, mouth open and a blank look about him.

"You're an amazing god, always trying your best for someone else's sake even when it's hard. I know of no other god that's willingly gone through as much pain as you have. Maybe I'm not the one to say it but, thank you! I mean it!"

"You're...thanking me?"

"Your sadness has helped many, and not just humans. Thank you." I put a tad more strength into my hug. I let go and looked straight into his dawn-colored eyes. "I have an idea! Let's write a continuation of your legend!"

"What? I...I don't understand."

"Your legend, Kurokami! Let's continue it! Maybe something like..." I began to gesture with my hands as I continued. "Kurokami, the god who created the Tsugaru Strait, changed after many years. He became a kind and considerate god. When the birds came, he aided them with his winds. And so, the birds loved the god and showed their gratitude by gifting him with lovely songs before their crossing... Something like that!"

This wouldn't be the legend of a Kurokami racked with grief but of a Kurokami who spent his days happily.

"Legends don't have to be unchanging. Whether those legends are folktales, myths, or something else entirely; they can alter with the passage of time and the changing of storytellers, especially during the era of oral storytelling. It might be harder now, with all the different mediums of recording information available, and it might take a really long time, but I believe that I can change your legend! And I won't be alone—I'll ask the spirits I know to help by continuing to tell your story long after I'm dead! If we succeed..." I gestured for Kurokami to finish my sentence.

"I won't have to keep crying forever?"

"That's right!" Beaming, I clenched my fist. "Please, let us help you. I can't promise results soon, but they will come! I'm sure of it. Spirits live long lives. Given enough time, this plan is sure to work. What do you say?"

Kurokami thought for a moment. "Why are you willing to go so far? We've only just met today."

I was stunned for a moment by his unexpected reply, but soon after broke into a smile. "What are you saying? It's because I've come to like you, duh!"

That instant, wind began to blow around Kurokami, hard enough to make breathing itself difficult. The windows rattled, and I heard something somewhere tumble over in the gale. The low-hanging clouds above were blown away, revealing the sky's evening glow and recoloring my world rose red. The winds passed, returning everything to silence. Out of nowhere, cherry blossom petals began to gently flutter down from the sky like rain.

"Ah..." For the briefest of moments, I was worried I'd angered him. But such worries proved groundless.

"You really are just as Shinonome described. Cute and adorable." The god before me smiled broadly, the evening sun reflected in his dawn-colored gaze. "I think I'll take you up on your offer. I look forward to the day when I can become a peaceful god."

The tears that flowed from his eyes had changed. Now, they shone with the radiance of gems.

"That was actually pretty terrifying... I thought my heart would stop for a moment," Suimei said.

"Me too..." Kuro said.

"I can't count how many times I was about ready to grab Kaori and run," Nyaa-san said.

"Well, I never lost faith. I believed Kaori would pull it off the whole time," Karaito Gozen claimed.

Suimei, Kuro, Nyaa-san, and I were making our way back to the spirit realm while Karaito Gozen tagged along to see us off.

"Sorry, did I make you guys worry with that whole thing at the end?" I asked. They stared off into the distance with exhaustion.

"To be honest, I'm not entirely surprised. You're always doing reckless stuff without thinking," Suimei said.

"What he said. I've long since given up on trying to stop you," Nyaa-san said.

"Yeah... It's like, 'Oh, there she goes again' at this point, honestly," Kuro said.

"Wha—guys?! You're joking, right?!"

They laughed back at me.

"At any rate," Karaito Gozen began, "you've successfully calmed Kurokami. We won't have to worry about him for a while, and I should be able to progress with my work now. I have nothing but gratitude, Kaori." She wore a friendly smile. "I am very impressed by your declaration that you intend to change the unchangeable. Incidentally, are you free this weekend?"

"I should be. Why?" I replied.

She smiled enthusiastically. "It occurs to me that your plan and all the ingenuity behind it was only possible because you've read so many books, so I was thinking maybe I should try reading some as well. Would you be so willing as to help me choose some?"

"But I thought you weren't interested in books!"

"I've been changed by you, it seems. Or is that not allowed?"

Wait. If I play this right, I might be able to make a new book-lover friend! Nodding my head furiously, I grabbed her hand. "I'd be glad to help! There are so many books I can recommend. I'm sure you'll be able to find one you like! I'll be waiting for you at our bookstore in the spirit realm!"

A gentle, briny breeze brushed past my cheeks. It was warm to the touch like all the wind that swept around the Tsugaru Peninsula in spring. The breeze continued toward the heavens and joined the soft clouds in the sky.

INTERMISSION
Moments Blending Together

Something fluttered in the air, illuminating its surroundings with a phosphorescent glow. It was a butterfly, one native to this mysterious and beautiful realm. It flitted about, basking in its newfound freedom after escaping its butterfly cage, and it made its way further into the eternal night.

This realm, a stranger to sunlight, was today in darkness yet again. What little starlight reached there failed to penetrate all the way into the backstreets, which were crowded with the undesirables. With a splash, a nameless spirit sipping muck by the roadside fled from the yellowish luminance of the butterfly. A cool breeze blew through. It rustled the leaves of garden trees and lifted the butterfly away, making the townscape below grow more and more distant by the minute.

The butterfly saw the town as it was in spring. Heavy traffic lined the streets between antiquated wooden buildings. An upbeat Tofu-kozo spirit hawked his wares as he carried tofu on a pole slung over his shoulder. A goldfish seller waited patiently as a little oni appraised his goods. An open-till-late ramen shop run by a Tsurube-otoshi spirit buzzed with customers.

The humidity the rainy season would bring had yet to arrive, and the fatigue of the previous winter was slowly being healed by the amiable spring weather. The butterfly enjoyed a leisurely waft through the air as it descended to the center of town. It flitted past many jovial spirits—practically brushing against them—before suddenly being crushed by an outstretched hand.

The bits of the butterfly fell unceremoniously to the ground. The hand that crushed it belonged to a man wearing a fox mask. The fox mask had thin, narrow eye slits and was white like clouds on a sunny day. Unlike a sunny day, however, the man wearing the mask was cheerless. He wore a British-style three-piece suit that gave him an air of elegance, belied by the piercing, cold stare behind the mask. It was a stare that betrayed his killing intent, sharp like a naked blade honed by cutting down dozens. He made no effort to hide this bone-chilling brutality, and an unnatural clearing formed along the glimmerfly-lamp-lit street as people swerved to avoid him.

Next to the man, a terribly polite youth stood. "The job proved easier than I first thought," he said. "All I had to do was wear the skin of their fellow Tsuchigumo and I was able to slip by unnoticed. You should have seen the looks on the faces of those fools as I walked up, cut them down, and made off with a few of their newborn children. Ah... Remembering it makes me smile! I don't think I'll be forgetting this anytime soon." The youth smiled broadly. Unlike the man, his clothes were of a modern style. He wore a hooded sweatshirt in place of an undershirt, over which he wore a dark-blue, hakama-less kimono woven with pongee. His kimono sash was fixed in place by a belt, and he wore a fedora hat at an angle. His face was slender, femininely so. He looked at the masked man with passionate eyes and a flushed face and asked, "I did well, right? I tried my best! Was I of any use to you, Master?"

The youth took his hat off, revealing hair with red highlights. He leaned forward, hoping for a pat on the head.

"Yes, you did well, Akamadara." The man reached out a gloved hand and gave the youth's head a perfunctory pat.

The youth beamed, making an expression that would make most women swoon. "Oh...! I'm so happy. I would do anything if it's for you, Master. Now, what will you have me do next? Ask away."

A pair of voices louder than the other passersby made themselves distinct.

"C'mon, Kinme! Hurry up! Nurarihyon's going to lose it if we're late!"

"Oh, please. You just want to look good for Kaori, don't you?"

"Wh-what?! Don't be stupid! Let's go!"

"Aha ha. Your face is beet red. You're so easy to read."

It was the Tengu twins, Kinme and Ginme. They weaved through the crowd of spirits on the street, joking around all the while. The man watched the pair through his fox mask.

"Ah, forget it! Go ahead and be late, you dork! I'm going ahead!" Ginme began to run, his face flushed. Kinme shrugged and looked at the masked man indifferently as he moved past, perhaps taking notice of the eyes on them. For a brief instant, Kinme's eyes narrowed into a sharp glare, but after a moment he trotted off after Ginme.

"...I've found a new toy." The man said.

"I understand completely. Please allow me, your loyal servant, to handle this." Akamadara sneered and locked his gaze on to the twins, his eyes the color of ripened pomegranate. He followed after them and faded into the crowd.

The man slowly pulled out a silver-colored hip flask from his breast pocket. He slid his mask up and drank from it, then licked his lips. His tongue was a dusky red, like the color of half-rotted innards.

SIDE STORY

Life in a World That Cast Us Aside

KINME AND GINME were abandoned as children. There wasn't anything particularly wrong with them; in fact, they were rather healthy compared to other raven chicks. Their nest wasn't attacked by any snakes or other beasts. The weather was good, and there were plenty of nuts and bugs around to eat. By all indications, they were on track to grow into perfectly ordinary ravens. And yet one day, their mother stopped returning to their nest.

The reason for their abandonment remained unknown. Their mother stopped coming to feed them one day, only watching them chirp at a distance. A few days later, she disappeared altogether. In Kinme's own words, it was like she had given up on raising children. The newborn chicks were left alone, unable to feed themselves and in an all-too-small nest built from bits of junk and twigs. There were only two things they could do: Wait for a mother that would never return and chirp until their voices gave out.

One day, Kaori asked the twins about that time.

Ginme said, "I kept chirping because I believed our mother would return. I thought, 'There's no way she would let me die; I still have so much more of my life to live!'"

Kinme, on the other hand, said, "I knew our mother would never return, but I kept chirping anyway. I was ready to die... But Ginme was chirping, so I had to as well."

Regardless of how differently they felt, they continued to chirp for their mother with all they had. They chirped through day and night, even as their voices began to tire, but their mother never came. Before long, they were too weak to chirp. A storm blew their nest down from its tree, and the twins huddled on the ground together and prepared for their end. They trembled as they looked up at the tree that had been their home and imagined the face of death creeping in from the dark perimeter of their fading vision. But their lives did not end there, for something peered into the nest. It was not a starving predator, nor the raven's natural enemy, the snake.

"Look, Nyaa-san, look! Birds! Baby birds!" Peering into their nest was a little girl with puffy, rosy cheeks. That moment was the turning point of their lives. The little girl would care for the twins and eventually entrust them to Sojobo of Mount Kurama to become raven Tengu.

The twins were born from the same mother, raised under the same circumstances, lived through the same struggles, and became the same type of spirit. The lives they led were exactly the same in every way, but their personalities couldn't have been more different.

"I owe my life to Kaori, so I gotta use it to help others as much as I can! It sucks that I was abandoned, sure, but I gotta live my life facing forward!" Ginme could smile in spite of his harsh past.

"Honestly, I'd rather Kaori didn't bother. I'd have been perfectly fine dying that day if it meant I could die together with Ginme. Ah, life's so boring. Won't something interesting come rolling along?" But Kinme hid behind a false smile, caging himself in a world too small for him.

It looks similar. So very similar...

Spring in the human world was remarkably agreeable. Its warm weather could easily lull someone to sleep, and its winds caressed one's cheeks without the smell of mold that lingered in the spirit realm.

A gentle shower from the heavens dampened the earth, the sight of which stung a pair of eyes that were accustomed to darkness. Kinme squinted his droopy eyes, scowling as he looked up. There stood a perfectly ordinary broadleaf tree. What sort of broadleaf tree it was, exactly, was a bit of a mystery; it was such a commonplace tree that nobody would bother to check. It was, however, certainly not an evergreen. The only thing at all distinct about the plain tree was that one of the thicker branches bore a resemblance to the branch that hosted the nest where the twins were born.

That tree is an eyesore. I should cut it down. Yes... I should cut it down right now.

"Heeey, Kinme!"

Kinme's troubling thoughts were interrupted by a carefree voice... No, perhaps a boundlessly sunny voice was a more accurate description. It was the other twin, Ginme. Ginme, with his cheery silver eyes and his face the spitting image of Kinme's, strolled toward his brother. He had a number of small cuts here and there on his face that were new to Kinme. His jet-black hair had spider webs and leaves tangled in it, and his entire body was sopping wet.

"Whoa. What happened to you?" Kinme asked.

"Ha ha ha! I was flying when I got some rain in my eye! Flew straight into a branch."

"Are you an idiot? What are you doing flying in the rain?" Kinme picked the leaves out of Ginme's hair and unintentionally let a laugh slip out. He followed up by scrubbing Ginme's face with a towel.

Ginme smiled bashfully. "Anyway, did you find anything? I came up dry myself."

"Har har," Kinme smiled. "Who do you think I am? Of course I found something."

"Whoa, you're awesome! Dang, I wish I had your smarts."

"I'm sure you could if you'd study for once. Not that that'll ever happen."

"Oof. Truth hurts. So, where's it at?"

"Right there." Kinme pointed to the base of a tree. Lying beneath the dense undergrowth was something roughly the size of a basketball. Its black and red color was out of place against the surrounding greenery, dyed darker by the rain.

Ginme slowly approached it, then let out a sad groan. "They were abducted and brought to the human world after all. Poor things." At the base of the tree were the remains of a spirit child. Their appearance was a mix between a human and a spider, and their guts lay spilled before them. Their still-soft cheeks were caked with dirt and blood, and remained locked in an expression of fear.

Kinme and Ginme had come to these mountain recesses in the human world on Nurarihyon's request. He wanted them to help confirm or deny an unsettling rumor that had been spreading across the town, a rumor that humans were kidnapping children. This rumor originated from the incident a month ago when Tsuchigumo children were abducted. Tsuchigumo were already a rather aggressive spirit, so it wasn't unusual that they sought revenge. This time, however, they were particularly bloodthirsty for two reasons: The first was that somebody had snuck into their carefully hidden village, and the second was that the chief's child was one of the abductees. The culprit left behind clothes that smelled of human, which led them to believe a human was behind the crime.

"I hear it's not just the Tsuchigumo; there've been kidnappings happening all over the place. This child matches the description of one of the Tsuchigumo children though. It looks like they were killed for resisting. You think maybe it's an exorcist's work?" Kinme looked over Ginme's head at the corpse. Looking at it gave rise to no particular feelings in him. To him, it was just a hunk of dead meat, not something he could feel for.

"Dunno about that. Look at this." Ginme smiled a toothy grin and pointed at the youthful face of the corpse. It had eight eyes. "Wouldn't an exorcist have plucked out the eyes?"

"Oh, you might be right. I hear spider eyes are the perfect catalyst for spells. We might not be up against an exorcist after all. Nice one, Ginme."

"Heh heh, I guess even I can figure stuff out sometimes!" Ginme said boastfully.

Kinme skritched his brother's head as a reward. But Ginme's head soon moved away from Kinme's hand. Ginme crouched and peered curiously at the corpse, a restless look on his face.

"Hey, Kinme..." Ginme gave his brother a sheepish look. "I'm actually kinda hungry. Can I eat this kid?"

As raven Tengu, the twins were omnivorous. They could eat normal food, but they also loved to eat the corpses of other living things. Ginme in particular loved carrion. The smell whet his appetite. He looked at his brother with the gleaming eyes of a spoiled kid eagerly awaiting permission. Kinme just smiled kindly and shook his head. "No, Kinme. We have to bring the body back to Nurarihyon."

"Whaaat... C'mon! It's not like he'll learn anything by looking at the body. And I'm sure this kid would've rather I didn't go hungry!"

"You could ask for the body after he's done looking at it."

"It won't taste as good then!" Ginme whined, puffing out his cheeks. "It's just the right flavor at this level of decomposition!"

Kinme snickered. "Jeez, Ginme. If you keep throwing a tantrum, I might have to tell Kaori about all this."

"Wh-what?!"

"You're trying to act human around her, right? I wonder what she would think if she found out you ate a dead kid," Kinme teased. He enjoyed the look of Ginme's paling face, albeit with some conflicting feelings. "What'll it be? Do you still want to eat it?"

Ginme shook his head and quickly stood up. "No, I'll wait until we get back home to eat."

"Good boy. I found some akebia fruit over that way if you want some."

"Oooh! Heck yeah!" Ginme beamed.

Kinme flashed a smile at his brother but shot a sharp glare toward a nearby thicket. "Come on out already. Didn't anyone ever teach you it's bad manners to eavesdrop?"

The third party who'd been listening in bolted.

"Ginme!"

"On it!" Ginme ran off, eager to show off the results of his training with Sojobo. Kinme watched as his brother disappeared into the thicket, and he strained his ears to listen. Minutes later, Ginme brushed the thicket aside and returned, but alone. Kinme frowned. It was unusual for his brother to let someone get away.

"Kinme..." Ginme called. He looked strange, his usual happy-go-lucky attitude was gone, and he seemed ready to break into tears instead.

Kinme followed his brother a short distance. There, among the dense trees, was a giant withered tree with a trunk so big you would need ten people linking hands to surround it. Inside, it was a hollow.

"Here?" Kinme asked.

"Mm-hmm..."

It appeared their mysterious observer had fled into the hollow. Thinking that still didn't explain Ginme's sudden change in manner, Kinme peered in. The rich smell of the forest—all its dead leaves, dirt, water, and trees—tickled his nose. A chill colder than the open air touched his skin. The hollow was deep, continuing for at least five meters.

"Goo-goo... Ga-ga..." Inside was a baby around one year old. No, that wasn't quite correct. A baby it appeared to be, yes, but its age couldn't be determined. Its round, cute eyes were a dark green. Its hair was a pale blue-green like the forests in spring, and vines coiled around it and stretched across the ground. Its skin was tinged blue. Its nails were a yellow-brown amber. It wore no clothes—a pitiable sight in the chill of the mountains.

To the twins, it was obvious this was a spirit, which meant its age wasn't discernible from appearance alone.

"Goo-goo..." The spirit seemed incapable of speech. It curled up in the hollow and trembled. Its body was thin, its lips were cracked, and dark shadows had formed under its eyes. It was clearly weak.

"What is this, Ginme?" Kinme asked.

"Dunno. It looks like this baby was what was watching us earlier though."

I have a bad feeling about this. Kinme frowned, and Ginme let out a sad sigh. The same thought ran through their minds, the way it did sometimes for twins. Ginme clung to the hem of Kinme's robe worriedly. "This baby might be like us."

Kinme's head began to throb. He rubbed his temple to ease it. He looked at his brother to see him waiting expectantly. Kinme was the one who made decisions for the both of them. Ginme acted wildly at times, but he didn't actually make decisions himself, since he'd learned through experience that it was best to leave things to Kinme's careful thinking. For today, though, Kinme resented this state of affairs. This was too heavy a decision to shoulder alone. So instead, he avoided making any decision at all. "Let's take it to the bookstore. We should at least find out *what* it is before doing anything." He figured the people at the bookstore would be soft enough to take the baby burden away from him.

"Oooh, good idea! You're a genius, Kinme!" Whether he actually knew Kinme's true intentions, Ginme smiled broadly. Kinme let out a relieved sigh. He looked at the baby within the tree hollow.

"Goo...?" It trembled, still curled up. He doubted that it understood its life was in the hands of the two strangers before it. Thinking about that kind of responsibility gave Kinme nausea, but he bore it and plastered on a friendly smile, reaching out to the baby.

"You must've been so scared, being all alone. Come here, we'll help you."

The baby looked up innocently at Kinme and tilted its head in wonder.

"Oh my. That's a child born of a union between a human and a nonhuman. Where could its parents possibly be?"

Ginme blinked with surprise. He assumed it would take some effort to figure out the baby's identity, but Noname had solved the mystery the very instant the twins stepped into the bookstore. "Whoa. You're amazing, Noname! I can see the wisdom of your years!"

"*Excuse* me?! Perhaps you'd like me to sew that thoughtless mouth of yours shut?"

"Oh, whoops! Ha ha, my bad!" Ginme guffawed.

Noname lowered her fist. While she did often raise her voice, it was rare for her to actually get angry. Her fury was reserved for those who did truly unforgivable things—although it did seem she let Ginme get away with quite a lot. *Noname can be a bit of a nag at times, but she's a good person,* Ginme thought. He grinned and tilted his head to the side, causing Noname to sigh and roughly tousle his hair.

"What're you grinning for? Oh, whatever. So, you're certain

their parents weren't around?" Noname asked, looking at the baby. It was eating rice gruel thinned with hot water and had regained some of its vitality. It didn't fuss, just blankly looked up at the face of the one holding it, Kaori.

"Of course I checked, who do you think I am?" Ginme said.

"I'm just asking," Noname said. "The more animalistic spirits sometimes abandon their children if a stranger's smell gets onto them, just like actual animals."

"Huh? W-wait, what?!" Ginme began to pale. He threw himself onto his brother and, through tears, exclaimed, "K-Kinme! You don't think it was abandoned because I touched it, do you?!"

Kinme, who had been quietly listening up until then, looked at the baby with cold eyes. "Don't be stupid, Ginme. If that thing had half-decent parents around, it wouldn't be nearly so skinny. Look, you can see the outline of its ribs. It probably hasn't had a real meal in a while."

"Oh yeaaah... So, it wasn't my fault. Phew." Ginme breathed a sigh of relief, remembering how surprised he'd been when he picked up the baby and felt how light it was. His mood soon soured, however, as he realized its lack of weight was, in fact, not a good thing. "Dang... You think its mother is out there looking for it right now?"

Kinme let out a grandiose sigh and put on a disgruntled face.

"Hm? Something up, Kinme?" Ginme asked.

"Nothing," Kinme replied curtly. He turned his face away. Ginme was about to pursue the matter further when something soft touched his feet.

"Ba-boo!" It was the baby, who'd escaped Kaori's arms and crawled to him on its elbows. It tried its best to climb onto his legs.

Unable to resist the utter adorableness of the baby, he picked it up. "Hey, mind telling us your name, little one?"

"Ba-boo?"

"Ha ha, figures that wouldn't work. Man, you really are small." He carefully brought the baby closer to his face. When he'd held the neighbor's baby the other day, it had this hard-to-describe sweet scent. The baby he held now, however, smelled thickly of the mountains. It smelled of water and dirt and leaves, and of all the creatures that made the mountain their home. The smell was familiar to Ginme—it was the same one that had been by his side his whole life. When he first broke free from his shell, it was there. When he strained his voice to call for his mother, it was there. When he went to live on Mount Kurama, it was there. It was a smell dear to him, yet one that dredged up bitter memories.

"Huh. You're a strange little guy," Ginme said. He drew circles on the baby's chest, causing it to laugh ticklishly. *It's weird how a living thing can be so small,* he mused. *It's so frail too, like a wisp of wind would be enough to make it fade away...*

"So...what's the plan, boys?" The owner of the bookstore, Shinonome, spoke up. His displeasure was clear from his tone, and his eyes had a clear "don't go causing me any trouble" glint to them.

The twins shared a look, their shoulders drooping. Ginme asked, "Uh, what should we do? We didn't really have any grand plan in mind when we brought it here."

"How irresponsible," Shinonome sighed. "Let me guess, you wanted us to take care of it?"

"Yikes. He's got us pegged right out of the gate," Kinme said. "What do we do, Ginme?"

"What d'ya mean?" Ginme replied, flummoxed. "I wasn't thinking of pushing the responsibility onto anyone or... Wait, were you thinking of that, Kinme?!"

"I mean, it's not like we can take care of it. Or do you really think we could?"

"Well... No, I guess not," Ginme said reluctantly. His brother smiled broadly. Ginme trusted his brother's judgment—he always admitted that Kinme was the smart one—but he still had to wonder how Kinme could be so indifferent toward the baby. Didn't he know the pain of abandonment? "What the hell..." Ginme grumbled, the baby still in his arms. He had thought Kinme wanted to help the baby, like he himself did, but it turned out his brother only saw the baby as a problem to foist off onto someone else. *Why, Kinme?* he wondered. *Don't the two of us understand this baby's suffering better than anyone?* He stared hard at the baby and felt that it looked like his own helpless self, calling for their mother so many years ago. His frown was pained, his chest tightened, and he whispered, "You poor thing. I'm sure you want to see your mother again." He looked up and met everyone's eyes with determination. "I want to find this baby's parents."

"I see." The first to respond was Kaori. Her chestnut-colored eyes softened as she looked at Ginme with a gentle gaze. In an instant, he began to blush. He was fond of that gentle gaze of hers, but being on the receiving end of it was a little too much to handle.

He looked down sheepishly, but a hand ruffled his hair. It was Noname, her smile slightly exasperated but proud.

The next to speak was Shinonome, taking a puff of his pipe and scratching his chin. "Hmph. I suppose it wouldn't kill me to look after the baby while you're out searching."

A small fit of laughter escaped Kaori who gave her father a warm look.

"Just don't expect me to take this one in like I did with Kaori," Shinonome said. "I still got my hands full enough looking after her."

"Yeah, yeah," Kaori laughed.

How nice... Ginme thought enviously. Even though they weren't biologically father and daughter, he could feel the very real bond between them. He longed for a bond like theirs: one where a parent protected, loved, and raised a child they considered their own, and the child entrusted themselves to the parent in return, while also supporting their parent in times of need. It looked so wonderful to Ginme, and how could it not? He had a twin he wouldn't trade for the world, friends he treasured, even a master who cared for him—but a parent wasn't something you could obtain so easily. Buried under Ginme's smile, that sad truth always remained.

That's why I gotta find your mother, he thought with resolution, looking at the baby in his arms. *Even if you were abandoned, there has to be a reason. I'll get to the bottom of it and fix the bond between you two.* There was no doubt in his mind that the others agreed with him.

"Wait, are you guys for real?" An apathetic voice immediately betrayed Ginme's trust. All eyes looked with disbelief at Kinme's annoyed face. "What's the point of finding the baby's parents? They've already abandoned it once. They'll just abandon it again." Kinme's eyes were more devoid of warmth than Ginme had ever seen. His smile was insincere as he shrugged jokingly. "Or do you mean you want to help the baby find its parents so it can take revenge on them? Yeah, I could see that. I imagine it'd *love* to lop off the heads of the parents who betrayed it and savor the blood from their corpses!"

"Wh-what the hell are you saying, Kinme? What's wrong with you?!" Ginme yelled.

"What's wrong with me? What's wrong with *you*? Why are you so obsessed with finding some living trash who'd leave their baby out in the forest to starve? Nothing could possibly come of this. You're just going to end up hurting yourself."

"But we have to at least try!"

"Forget it, Ginme. Reality isn't as kind as you want it to be."

I know that well enough already! Ginme opened his mouth to protest but was too worked up to speak. He wanted to lash out angrily but hesitated to yell at his dear brother. *Goddamnit... How can you say such things, Kinme?!* "I...I thought you'd feel the same way as me," Ginme said, preparing for the worst. How could Kinme not agree with him? They were twins. Save for some slight differences, they should have been alike in every way imaginable, even in thought. He looked into the eyes of his other half, hoping he'd get an apology. To his dismay, Kinme averted his gaze.

"That's enough," a soft voice interrupted. A floral scent tickled Ginme's nose as a well-toned arm wrapped around his neck. He looked up to see Noname looking sorrowful. "There's no point arguing when we don't even know what the parents are like. First things first: we find the parents."

"Sh-she's right," Kaori quickly jumped in. "Let's calm down a bit, okay? This is a child's future we're dealing with; we should think this through carefully."

Future. That word resonated with Ginme, allowing his anger to fade. He took a deep sigh and thought: *That's right. This baby's future is on the line. I gotta pull myself together here.* He hugged the baby in his arms tightly and nodded. "Yeah, you're right, Kaori. We can figure out what to do *after* we find this kid's parents. Sorry, I got a bit heated there."

"Ginme…" Kinme called his brother's name. When his brother got flustered, he always turned to him for help. That was simply the way things were between them. Kinme was their decision maker. At least, he was supposed to be.

Without so much as a glance toward Kinme, Ginme bowed his head to everyone. "I swear, as the one who first found this baby, I'll do everything I can to find its parents. Only then will I worry about returning it."

The others looked around at each other and nodded.

"Very good, dear. We'll make sure to look after the child while you're out looking," Noname said.

"Let's hope we can find them soon," Kaori said.

"Hmph. Like I said, I'll help out too if I must," Shinonome said.

Kinme didn't say anything, but Ginme could have sworn he felt the hole his twin was boring into him with his stare. Even so, Ginme ignored him and flashed his usual grin.

Ginme consulted with the others a bit, and it was agreed that he would search for the parents starting tomorrow. He ate dinner and took a bath, but Kinme was nowhere to be found when he got out. Worried, he left the bookstore in search of his brother but ultimately couldn't find him.

"Kinme, where are you? Kiiiinme!" Ginme's voice echoed vainly throughout the town, fading away into the springtime night. "What's with you, Kinme?"

Ginme spent the night without his twin for the first time in a long while.

When Ginme awoke the next morning on the second floor of the bookstore, his brother was still missing. The bed he had laid out for Kinme showed no signs of being used. He scratched his head in frustration. "Damn it..."

Suimei, not as sound asleep as he'd appeared, opened his eyes a smidge. "Did you two have a fight or something?"

His words made Ginme think: *Did* they have a fight? No, that couldn't be. Fighting involved slinging mean words at each other and brawling. What happened yesterday couldn't possibly be a fight.

A myriad of thoughts and emotions filled his mind:

But I did ignore him yesterday...

No! It's his own fault for saying the things he said!

Why was he so against what I wanted anyway?

At his wits' end, he groaned loudly. "Gaaah! Suimei, what do I do?!"

"Pipe down. You'll bother the neighbors," Suimei calmly replied. His words went in one ear and out the other though, since Ginme was too racked with worry to listen.

"Suimeiiii! Help me!" In tears, Ginme clung to Suimei on the ground.

Suimei threw him off. Dark circles were under his eyes from a lack of good sleep. "Get off me. Think for yourself; you're not a child. Good grief, is this what Kinme has to put up with?"

"Ngh... How can you be so cold?! We're friends, aren't we?!"

"Since when did I agree to be your friend?" With that, Suimei pulled his blanket over his head.

"It wouldn't kill him to be a little nicer, would it?" Ginme muttered. Nobody was around to reply.

What the hell am I doing? Ginme thought, bitter at his own inability to think for himself. He had always left anything troublesome or difficult to Kinme, and now he was paying the price. *But I can't just do nothing. I swore I would find that baby's mother.*

Sluggishly, he put away his futon and dressed himself. He ate breakfast and got ready to leave in search of the baby's parents. The baby had been temporarily named Ao so that they had something to call the kid other than "the baby." Ao was left in the care of Kaori for the day, much to her joy, as she had little else to do, what with being stuck inside and all. "Take care, Ginme," she said.

"Ba-boo!"

"Y-yeah." Ginme blushed. He left, practically fleeing from the bookstore. With his face hot and the image of Kaori holding Ao seared into his mind, he'd already started to ask, "Hey, Kinme, why—" Before he remembered the fact that his brother wasn't around to help decipher his feelings. "...Right."

With a morose frown, he journeyed straight to the place where he'd found Ao.

There was no wind, only an endless, obscuring drizzle that hung in the air like fog. The forest where he'd found Ao was absent of sound, save for the pitter-patter of rain. Not a single bird or bug made themselves heard. It was too early in spring for the cicadas to cry, but that alone didn't explain why the forest seemed so devoid of life.

Huh. I didn't notice the last time I was here, but this place is kinda off. Ginme tried his hardest to think of a reason to explain the unnaturalness, his brain firing on all cylinders for the first time in ages. He soon gave up, however, once no good ideas came to mind. *Well, whatever! Maybe I'll figure something out if I keep going.*

The rain continued to pitter-patter against the ground. Something about the lack of sound other than rain amplified Ginme's loneliness. His wet clothes weighed on him.

Before long, the giant tree where Ao had been came into view. It was around twice the size of the surrounding trees. Ginme stared up at it and thought, *Wait... Do these kinds of trees grow this big...?* He could faintly recall the name of the tree: Japanese snowbell. It was a deciduous tree found all across Japan. They typically only grew to be around ten meters tall and had oval-shaped fruits that foamed when crushed and put into water, which was why they had been used as a soap in the past. Their fruit wasn't fit for consumption since it had a harsh taste and was toxic, something Ginme would never forget after receiving a nasty scolding from Sojobo for eating one.

It doesn't look like this tree's doing that great though. The massive tree was half withered: its leaves were speckled with holes, presumably from bugs; gall had formed on the edge of its branches; and its buds were tiny despite the imminent flowering season. Ginme could tell at a glance that many diseases and pests plagued it. Its days were numbered. He gently stroked the tree's bark and whispered to it. "You have it rough, yet you still protected Ao. Thank you."

He entered the tree's hollow. It was dim inside, and the air was damp. He searched carefully for any clues. He didn't know *what* Ao's parents were, but he figured they had to leave some kind of footprint behind. In the end, however, all he managed to find were the tracks Ao had left from crawling.

Hm? Ginme noticed a long, thin vine dangling from the ceiling. Its end was strangely soft. He touched it, and a tiny amount of fluid oozed out. He brought his fingers close to his face and thought it smelled vaguely sweet. *Maybe Ao was suckling on this like a pacifier?* Young children often put things in their mouths, so that made sense. He nodded, convinced. He felt some uncertainty in the back of his mind but couldn't understand why.

Finished with his investigation, Ginme lay down flat on the ground. He took a deep breath and filled his lungs with the thick scent of the tree. Quietly, he muttered to himself. "I wonder what Kinme's doing..."

He slowly closed his eyes and listened to the sound of rain quietly drumming in his ears.

"This rain won't let up," Kinme muttered, focusing on the sounds of the weather. It had continued unabated since yesterday and showed no signs of stopping. It drenched the trees, seeped through the earth, flowed into the rivers, raised the water level, and alarmed the humans by setting a rainfall record.

Kinme was on the same mountain as Ginme, but he was quite some distance away—right by a simple, old clinic run by an elderly physician. Kinme hid in a tree behind the clinic, carefully watching people come and go. The soft smile he usually wore was gone, and his eyes were bloodshot with dark circles underneath.

"What am I even doing here...?" He sighed and rubbed his throbbing temples. The image of Ginme's bewildered face, near tears, lingered at the forefront of his mind, as well as the way his brother had refused to look at him. Because of it, Kinme had been unable to sleep a wink all night. Never in his life had he felt this conflicted.

"Ginme, you idiot," he muttered, not that Ginme was around to hear. "Maybe I'm the real idiot." Kinme lay down on the branch, regret swirling inside his heart. Ginme was his light. No matter how rough or tough things got, Ginme was always there to illuminate his way forward. Kinme might have been the decision maker between them, but the one who kept him from wandering onto the wrong path was Ginme. Kinme was sure he would have gone morally astray at some point without his brother. He loved Ginme for that, and yet he'd still hurt him.

"How can you be so positive? I don't understand you." The reason Kinme had been so stubborn yesterday was because this whole baby situation reminded him of what his own mother had done. In Kinme's mind, abandoning a child was an unforgivable act, so seeing Ginme willing to give Ao's parents a second chance infuriated him. "You're too naive, Ginme. Not everyone in this world can be trusted." He sighed again. "If you keep opening your heart to others without thinking, you'll just get tossed aside again. You fool…" But no matter how he berated his absent brother, it wouldn't fix a thing. In fact, the only thing it achieved was lowering his own spirits. Kinme smiled derisively to himself at that realization.

Just then, he heard two voices.

"Thank you for all your cooperation. I'll come by again."

"Please do. Take care on your way home."

Kinme watched as the door of the clinic swung open and a person—a police officer—stepped out. The officer bowed to the elderly physician, threw on a raincoat, and got on their motorcycle. Kinme swiftly hopped off the tree and spread his jet-black wings, following the officer.

"I won't let anyone hurt Ginme," Kinme whispered with determination. His words reached nobody, drowned out by the rain.

A week had passed since Ao was found. Ginme was beginning to grow worried, but it wasn't just because he hadn't found Ao's parents.

"Agoo! Manma!"

"No! It's dangerous!" Kaori's voice echoed throughout the living room of the bookstore. She rushed forward and wrapped her arms around a child that looked about five years old and wore a navy-blue yukata. The child seemed to want to leave the room and tried their hardest to break free from Kaori's grasp. Unfortunately, children didn't know their own strength: The child's flailing bruised Kaori greatly.

"H-hey!"

"That's *enough*! Cut that out!"

Ginme was about to step in and help, but Suimei beat him to the punch. He grabbed the child from Kaori's arms and hugged them tightly to prevent any more thrashing.

"Calm down. Everything's okay." He patted the child's back and soothed them. After a few minutes passed, the child finally began to calm down.

"Uuhn... Manma... Manma..." The child wrapped their arms around Suimei's neck and began to nod off.

Kaori breathed a sigh of relief. "Thank you, Suimei. I definitely couldn't have handled that on my own."

"It's fine," he replied, swaying gently to lull the child to sleep. "Surprisingly, this kid's quite the handful."

"They must really miss their parents," Kaori mused.

The child was Ao. Ao had grown explosively in the short week they were at the bookstore, their toddler's physique changing to resemble that of a child several years older. However, the same couldn't be said for the child's mind. While Ao had grown physically, they were still the same baby inside.

Spirits had incredibly short childhood developmental stages, more similar to a wild animal's than a human's. But even considering that, Ao's growth was still abnormally fast, leaving everyone perplexed.

"I'm sorry, none of this would have happened if I hadn't brought the kid here. Are you okay, Kaori?" Ginme asked. He reached out to touch the bruise on her cheek but stopped halfway there and cast his gaze downward instead.

"It's fine, I'm the one who agreed to look after Ao," Kaori said with a smile. Her expression clouded as she looked at the cherubic face of Ao, sleeping in Suimei's arms. "And, well... you're not the only one who wants to reunite them with their parents."

"...Right." Ginme gritted his teeth. He remembered Kaori had also grown up separated from her mother.

"Ugh, it's no good. I can't figure out what spirit this kid's parent is." Shinonome appeared, a disgruntled look on his face. In his hands was a large stack of books, presumably the ones he had gone through in the hope of finding some sort of clue. "Clearly, trees are involved somehow, so I initially thought they might be a Kinoko or something."

He sat himself down at the low dining table and began leafing through one of the books with a sour look on his face. Kinoko spirits were a type of mountain-dwelling child spirit with origins around Yoshino in Nara Prefecture. They were said to look around three or four years old and wear either leaves or blue clothing.

"But I've never heard of a Kinoko mating with a human. What's more, this kid's growing far more than what's described in Kinoko tales. Kinoko are child spirits *precisely* because they don't grow past childhood. Ao's parents must be something else entirely." It seemed not even Shinonome, with all his spirit-related expertise, could figure out what type of spirit Ao's nonhuman parent was. He scratched his head roughly, vexed, and packed tobacco leaves into his smoking pipe with an air of defeat.

I feel like I've caused a lot of trouble for everyone... Ginme thought. He was frustrated by his inability to find so much as one clue as to the identity of Ao's parents. As the days continued to pass fruitlessly, he felt a creeping, growing conviction that things would have turned out differently if Kinme were around. "I'm sorry, everyone. I can't do anything without Kinme." He hadn't seen Kinme since the day he vanished. Kinme had apparently swung by Mount Kurama to see Sojobo, but he hadn't come anywhere near the bookstore. This was the longest the twins had been apart, and that fact hurt Ginme a lot.

"What the heck are you saying?" Suimei said, shooting Ginme a puzzled look. He had just put Ao to sleep in a futon laid out in the corner of the room. "That's not anything new."

"Urk... That's harsh, man..." Shocked, Ginme crumpled onto the floor, eventually falling flat on his side. He felt the cool touch of tatami mat on his cheek and glared at Suimei.

Suimei returned the glare with a mystified look. "C'mon, where'd that backbone go? The one you had when you attacked me on our very first meeting?"

"Hey, that was a misunderstanding. I even apologized."

"You're not listening. I'm asking where the Ginme who didn't give a damn about the trouble he caused others went. You've never been the type to behave."

"What...? Really?" Ginme mumbled. *Whoa. I had no idea I was such a jerk.* He felt the urge to cry begin to rise as Suimei continued on, expressionless as always.

"I don't know what you two are fighting about, but the twins are meant to be together. Rather than moping around, you should hurry up and make up with him." Suimei gave Ginme a chop on the head. "Oh, and you're not the only one who can't do anything without the other. In fact, I'd say your twin's more useless without you than you are without him. Man, you really need to learn to think for yourself. How am I teaching you about your *own* brother, you birdbrain."

"...What?" Ginme blinked. *Kinme's useless without me...?* Ginme had a hard time believing Suimei's words. Kinme was amazing, clearheaded, calm... He could do—

"*Ginme...*"

Ginme heard a voice call out from the depths of his mind. It was the voice he'd heard when he proclaimed his intention to find Ao's parents, the very one he ignored out of sheer stubbornness. He tried to recall how his brother's voice had sounded: Was it the same as always? It certainly didn't sound shaky, nor did it sound worried. Ginme thought back to the look of his brother's face then: the same forlorn look he had when they were calling for their mother from their nest.

Ginme bolted upright and stared at Suimei. Seeing that new life had been breathed into him, Suimei gave a rare smile. He spun around and said, "Go. Don't leave him waiting long."

"R-right!" Ginme replied, still finding his bearings. A surge of emotion rose in his chest, and he hugged Suimei from behind.

"Wh-what the hell are you doing?!" Suimei resisted the hug, twisting his body and pushing against Ginme's face.

"Suimei, you rock! You really are my friend!"

"I said I'm *not* your friend! How many times do I gotta tell you?!"

"Aww, don't be shy! Once I make up with Kinme, let's all go hang out together somewhere!"

"No way! Not in a million years! And hurry up and get off me! You'll wake up Ao!"

"Sorry, pal, but I'm the Ginme who doesn't care about causing problems for others!"

"Don't you dare use my own words against me!"

Sure enough, Ao began to stir from the noise. The pair froze. Meekly, they looked over and saw Ao resume sleeping peacefully. They breathed a sigh of relief together.

"Get going already. Jeez," Suimei said with a weary look.

"Heh heh! I'll be off then." Ginme grinned. He made for the veranda past the sliding door, moving quietly so as to not wake up Ao. He slid his zori thonged sandals on and stretched his back. *Aaah... Racking my brain trying to think really isn't for me! I should hurry up and find Kinme...then tell him how I feel!*

"Stay safe, Ginme!" Kaori said.

"Will do! Sorry for making you all worry about me!" Flashing Kaori a bright smile, he spread his jet-black wings and took to the clear spring sky.

"Huh...?"

"What in the world?!"

But the instant he left, he heard two panicked voices behind him. He quickly spun around and saw Suimei and Shinonome looking at something, flustered. Worried, he flew back into the bookstore and looked past Shinonome.

"WaaaaAAAAAH!"

Ginme froze in horror. He saw Ao's body stretch and creak as the child grew at a far, *far* more rapid rate than ever before.

"Has her memory still not returned?"

"No. She doesn't even seem to remember entering the mountains. It's a mystery how she could have gotten stranded so far in—she didn't use any car, and no buses come this far. She didn't have any identification either, and she was even barefoot. I suspect something criminal occurred."

Inside the waiting room of a clinic, a police officer and an elderly physician talked together as the rain showered incessantly outside. Kinme listened in from outside the window, using a giant butterbur leaf in place of an umbrella.

"She doesn't seem to want to remember what happened, since whenever I ask her about it, she becomes unstable. She even tries to escape whenever I take my eyes off her. I'm honestly not sure what I can do to help her," the physician said.

"For now, let's have her stay here until she calms down. She seems exhausted anyway. I'll wait until she recovers more to question her," said the police officer.

"Of course. Now, for the paperwork…"

Having heard enough, Kinme left that window. He made for a new destination, avoiding the large puddles of water pooled along the way. Unlike Ginme, Kinme succeeded in finding leads by searching for the human parent, not the spirit one. He'd gone to the human village nearest to where they found Ao and looked for anything unusual there.

This isn't a fairy tale; a union between a human and a spirit isn't likely to be consensual. Someone has to have kicked up a stir about it somewhere, he'd thought. Sure enough, there was some gossip going around the village: An unfamiliar woman was found wandering the mountain with nothing but the clothes on her back. Apparently, she wasn't from any of the other surrounding villages either. Nobody knew where she came from, as though it was a modern day case of someone being spirited away. Kinme was certain the woman was Ao's mother.

With a splash, he jumped over a large puddle. He continued through the well-managed clinic courtyard and came to a stop before the window of the hospital room right at the end of the clinic. Looking through the lace curtains, he saw only a single bed. Lying on it was a young woman in her twenties. Her flowing black hair fanned out on the bedsheets below her. Her face was remarkably average, and she stared emptily out into space.

After confirming the woman was there, Kinme picked up a rock off the ground. He stared at it for a moment, expressionless, before taking a step forward to throw it.

"What're you doing?"

But before he could, somebody grabbed his arm. Slowly, he turned to look and saw Noname there, a troubled look on her face, and her moss-green hair wet from the rain.

"I've been looking for you. Next time, tell someone where you're going before you leave," she said. She smiled and held out something with her other hand. "Are you hungry? I brought a bento."

Kinme let his gaze drop to the bento, then wordlessly stared down at the ground.

They went to the tree where Ao was found, simply to use the hollow as a shelter from the rain.

"It's fried chicken flavored with salted rice malt, asparagus meat rolls, meatballs, and hamburger meat. Heh heh, the bento's all brown because I packed it with your favorites. I also packed some rice balls for you here; the round ones have fried cod roe, and the bale-shaped ones have salmon. I didn't put any plum in them because I know you still haven't gotten over your distaste for sour things—as well as spicy things, for that matter. Here, your chopsticks!" Noname smoothly explained the entire spread she had prepared, but Kinme didn't respond. She reached out and brushed the dark circles under his eyes. "When was the last time you slept properly?"

"...I don't know. But I have tried to sleep."

"I see..." Noname smiled softly, moved a few pieces of food to a plate, and passed it to him.

In truth, Kinme didn't have any appetite at all. But he figured refusing to eat would lead to more hassle, so he reluctantly obliged her. It didn't matter, though, because Noname could see right through him.

"Oh, don't make that face," she said. "Just a little is fine, but you *do* need to eat something. I'll bet you haven't had anything substantial to eat in a while. Bugs and wild fruit can only sustain you for so long, you know."

Kinme grimaced. She'd exactly nailed his eating habits for the past week. "Oh, stop it. What are you, my mother?"

Noname's amber eyes went wide. She blushed and cheerfully said, "Oh my. Should I take that as a compliment? I *did* raise Kaori and you twins like my own, or have you forgotten?"

"Urk…" Kinme blushed too and hung his head.

Noname looked at him as she would at anyone she cherished and took a piece of fried chicken for herself. "Mmm! Delicious! Came out rather well if I do say so myself. C'mon, try one. Open wiiide."

"Mgh?!" A piece of chicken was forcibly pushed into Kinme's mouth and took him by surprise. Left with no recourse, he chewed, tasting the euphoric flavor of savory chicken and sweet soy sauce for the first time in a long while. His expression loosened into a smile.

"Yeah, that kind of face suits you a whole lot better," Noname said with pleasure.

"Don't talk like you know me."

"Oh? But I *do* know you. How many years do you think we've been together? I know all about how negative you can be, how spoiled you really are, and how you hate being alone." Noname hugged his head and nuzzled her cheek against him tenderly. "I even know you haven't once opened your heart to Shinonome and me."

Kinme pulled himself away from Noname abruptly and stormed out of the hollow. Paying no mind to the rain that poured down on him, he glared back at her, his wariness on full display.

"Oh, my goodness. Did you really think we didn't know? You're an open book to us," said Noname, feigning surprise and laughing. But her expression turned serious, and she met Kinme's eyes with a cold stare. "How long do you intend to stay a baby chick? Don't you think it's about time you left your nest?"

Kinme could feel tears of frustration coming on. He wanted to yell that he wasn't a baby chick, but the words wouldn't come out. He began to doubt himself: Maybe she was right about him. Was he a baby chick?

Kinme's world was terribly small. He could count the number of people he trusted on a single hand: There was Ginme, his twin; Sojobo, his master; and Kaori, to whom he owed his life. Anybody else might as well be a stranger to him. His world hadn't expanded a single millimeter since that fateful day when his mother left him. It remained the size of a tiny circle with the circumference of an all-too-small nest built from bits of junk and twigs.

He heard Fuguruma-youbi's words echo in his mind: *"And you there, you're the most troublesome of them all. You consider your world complete."*

He lived moving in circles, rotating between the same places endlessly. He couldn't go anywhere else. He didn't *want* to go anywhere else. All he needed in his life was Ginme by his side, so he reserved his heart for a select few. But out of nowhere, things had changed.

His brother's words came to him as well: *"I...I thought you'd feel the same way as me."*

Ginme had left Kinme behind; his most trusted companion had left him behind, and so effortlessly at that. It was as though his brother had declared the confines of their nest suffocating and flown away. Kinme knew his brother would soon learn how open the sky was and come to adopt its values. He would learn things Kinme himself could never hope to learn, he'd let new emotions flourish in his heart, and in the end, his twin wouldn't even look the same as Kinme anymore.

No! No, no, no! I can't accept that!

He finally realized that after all this time, he truly was still a baby chick on the inside. A powerless baby chick that could only chirp in the face of its own powerlessness.

Stop it! You can't leave me too, Ginme! Don't... Don't abandon me too.

Those were his true thoughts laid bare. But it was exactly because he felt that way that he chose to put on a brave front. "What's so wrong about it?" The voice he finally managed to muster was shaky, and he was near tears. But he wouldn't allow himself to back down. If he didn't stand up for the narrow world he lived in, it would crumble around him faster than a half-made nest. He clenched his rain-drenched fists defiantly. "If you want an apology, I'll give it to you. But I'm fine the way I am. I'd rather be wary of everyone than trust them blindly."

"Oh, my." Noname opened her eyes wide. She furrowed her brows with worry and chuckled quietly. "Well, that's fine. As long as that's what you want."

"...What?" Kinme was taken aback. He'd expected her to try and persuade him to open his heart. This was just anti-climactic.

"What, did you think I'd give you a sermon or something? You're the only one who can decide to let others in. The door to your heart isn't something that can be opened from the outside, nor by the words of another." Noname winked at him. "Besides, you're only a fifteen-year-old child. We spirits live lives longer than we know what to do with. You're free to take your time choosing who you want to trust, and you're also free to stay in your nest forever, if that's what you'd like. Unlike humans, we spirits enjoy many freedoms!"

Argh! What is with her?! Her words were kind yet oddly distant. Kinme was greatly confused. He felt himself falter. "Just stop. What are you even here for?! If all you want is for me to make up with Ginme, then say so! I don't need you to act like you care about me! Being abandoned by someone I don't even trust doesn't hurt at all, so just leave me alone!" Kinme let his emotions take hold and yelled, desperately hoping Noname wouldn't back him any further into a corner. Ginme was the one who was good with the emotional side of things. Kinme couldn't process this many feelings.

Noname stuck her tongue out. "No way. Didn't I say I think of you as my own child? How could I leave you alone, much less abandon you, when you're clearly suffering?" She eased herself out of the hollow and approached Kinme. "Such a clumsy child you are. Are you that afraid of being abandoned?" The rain began to drench her Chinese-style clothes. As it did, her expression drastically changed. Her beautiful face, perfect like a sculpture, took on the visage of a predator about to strike. Overwhelmed, Kinme took a step back. Noname continued to stalk forward, finally stopping just in front of him and grabbing his collar. Her furious amber eyes bored into him. She yelled, "Don't screw with me! Do you really think I'd turn my back on you just because you won't open up?! I'm not so damn cruel!"

"Eek..." Kinme froze. This was the first time Noname had ever been angry at him. Usually, she only had to scold Ginme or Kaori. Faced with such direct, unfiltered anger, he felt tears fall from his eyes. His mind was still a mess. All he wanted to do was bawl his eyes out like a child. "D-don't be angry... It's my fault. I'm sorry. I'm sorry..."

Noname's expression softened. She hugged Kinme and said, "I'm sorry. You're not the only one to blame. I am too. In all our years together, not once did I earn your trust."

Kinme sniffed.

"It's the fault of us adults that you felt so cornered. If we had protected you better, maybe you wouldn't have grown up so hurt. But listen, I am *different* from your mother. I want you to be happy. You don't need to live your whole life afraid to trust people."

Kinme couldn't move. His shoulders trembled. His clothes were heavy from the rain. His mind was a whirlpool of emotions. There wasn't a single calm thought in him, only confusion and a morass of feelings.

Is it really okay for me to not be afraid of abandonment anymore? he wondered. The spring rain sapped his heat. Oddly enough, though, he didn't find it unpleasant. It was as though the rain were washing away something that had clung on deep inside him. His face scrunched into a frown as he buried it in Noname's shoulder, sobbing.

She patted his back with a dainty hand. It was a gesture of love from someone who'd sworn she would never abandon him. "Can I ask you something?" she said.

Kinme nodded.

"Were you looking for the baby's parents so you could kill them before Ginme found them?"

He swallowed and nodded again.

"I see." Noname put her hands on his cheeks and looked him in the eyes. "Why? I want to hear it from your own mouth."

Kinme winced. More tears streamed down his face. "I did it for Ginme's sake. He acts so carefree, but he's actually soft. I know he'd get hurt if he met someone awful enough to abandon their child, so I figured I'd get rid of them before that could happen."

"Goodness..." Noname frowned upon hearing him say that he was willing to dirty his own hands for the sake of his brother. She looked off into the distance thoughtfully, still patting his back as he wept. Suddenly, she smiled like she had an idea and pushed him up off her shoulder.

"Huh...?" Kinme frowned, afraid Noname had turned her back on him. His heart would be ripped to pieces. *After all that talk, you're betraying me?*

"Kinme!"

But the very next instant, he felt a familiar warmth against his back. In stunned silence, he turned around and saw a face just like his own, covered in snot and tears.

"It's all, *hic*, my fault! Kinmeeeee!"

"Ginme?" Kinme looked to Noname for help.

She ran a hand through her wet hair and smiled impishly, proud of herself. "Heh heh heh! Well, would you look at that. It looks like all your feelings got across to your brother."

"Huh...?" Kinme said.

"I'm impatient, you see... Even when I read romance, I complain all the while that the characters are taking too long to get together."

Wait... That means Ginme heard everything? As Kinme's confusion subsided, his mind became clear. His cheeks went red with embarrassment. "Y-you're evil!"

"Oho ho ho! It's your own fault for spilling the beans so easily!" Noname roared with laughter. She looked at him affectionately. "But what I said earlier wasn't a lie. I would never abandon or turn my back on you."

"N-ngh...!" Kinme glared at her as hard as he could, unable to muster any words.

Ginme, still gripping his blushing brother in a bear hug, smiled. "Sorry. Really. I was so single-minded, thinking about finding Ao's parents so much that I didn't consider your feelings at all."

Kinme looked down at his feet. "I'm sorry too. I was forcing my own beliefs onto you. You didn't do anything wrong. I went and saw our horrible mother in some stranger for no good reason."

"Kinme..."

"Aw, don't make that face. And do something about that snot already." He wiped his brother's nose with his own sleeve.

A bit embarrassed, Ginme flashed a toothy grin. His nose and eyes were red and puffy, as though he'd been crying the whole time Kinme was talking to Noname. Kinme laughed at his brother's absurd face and then Ginme began to laugh too.

"Hey, Ginme. Do you think maybe we haven't been properly telling each other about ourselves because we're twins?"

"I guess so. We're always together, so maybe we thought we already knew everything there was to know about one another."

"I always thought we were the same, Ginme."

"And I always thought we were the same, Kinme."

They looked each other in the eyes and spoke at the same time. "But that won't work anymore, will it?"

"We're different now, aren't we, Kinme? When we get home, let me tell you about who I've become."

"We're no longer the same, are we, Ginme? Once we get home, let me tell you about how I haven't changed for a long time."

"Promise?"

"Yeah."

Ah... With this, we don't need to hide anything from each other, Kinme thought, feeling his chest grow warm.

Ginme messily wiped the tears from his face. "Hey, Kinme?"

"Yes, Ginme?"

"Why don't we go discover what she's like now?"

"Huh? What are you talking about?" Kinme said, confused.

Ginme smiled and pointed past Kinme. "I'm talking about Ao's mother of course!"

Kinme spun around and saw an unfamiliar figure about two meters tall. They looked exactly like what one would imagine a giant baby to look like and had a semi-transparent body that gave off a spectral blue glow. Various forest plant life swayed inside their body like a giant herbarium, and with each step they took, the surrounding trees swayed without wind. Small animals that had been hiding appeared and bowed their heads to the figure as though welcoming the return of their lord.

Ignoring Kinme, who was frozen stiff with his mouth hanging open, Ginme greeted the giant person. "Ao, you're here! Took you long enough!"

"Ao...?" Kinme said.

"Oh, that's what we named the baby we found."

"Wait, whaaat? Why do they look like that now? Explain!" It was incomprehensible to Kinme that Ao, who looked around one year old when he last saw them, could have grown to this size in a week.

"Allow me," said Shinonome, brushing aside some leaves to appear with Kaori and Suimei. "Ao is a Kinoko, a child spirit that lives in the mountain forests and loves mischief."

"That can't be," Kinme replied. "There's no way a child spirit could get that big!"

"Normally, yes, but Ao is special. They're born from divinity."

Shinonome went on to explain that Ao was a native god in the making. Native gods were souls that dwelled in large trees, giant boulders, lakes, and other things that had stood since time immemorial. What made them different from Tsukumogami, spirits that dwelled in objects, was that native gods were often violent. If a road was being cleared of fallen trees or boulders, and a person was hurt in the process, it was said to be the work of an offended native god.

Shinonome continued. "One known characteristic of native gods is that they are not immortal. I don't know if it's because of decline, the end of their life span, or disease, but it's likely that the large tree you found Ao in borrowed the womb of a human woman to create Ao as a replacement for the old god." Stories of gods using the wombs of women, particularly virgin women, to create proxies without actually mating with them were common. The Christian tale of the Virgin Mary was a famous example of this.

"So the tree made a successor? But why was Ao left abandoned and hungry?" Kinme asked.

"About that..." Shinonome prompted Suimei to continue.

"Ginme found a vine in the hollow that we think was something resembling an umbilical cord between the tree and Ao. Chances are, Ao was removed from their mother and was supposed to be connected to the tree's 'umbilical cord' so Ao could grow in the hollow. But that's not what happened. Kinme, can you see that there, right on Ao's stomach?" Extending from Ao's midsection was a long, tube-like protuberance. It glowed a pale, translucent light and extended farther than the eye could see.

"What...is that?" Kinme muttered. "It looks like an umbilical cord..."

"Exactly. We think it's still connected to the birth mother." The color drained from Suimei's face. He looked down somberly.

Seeing how uncomfortable Suimei looked, Kaori took over explaining. She said, "It's likely because of the long rain. There are landslides throughout the region, and the rivers are flooded. The mountain's going to die at this rate."

It seemed that not even the native god had predicted that the rain would continue so long. In its haste to make a successor, it failed to completely separate Ao from their mother. Consequently, it was unable to connect its own "umbilical cord" to Ao to sustain them.

With Kinme stunned into silence, Kaori sadly said, "Kinme... You know what we have to do now, right?" Her expression was stiff, her lips were pale blue, and her small hands trembled.

In that instant, Kinme finally understood. *Heh. How strange. And the four of us all had our own problems dealing with parents.* Kaori had been separated from her mother before wandering into the spirit realm, and Suimei had lost his mother young and had his emotions suppressed by his father. Knowing their histories, he pressed on to give his answer. "We need to cut that umbilical cord and separate Ao from their mother, right? As things stand, Ao won't become a god or a human. We need to connect them to the native god so that they can become one themselves."

Kaori nodded, near tears. "Right."

How ironic, Kinme thought. Suimei and Kaori, who had never once stopped missing their mothers, would have to sever the bond between this child and their mother. Kinme understood the reason for their pained expressions, yet found it amusing all the same. To think they would willingly hurt themselves, all for the sake of a child they had only just met. *They're too kind for their own good. I don't see the problem, so get it over with and cut the cord.* Surprised by his own cruelty, he stifled a smile and thought, *Wow. I really don't change. As negative as ever and stuck in my own world.*

Compared to the others at the bookstore, Kinme was a realist. He didn't adhere to lofty ideals for the sake of helping others like Kaori and the rest, and that meant he could do things they couldn't.

Every now and then, somebody cold like me is exactly who's needed. Kinme beamed at the pale Suimei and Kaori. "I'm surprised you two realized what Ao was, with gods being outside Shinonome's expertise and all."

"It was pretty obvious once we saw them looking like that. Ao's clearly different from any ordinary spirit," Suimei said.

"So, what's the plan? Are we cutting and reconnecting their umbilical cord after all?" Kinme asked.

Kaori and Suimei froze again.

Ginme appeared beside his brother and hugged Kinme. "Sorry, but do you mind waiting a bit on that, Kinme?"

"Ginme…?"

"No, no, don't misunderstand. I'm not going to tell you *not* to cut the umbilical cord or anything. But I think we should see what's up with Ao's mother first, y'know? I want to let them meet. It shouldn't be too late to cut the cord afterward." Ginme smiled sadly and looked up at Ao, who stood gazing blankly off into the distance. "It sucks, but I do understand that this kid can't stay with their mom. They won't be able to live among humans no matter how hard they try. I feel bad for them, Kinme. I had you, but this kid has nobody."

"You feel sympathy for Ao?"

"'Course I do. They remind me of myself back when I was all helpless in that nest. But there's nothing wrong with feeling sympathy. Sympathy can be the kickstart needed to take action."

Ginme grabbed Kinme's shoulders and grinned his usual carefree smile. "I know I'm doing this for my own sake. Hell, I'm sure this'll cause trouble for everyone. But I still want to do it." He let his gaze wander to the side. "I think a miracle might happen if Ao and their mother can meet."

Kinme could easily imagine what kind of miracle Ginme was envisioning. It was a moving image, like something from a fairy tale or a movie. The mother would recognize their child at first sight, and the child would leap into their mother's arms—a scene as beautiful as a work of religious art. But such a thing was impossible. Reality wasn't so kind. Ginme should at least be able to understand that.

Ginme grinned mischievously and gripped Kinme's shoulders, the latter's thoughts clearly visible on his face. "I know what you're thinking," Ginme said. "Such a thing can't be possible. But I have you with me, don't I? If a miracle won't happen, we'll have to *make* it happen. I mean, you're smart. I'm sure we can figure something out!"

"...The heck? You're basically pushing all the responsibility onto me." Kinme sighed.

Ginme let out a boisterous laugh. "Hey, I'm the brawn, and you're the brains. Compared to me, you're a genius! I believe in you. So, go on, figure this out for me, will ya?"

Kinme cast his gaze down. He didn't hate being praised. He raised his hands in defeat. "All right, fine."

"Woo-hoo!" Ginme cheered like a little kid.

I'll show you what the brains of this operation can do. Kinme smiled, addressing his brother, who was still hugging him from behind. "I already know where Ao's mother is."

"Whoa! Kinme, you're a genius!"

"You bet I am. Some humans found her wandering around on the mountain in a daze, and they took her to a clinic. And get this...they say she was a modern day case of being spirited away."

Ginme froze. After some silence, he peered over his brother's shoulder and scowled. "Ugh. Not sure how I feel about that."

"Whoa, that's quite a face you're making. But yeah, I get it. I had the same reaction when I first heard it." Kinme grinned and patted his brother's head. He seemed to have a bright idea and smiled maliciously.

"Sorry to cut in, but what exactly is the plan?" Suimei asked with some unease.

Kinme sneered and said, "Really, Suimei? Did you forget what we are? We're raven Tengu, and spiriting people away is a Tengu specialty. We can't exactly do nothing when our specialty was half-assed by some god. Let's perform a *real* spiriting away."

Suimei frowned. He shot Kaori and Shinonome a worried look, but they merely shrugged—it looked like they'd already accepted what was to come.

"It's not a true spiriting away if the victim doesn't have a strange, unexplainable experience, so that's exactly what we'll give Ao's mother!" Kinme said. "At any rate, you can trust Ginme and me. We're not going to do anything bad! Really! Oh, and I need you to do something for me, Shinonome!"

"This better not be too much trouble..."

"No, no! Knowing you, it should be no problem at all!"

Shinonome and Suimei shared a deeply worried look. Together, they let out a heavy sigh.

The woman woke up and blinked a few times. Uncertain where she was, she explored her surroundings with her eyes, not daring to move her head. It was dark—dark enough that she couldn't see past an arm's length away into the gloom. The stifling smell of trees stung her nose. Beneath her was a bed of soft fallen leaves.

She realized she was, at the very least, not tied up and pushed herself upright. "Where am I...?" she mumbled.

Just then, she sensed somebody's presence and looked up.

"Oh, you're awake! Good morning! Er, good afternoon? Good evening...? I dunno, but you're up and that's all that matters!"

A blinding light suddenly shone down on her. She reflexively squinted and covered her eyes, struggling to make out the source of the light: it was a lamp held by a youth in unusual garb.

The young man wore black monk robes with blue puffballs on the front. On his head was a small cap often seen on mountain ascetics. He looked exactly like a yamabushi mountain monk, save for the mask he wore that covered half his face—it seemed to be a bird mask, given the black beak.

The young man pranced forward with spring in his step and grabbed the woman's hand. "You were asleep so long, I was beginning to worry! You all right? Not hungry, are ya?"

"Huh? Oh. Um... I'm okay. Thank you."

"Not at all, not at all!" The man's eyes smiled from behind the mask.

Who is this man? At least he doesn't seem like a bad person, the woman thought. A swirl of other thoughts flitted in and out of her mind—*How did I get here? What is my name? Where am I?*—but they all faded without causing her any lingering worry. She felt as though she were in a dream. She looked around. "It's pretty dark... How did I get here?"

The man tilted his head. "You don't remember? There's something important to you here; something that's more important than anything else."

"There is?"

The man grinned toothily. Another man appeared beside him, this one with red puffballs on his monk robes instead of blue.

"Helloooo! I hope you had a nice nap!" Unlike his more energetic, blue-puffed counterpart, the man with the red puffs spoke with a slightly sleepy cadence. He approached the woman and patted her back, giving her a warm smile. "I was beginning to think you wouldn't wake up! Now let's waste no time getting down to business. We have something important to return to you. Will you accept it?" He gently took her hand and pointed.

"Huh?" The woman couldn't believe her eyes.

"Manma!"

From within the darkness, a baby appeared. The dazzlingly bright lamplight shone on them, illuminating their soft and plump arms, legs, and cheeks. Sparse hair sat gently atop their head. It looked like a baby of only some-odd months, one that would still drink their mother's milk.

"A child...?" the woman said. "What are they doing out here?"

The two young men behind her each put a hand on her shoulders. They began to speak to her, practically whispering.

"What's the matter?" the one with the blue puffs said. "That's the thing most precious to you, isn't it?"

"That's right," the red-puffed one said. "You must be really exhausted if you've forgotten what your own child looks like."

"Huh...?" The woman whipped up her head, surprised.

"This is the child you bore yourself, remember? Go on, take a closer look," the red-puffed one said.

"They want to be held in your arms. See? They're reaching out for you."

"That's...my child?"

"What's wrong? Don't tell me you don't recognize them. Put your hand over your heart and try to remember," the red-puffed one said.

"While you're at it, look at how darn cute they are. Aw, they're tearing up because they want their mommy. Hurry, before they cry!" the blue-puffed one urged.

"Oh, r-right." The woman nodded, still a bit bewildered, and awkwardly approached the baby. *I really don't recall ever bearing a child,* she thought. Still, she couldn't bring herself to ignore the baby. She got on her knees and hesitantly reached out to pick up the child, but their soft body slipped from her arms. "Ah!" she yelled. She quickly caught and repositioned the baby in her arms, then let out a long sigh of relief. But a doubt had formed in her mind: If she had a baby, shouldn't she already know how to hold it properly? "U-um... I think this child might not be mine after all."

She turned around and froze, for the air around the two young men had completely changed. Gone were their warm smiles, now they wore grim, taut frowns. They stared down on her imposingly, and from behind their masks the lamplight reflected off their silver and gold eyes. Within those eyes, she saw a glimmer of anger.

"Ah!" The woman recoiled, sliding herself backward on the ground. Sensing danger, she instinctively hugged the baby to protect them.

With leisurely steps, the two young men came forward and knelt by the woman's side. She was certain she was done for, when...nothing happened. She raised her face, confused, and saw the pair begin to talk to the baby.

"Well, aren't you a lucky little thing," the one with blue puffs said. "You have a mom who'll protect you."

"Yeah. How nice..." the one with the red puffs said.

"Huh?" The woman was taken aback by the kindness in their voices.

With softness back in their eyes, they poked the baby's cheeks and smiled.

"Look, they're all calm now! It must be because their mother's holding them," said the red-puffed one.

"Oh, you're right! Wow, and to think they wouldn't even make eye contact with us!"

"Heh heh, they're holding on to their mother's clothes as tight as they can, like they're saying 'don't go anywhere.'"

"Yeah... Of course, they would. They finally found their mother, after all."

The two young men looked at one another before looking at the woman. Together, they said, "Please stay by your baby's side, if even just for a little while longer."

Without another word, the young men left the cave. She watched them leave, bewildered. The baby began to fuss.

"Manma! Agooo..."

The woman quickly turned her attention down to the baby and began to clumsily soothe them. She tried every method in the tiny book of tricks she had, and after a few minutes of struggling, succeeded in lulling the baby to sleep. She breathed a sigh of relief and gazed at the baby in her arms. She still didn't have any instinctive feeling they were hers, but that didn't change the fact the baby was so very warm, small, and soft. "...How adorable." She gently brushed the baby's cheeks and began humming a lullaby her mother used to hum for her.

The rain came to a complete stop, and so the sound of the woman's lullaby drifted outside the hollow and into the forest. The wet leaves of the giant tree, the native god itself, dripped water rhythmically—the soft splashing sound it made joining in as accompaniment.

Ginme rested against the giant tree and listened to the lullaby, his eyes gazing upward at the twinkling stars above. "Heh... Good for you, Ao."

The baby inside the hollow was Ao, at least, for the most part. The twins had used Ao's spiritual power to cast an illusion that made Ao look like an ordinary baby. This was the only way they figured they could get the mother to dote on Ao, whose true appearance was both larger than the mother and more foreign to her.

The twins were staging something akin to a Tengu abduction, a phrase with roots in the Edo period. Back then, whenever children went missing, people would say it was the work of a Tengu. Unlike normal cases of spiriting away, however, children that went missing from Tengu abductions would return days, sometimes years later.

A famous account was written by Hirata Atsutane, a scholar from the late Edo period. He details the story of a boy named Torakira in his book *Tales of the Mystique*, in which Torakira returns from a Tengu abduction and uses the knowledge he gained from the Tengu in his day-to-day life.

Similarly, the twins planned to return Ao's mother after she'd spent ample time with Ao.

Suimei objected greatly to the kidnapping, but the twins decided to go ahead with it anyway. After all, human logic didn't apply to spirits, and they figured it wasn't really that awful a thing to kidnap someone if it was for the sake of them spending some time with their child, however brief. "You guys are being too irresponsible! ...Not that that's anything new," Suimei had complained in his attempt to dissuade the twins. He failed to do so, however, as the twins were intent on making sure Ao didn't grow up harboring the same feelings they did.

"You're incredible, Kinme. You managed to show me exactly what I wanted to see, and so easily too," Ginme said. He recalled the deeply stirring scene, like something pulled straight from a movie, and it warmed his heart. *With Shinonome clearing the clouds away, we should be good on rain for a while!* Ginme smiled as he also thought back to the sight of Shinonome parting the clouds, albeit not without some grumbling. Shinonome was the Tsukumogami of a hanging scroll depicting a dragon, so he could fly through the air and such.

Ginme removed his mask and fell into deep thought. He listened to the soothing lullaby and, feeling a little restless, peeked into the hollow. There he saw Ao curling their large body up as much as they could and hugging their much smaller mother tenderly. *How nice...* he thought with a tinge of envy. "...Ah." Ginme felt his eyes had grown hot. He cast his gaze downward and slumped onto the ground. *Don't cry. Don't you dare cry! This is supposed to be a happy moment!* He resisted the urge to cry as hard as he could. He was an upstanding raven Tengu; he couldn't allow himself to cry like a child. Especially since there was a chance Kaori might see.

"Are you okay?" Kinme said, coming to his brother's side. With a kind look in his eyes, he rubbed Ginme's head. "It's not good to bottle things up. It's okay. Let it out."

Ginme lasted one more moment. He desperately told himself not to cry, but the dam couldn't hold in the face of his beloved brother. With trembling lips, he hugged Kinme and said, "I-I... I'm jealous."

"I know."

"I want a mom I can hug too."

"...I know."

A single tear rolled down Ginme's cheek. With the floodgates now opened, many more tears soon followed, and he was helpless to stop them. "I want to eat food made by a mom, to sleep in the same bed as her, to hold hands and walk with her..." He sniffed. "I want to get praised when I do something good. I want to get scolded when I do something bad. I'm jealous, Kinme. I'm jealous of Ao. I want a mom..."

Hah. "I want this." "I want that." What am I, a child? Ginme felt exasperated by his own immaturity, but the words wouldn't stop coming. He continued, "What would a mom feel like? Would she feel warm? Cold? Soft? Maybe a little firm? What would she smell like?" Ginme buried his face in his brother's shoulder and continued in a shaky voice. "How would she smile? What would she sound like? I don't know anything, Kinme. Why don't I know? Everyone else knows these things, so why do I alone not know?"

His vision blurred with tears, scalding hot like they'd melted the ice around his heart. They stood ready to trace down his cheek but fell straight down onto the blue monk's puffballs on his chest instead. "Mom... Why did you abandon us?!"

What was so wrong with me? Was it something I did? I wanted nothing more than for you to come back. So why, why could I not even have that?

"It's okay, Ginme. I'm here." Kinme tried his hardest to soothe his brother.

Ginme felt safe in his brother's arms; his brother's smell was the most familiar thing in the world to him. But a brother couldn't fill the gap a missing mother left, not in his heart, and not in Kinme's. Despite being twins, they were different in many ways. But at their core, they *both* never stopped longing for their mother, or grieving the fact that their beseeching voices couldn't make her return.

Deeply aware he could never truly get over his mother's absence, Ginme couldn't stop the words he'd sworn he would keep locked away in his heart. "If I was just going to be abandoned, I'd rather not have been born at all."

Kinme went wide-eyed. He looked at his brother, hurt.

Ah... I shouldn't have said that. Ginme regretted it and began thinking of an excuse to make, something unusual for his generally unapologetic self. A sweet smell tickled his nose. He looked up, surprised to smell such a sweet aroma in the forest of all places, and spotted something white above their heads. "You're kidding."

"Ginme?" Kinme questioned.

Ginme separated from his brother, looking upward in a daze all the while. Above them were clusters of small white flowers hanging off the ends of branches. The buds hadn't been even close to blooming just the other day, and yet here was the giant Japanese snowbell in full bloom.

"That's so dumb. Why? What's the point of this?" Ginme said.

The countless flowers wafted sweetly. The smell would draw birds and bugs in search of the flowers' nectar, pollinating the tree and granting it plentiful fruit come winter. Those fruit would be eaten, and its seeds would travel far and sprout new life elsewhere. Such was, and always has been, the cycle of life for plants. But for the giant tree, the native god, such a cycle should be meaningless now that its legacy was entrusted to Ao. And yet, it shaved away at what little life it had left to make these flowers bloom. Could such an act be considered anything but suicidal?

"I don't understand. You're going to die soon. Your next generation is secure. What's the point of trying to make children now?!" Ginme wailed. Then something light fell atop his head. He looked up and was shocked to see white flowers fluttering down through the air, one after another. Reminded of the tree's name, he muttered, "Snowbell." The flowers drifted down and blanketed the ground like snow. They had an ephemeral quality, but they also evoked the abiding drive that life had to create the next generation, no matter the circumstances.

"Aha ha...aha ha ha!" Without warning, Ginme doubled over in laughter. He fell onto the flower-blanketed ground, gasping for air, and roared with laughter.

Kinme watched him, utterly confused. He couldn't figure out for the life of him what his brother was laughing about.

"So that's how it is. I get it now…" Ginme said.

"Are you feeling all right?" Kinme asked. He scratched his head and knelt down to put his hand on Ginme's forehead.

Ginme snickered and brushed his brother's hand aside. "I'm not running a fever or anything, relax."

"How am I supposed to relax when my one and only brother is acting insane?"

Ginme blinked a few times and then broke into a toothy grin. He reached out and swiftly pulled his brother down into the fallen blossoms.

"Hey! What was that for?"

"Aha ha ha! Sorry, are you hurt?" Ginme hugged his confused brother. "Kinme… We mustn't forget: While we may be raven Tengu now, we used to be ordinary baby chicks."

"…Okay?" Kinme said, totally clueless as to what his brother was getting at.

Ginme giggled. "That means our mom was an ordinary bird too. A small life in a vast world. Not a raven Tengu. Not a human. Just a run-of-the-mill bird. She couldn't fight against nature." As he spoke, his own thoughts grew more and more lucid. His mind became clear, and his usually slow wits sharpened. There was nothing wrong with Ginme and Kinme, yet their mother had abandoned them all the same. The reason remained unclear to this day, but perhaps she hadn't had a choice. Such was nature. One had to do everything in their power to survive, even if that meant doing the unforgivable. "Mom probably abandoned us because it was necessary," he said.

Kinme frowned. His eyes wandered aimlessly, as though he struggled with a hard truth. A bit hesitant, he said, "Even if that were true, does that change anything for us?"

"Nope!" Ginme replied without hesitation. He began to softly pat his brother's back. "Nothing can change the fact we were left for dead. The wounds on our hearts can't be healed so easily. We had to grow up not knowing the smell, the touch, the sound, the everything of a mother. But I think we just have to accept that. After all, we're both a part of nature too, aren't we?" Ginme made a fist and raised it toward the native god raining petals from above. "I forgive our mom. She did what she had to. I'm sure she made new life somewhere out there to make up for abandoning us."

Kinme began to shake his head side to side. "Don't be stupid! We only managed to survive by sheer luck! I wouldn't care if I died, but not you! I can't forgive her!"

"Hey now, Kinme. You can't badmouth yourself like that." Ginme pinched his brother's cheek, making an angry frown.

"Ow..." Kinme looked away sheepishly, and Ginme's face quickly loosened into a smile.

"I forgive mom, and you don't. That's fine. That's totally fine," Ginme said a bit thoughtfully. He took his finger off his brother's cheek and hugged him tightly. "The two of us are one. But we're also different. That's why it's okay for us to have different feelings. You got that, Kinme?"

For a moment, Kinme stiffened. Then, like his exhaustion had finally caught up with him all at once, he let his body slump onto his brother's. "What the hell... I don't get you one bit. You better not be growing smart all of a sudden and leaving me behind... Birdbrain."

"What're you saying? I would never leave you behind! Let's take our time and grow together. We can let our world expand bit by bit."

Kinme opened his eyes wide. After a brief pause, he replied, "Yeah."

They sank into silence together. Ginme patted the back of his brother's head and gazed up at the canopy above. He saw the leaves of the large, wide-reaching Japanese snowbell tree, as well as its flowers that drifted down like a flurry. From the bottom of his heart, Ginme loved this grand and cruel world. He lent an ear to the mother's faint lullaby and let his eyes fall shut. His heart, like the skies freed after the long rain, was clear.

INTERMISSION

Life in a World Still Too Small

THE SOUND OF GENTLE SNORING reached Kinme's ears. He sat up slowly and saw his brother fast asleep on the ground.

"Let our world expand, huh...?"

He brushed aside the petals that had fallen on Ginme's face and took the time to fix his brother's messy hair as well. He sat there for a while, watching Ginme sleep. Eventually he stood up, careful not to rouse his brother.

Kaori and the rest would be waiting for them, eager to hear how things were going. Kinme decided to go report to them before they grew impatient and crowded in here first—or at least that was what he intended to do. His feet came to a sudden halt. His usually sleepy eyes sharpened into a glare aimed at what looked like a perfectly ordinary thicket. Fanning out his wings, he took a step forward.

"Oh, you found me! You really are keen-eyed!" A man with black hair and red highlights stepped out from the thicket. It was almost as if he had no intention of hiding in the first place.

He bowed, holding a fedora against his chest. "I am known as Akamadara. I must say, that was quite the charade you put on."

Kinme's eyebrow twitched at the word "charade."

"Oh, do forgive me. Being too direct with my words is one of my little foibles." Akamadara showed surprise with his hands and face in an exaggerated manner, like a stage actor. He smiled meaningfully and approached Kinme, staring him straight in the eye. "I've come to offer you a deal you can't *possibly* refuse." He reached into his breast pocket and pulled something out. With a sly look, he continued. "This is nothing more than a proposition, of course. But I do think you'll prefer my offer to any harm coming the way of your precious brother." His eyes, red like ripened pomegranate, seemed to size Kinme up. He laughed. "I simply want to grant my master's wish. That is all. Now, what'll it be?"

Kinme narrowed his eyes and stared back at Akamadara. He sighed deeply. His heart, unlike how it had been moments earlier with Ginme, was cold like midwinter.

CHAPTER 3
The Bookstore Ghost

*W*ELL, THIS IS *a weird turn of events,* I grumbled to myself. I was sitting at a counter with a sushi tray before me. Across the counter was a sushi chef, and between the chef and me was a glass case full of fresh seafood. We were at a sushi restaurant, and not the kind where sushi came served on a conveyor belt but the high-end kind of place where they prepared the sushi right before your eyes.

An assortment of glossy, high-grade sushi sat atop my sushi tray waiting to be devoured. The fatty tuna in particular seemed to be saying, "Eat me! Eat me!" Which was exactly what I wanted to do that very moment, but I refrained, as the cheerful gentleman to my side wasn't yet ready with his sushi.

"I'll take some blackthroat seaperch, lightly seared. Hm, brown prawn sounds rather nice too. Kaori, you'd be surprised by how good brown prawn tastes; don't let its appearance fool you. Ah, yes, some brown prawn for the girl please."

"Right away," the sushi chef said.

"W-wait, hold that order! You don't have to treat me to that much," I said to the gentleman.

He raised an eyebrow at me. "You've come all this way to Kanazawa; you have to at least try *some* of the local sushi."

"Well, I'd love to, but...maybe some of the cheaper stuff?"

"No, no, that's no good. As a young'un, you have a duty to let your elders treat you. Or are you saying it's too uncool for you to share a meal with some old fogey like me?"

"N-no, not at all, Seigen-san..."

"It's settled then!" He nodded enthusiastically, passed me a bottle of sake, and held out a small drinking cup. "If you would, please. Sushi tastes best paired with sake poured by another."

"Um, sure..." I poured him a cup, which he drank in one gulp.

His cheeks now flushed, he said, "Delicious! Go ahead and eat, don't hold back on my account. Let's make the most of this wonderful day!"

"R-right." I timidly reached for the fatty tuna. *Mmm! This is mind-meltingly good! I wish Shinonome-san could try some of this!* I was moved to tears by how delicious the fatty tuna was. I continued to eat piece after piece, no longer holding anything back. Seigen-san happily watched me eat.

I was in Kanazawa city, in Ishikawa Prefecture. As for why I was there, we need to go back a few hours to explain.

The town was under a dense fog that morning. I woke up early, something I had grown accustomed to as of late, with the more mouths to feed—and ravenous ones at that. I rubbed my tired eyes and prepared breakfast in the kitchen, the house completely devoid of sound.

"All right, next I need to add the soup stock..." I rolled up my sleeves and pulled the bonito flakes out of the cupboard. Then there came a knock at the door of the bookstore. It was still only five-thirty in the morning, too early to open for business.

What should I do...? I took a peek up the stairs leading to the second floor. Suimei had warned me a dozen times over to call for him if someone came, but it was still really early in the morning. Knowing what a light sleeper he was, he definitely wouldn't be able to fall back asleep if I woke him up now. It felt kind of wrong.

There was a knock again, this time more urgent. Perhaps whoever it was had really important business?

"Zzz..." I heard Shinonome-san's loud snoring and thought about maybe waking him up but quickly decided against it. By the sound of things, he hadn't been asleep long.

Where's Nyaa-san when you need her? I thought to myself. *It's almost like she knows when to make herself scarce.* I took off my apron and quickly made my way through the bookstore. It was dark, so I put a glimmerfly into a paper lantern, casting a yellowish glow onto surrounding shelves. I put on some sandals and continued to the front door. As I walked, the click-clack of my sandals echoed, intruding on the silence of the store. Beyond the frosted glass of the door, I could make out the outline of a woman. I asked, "Who is it?"

There was no reply. The woman's outline swayed, like the leaves of a willow tree.

Maybe she didn't hear me? I thought. I was about to repeat myself, but abruptly, the woman pressed herself against the frosted glass, her entire body becoming distinct. I let out a scream. Her face was pale, almost deathly pale. She had creepily large eyes that darted about wildly, scanning the bookstore. Her long, unkempt black hair reached down to her waist and stuck nauseatingly to her skin. Dark shadows were drawn under her eyes, and her lips were lusterless. She wore some sort of white garb, which only made her pale skin look paler.

"A-ah…" I accidentally made some noise, and the woman finally noticed my presence.

Her lips curved into a sickening crescent smile. In a hoarse voice, she said, "I would like to rent a book."

Her words brought me back to my senses. Hoping to end this quickly, I said, "W-we open at nine. Could you come back then?"

"Whyyyyy?!" The woman slammed her head against the frosted glass.

"Eeek!"

She continued repeatedly slamming her head. The old door showed no signs of breaking, but it rattled worryingly.

"Um, p-please stop!" I said.

To my surprise, she did just that, freezing in place. She tilted her head unnaturally, like a mechanical doll. In a weak voice, she said, "It took me a great effort to travel all this way here… I won't take long… Could you please let me in?"

"O-oh, um..." I considered it. Transportation in the spirit realm wasn't as advanced as it was in the human world, so trips did often run long, and while there were travelers' inns in town she could stay at, they likely wouldn't be open at this time. Ultimately, however, what forced my hand was the fact that it wouldn't feel right to turn someone away who just came to borrow a book. Having made up my mind, I reached for the door's lock. Our door had an old-fashioned screw-type lock. Its metal grated as I twisted the bolt all the way out. Slowly, I slid open the door. A breeze, quite warm for such an early morning, caressed my cheek. The smell of incense wafted over me, and the fog outside began to pour into the store. "Come on in," I said.

"Thank you..." There she stood, a young woman who looked to be in her mid-twenties. She wore a white yukata with a hydrangea design and held her belongings, wrapped in a red cloth, close to her chest as if they were precious. Her slender, willowy neck was wrapped in gauze dressing that was so white it looked transparent. She slowly bowed her head, then entered the bookstore, her wooden geta clacking against the ground.

"Is there a specific book you're looking for?" I asked as I moved the glimmerfly lantern to a fixture.

She slowly turned her head to look at me and said, "I want something I can read to a small...baby. Yes, my baby... Something like a picture book." She looked down at the belongings in her arms. They were large enough to hold a doll.

"I see!" I smiled and went farther into the store. Only yesterday we had created a special picture book section. Thrilled to put it to use so soon, I spun around and said, "You can find what you need right...here?"

The woman was gone. Vanished like smoke.

"Huh? Hello?" I searched the store but found no trace of her. "Huh. I guess she left." Confused, I walked back to the picture book section and went wide-eyed with surprise.

"...Then lo and behold, this money was there in place of one of the books!"

A week after I first met the mystery woman, I was holding up a bag and telling everyone the story of what happened. The bag I held was covered in brown stains. Inside it were copper coins from the Edo period—six of them, to be exact.

"Six copper coins... Isn't that the fee to cross the Sanzu River? This bag must be one of the ones they hang around the necks of the deceased," Shinonome-san said, scrutinizing the bag.

"That means that woman was a ghost, right? Whew, scary stuff!" Kinme said, cackling.

Ginme hugged his brother tight and said, "K-Kinme?! Don't say that, I'll freak out, seriously! It's your fault if I can't sleep tonight!"

"What kind of spirit's afraid of ghosts? And you, get away from me, mutt." Nyaa-san whacked Kuro with her three tails.

He didn't unglue from her side. "N-n-n-no! I'm, uh, worried you might be scared too!"

Only Suimei remained silent, arms crossed and eyes shut. He had a sour look on his face.

I continued, "That woman has visited a number of times since then, but she always vanishes the moment she enters the store. The books she borrows are always suddenly back where they belong afterward, while a new book is replaced by more coins."

"What a weird customer," Shinonome-san said. "Nyaa, haven't you seen her around?"

"No, she always seems to come on days when I'm not here," Nyaa-san answered. I had met the woman three times so far, and each time I was the only one in the store.

Ginme was in tears and still clinging worriedly to his brother. "Are you okay? Wasn't it scary? Next time she comes around, call for me and I'll chase her off!"

"Aha ha, don't worry, I'm not scared at all!" I waved my hands and smiled. "I mean, I was a little scared at first. But now I'm happy we have another repeat customer! It's actually become something of a game for me to try and catch her when she disappears!"

"Oh, I see!" Ginme said cheerfully.

Kinme's face was exasperated. "Jeez, Kaori. You become a whole 'nother person when books are involved."

"Yes, well, I simply can't bring myself to hate a fellow book-lover. That said..." I rested my elbows on the low dining table and sighed. "The money's a bit of a problem."

"Really?" Kuro said. "But it's old money, right? Can't you sell that for a whole lot?"

"You'd think, right?! But no..." I began to explain how I brought the old coins to Toochika-san to learn their value.

With a shrug, he had said, *"These here are just really common mon coins. You probably wouldn't fetch the price of a bottle of tea for all of them."*

I was speechless when he said that. I'd bolted to a nearby internet café, found an online old coin market, and saw a couple hundred of these coins being sold for a paltry two thousand yen...

"Ugh. You're kidding..." Shinonome-san groaned bitterly when I told them all about it. Allowing one customer to get away with cheaper prices was a disservice to all our other clients.

"Actually, that's why I gathered you all here today," I said. I fixed my posture, then bowed my head. "I want to ask the woman to pay the normal fee, but could one of you be with me when I do? Her face is a little too scary for me alone, but I'd totally be able to do it if someone were there with me!"

Shinonome-san looked a bit skeptical, like he had something he wanted to say to that. The others avoided eye contact, clearly not too thrilled to help.

Only Suimei gave me a proper response: "No," he firmly stated. He looked almost angry about it. "Don't let that customer in anymore. How many times do I need to remind you that you might be in danger? Do you have any idea how hard we've been working to keep the spirit realm safe? Speaking of which, how could you let them inside in the first place when you don't even know what spirit they are?"

On Nurarihyon's request, Nyaa-san, Kinme, Ginme, and Suimei had been leaving the house a lot recently to help out around the spirit realm. I knew that they were working hard, but

I couldn't back down without one last push. "Y-you say that, but I actually *do* have an idea what spirit they are. They're likely the spirit known as 'the candy-buying ghost.'"

The tale of the candy-buying ghost was known all across Japan. While certain details varied from place to place, the main gist of the story always remained the same: A pregnant mother passed away and was buried, but her unborn child was born soon thereafter, in her grave. And so, her ghost walked the town every night, paying six copper coins—the fee to cross the Sanzu River—to buy candy to feed her baby as a substitute for milk.

"I'm pretty sure the woman is buying books for her child," I said. "I don't know why she's buying books instead of candy, though... Maybe she needs to soothe her child instead?" I could tell the woman really cared for her child, so I wanted to help by continuing to do business with her, if possible. Perhaps that was naive of me, but as someone raised by spirits, it felt only right to help spirits in need. I lowered my head again. "Please, I know you're all busy, but—"

"*No.*" Suimei said, coldly cutting me off.

"Why?!" I yelled. The stress of not being allowed to do anything was starting to get to me. "I'm just asking for one of you to be with me the next time she appears!"

"And I'm saying you shouldn't let her in at all anymore. Tell her the store's not open yet and chase her off."

"That's not fair! Ngh... Suimei, you're a meanie!"

"Yeah? Well, you're too kind for your own good!"

We glared daggers at each other.

"Okay, that's enough, you two." Kinme said, pulling us apart. "It's not like you to fight with each other." Smiling, he grabbed both of our hands. "There's no need to be so hotheaded, Suimei. I know you care about Kaori more than anything in the world, but you could do to phrase things a little nicer."

"Wh-what did you say?" Suimei said, blushing.

Kinme continued. "And you're being a little too willful, Kaori. It's nothing new for you to get all worked up when books are involved, but even I think it's weird to go through all the trouble of opening the store well before opening hours. Besides, how can you worry about fees when you're not even upholding our schedule at all?"

"Urk..." He had me there.

Seeing us now quiet, Kinme smiled. "At any rate, it's a fact that this woman's been borrowing books without paying the full fee, so we're going to need to talk to her regardless. It shouldn't be that hard, right, Shinonome?"

"Hmm... I suppose," Shinonome-san said, somewhat unsure.

"There you have it—the boss has given permission." Kinme pulled me and Suimei close. "Now make up, you two!"

We looked one another in the eye and awkwardly shook hands.

"I'm sorry for being so willful..." I said.

"I'm sorry for not hearing you out..." Suimei said.

"Honestly, you two fight like a married couple," Nyaa-san sighed.

"I'm happy you could make up with Kaori, Suimei!" Kuro said.

The animals gave us knowing grins. Suimei and I quickly withdrew our hands, embarrassed.

It was decided that starting the next day, someone would wake up and help prepare breakfast with me. I felt bad imposing on everyone, but it was also nice to have an extra hand around to help finish cooking earlier than usual.

Three days had passed since the mystery woman last came. I had my part-time job in the human world to go to, and my shift just so happened to overlap with Kinme's, so we decided he would be the one to wake up and accompany me.

"I'm still a bit sleepy." Kinme yawned, rubbing his eyes.

"Sorry about all the trouble. Here, have some of these." I handed him a plate of freshly cooked rolled omelet.

He beamed and took a huge bite. "Mmm, delicious! Man, I think your omelets taste even better than Noname's."

"Is that right? Heh heh... Here, want a sausage too?"

"Woo-hoo! Perks of waking up early!"

I smiled, thinking how funny it was that boys his age always had such huge appetites, even first thing in the morning. Kinme smiled back, then moved behind me to rest his chin atop my head.

"You're kinda making it hard to move, Kinme."

"Not my fault you're the perfect chin-rest height."

"Hey! I'm still growing! And what am I supposed to do anyway, not be this short?"

He snickered. "More importantly, you got a jellyfish from Nurarihyon, right? What'd you do with it?"

"Oh, that little thing? I've been meaning to return it, but he hasn't come by lately. I've put it in a goldfish bowl for now." I glanced toward the corner of the kitchen where a goldfish bowl I pulled out of the shed sat. I had somewhat neglected the jellyfish inside, but it didn't seem to mind, as it floated around just as lively as ever. It probably wasn't really a "living" creature, strictly speaking.

"Ah, so that's where it was. Oh, that gives me an idea. Take these," he said. Kinme rummaged around his breast pocket and pulled out a few raven feathers.

"Whoa, are you balding?"

"Pfft, ha ha! I guess these *are* my feathers, yeah." He cackled and shoved the feathers into my pockets. "Something good will happen if you hold on to these feathers... Probably."

"What's that supposed to mean? Are Tengu feathers a lucky item or something?"

"Yeah, totally, for sure. And if not, then let's just say I put my supernatural power into them or something."

"Ha ha, all right."

Suddenly, the long-awaited knock arrived. After Kinme and I shared a look, I turned off the stove and removed my apron. I was about to head to the store when I noticed Kinme heading off in the opposite direction. "Where are you going?"

"I'm gonna loop around from outside." With a grin, he slid open a glass door, stepped out onto the veranda, and took flight.

I took a deep breath the moment he left my view and pumped myself up. *This time for sure!*

I grabbed a paper lantern and picked up a fee chart I'd prepared beforehand. As I made my way to the entrance of the store, the click-clack of my sandals intruded on the silence. It was brighter than usual, perhaps because of the full moon. The yellowish luminance of the glimmerflies and the pale glow of moonlight mixed together, bathing the cold store in soft illumination. Already knowing who was beyond the door, I asked, "Who is it?"

Through the frosted glass, I saw a figure sway like the leaves of a willow tree. Like every time before, she replied, "I would like to rent a book."

"Okay, give me a second to open the door."

A tinge of worry surfaced as I remembered Suimei's words: *"Don't let that customer in anymore. How many times do I need to remind you that you might be in danger?"* I soon collected myself, though. If the woman wanted to hurt me, she would have done so on one of the previous three times we met. I should be fine.

"...Let's do this!" I remotivated myself and undid the door's lock. The moment I slid the door open, a warm breeze blew in, wafting over the scent of incense.

The woman's face looked devoid of vitality yet again today. In her hands was the same red cloth bundle she had last time, held dearly.

"Um, there's something I'd like to talk to you about today." I made my move immediately, before she had a chance to disappear. She stared back at me with lifeless eyes. My heart raced.

Choosing my words carefully, I continued. "It's about the fee for our book lending. Um... The payments you've made up until now have actually not been anywhere near enough." For a brief instant, I looked away from the woman and down at my hands to unfold the fee chart. But then I screamed and recoiled. "Eeek!"

A mass of jet-black hair had fallen onto my hands.

"E-ew! What is this?!" I yelled. I tried to shake the sticky, greasy hair off my hands but couldn't, and I panicked even more. My skin broke out in goosebumps as I fought the urge to shriek in sheer revulsion.

After some struggle, I finally managed to shake the hair off and breathed a sigh of relief. No sooner had I freed myself, however, than I froze stiff. The scent of incense was stronger now. Without my notice, the woman had moved close enough for me to hear her breathing—even though I could swear I hadn't heard the sound of her geta clacking against the floorboards. I heard a pounding noise in the depths of my ears, which took me a few seconds to recognize as the thudding of my own heartbeat. Sweat began to collect across my body.

Why am I so afraid? I thought to myself. I had been raised in the spirit realm and had met countless spirits over my lifetime. Sure, I still felt an instinctual fear when meeting enormous spirits, but that fear always faded after I got to know them. So what set this woman apart? I had met her a number of times already—it didn't make sense that I was still afraid of her every single time.

"Um..." I took a deep breath and worked up the courage to lift my head. I saw her eyes, staring back at me through a curtain of pitch-black hair, and immediately lost what courage I'd managed to scrounge.

She smiled stiffly and reached her rough fingers up to the gauze dressing around her neck, her pale red lips trembling. Bit by bit, she unwrapped the gauze to reveal a fresh scar that stretched all the way around her neck.

"A-ah..." I fought down a shriek.

Kinme's booming voice rang out. "What do you think you're doing?!"

The woman spun around with a swiftness she'd never shown me before. She saw Kinme standing with his arms crossed in the middle of the street and clicked her tongue, then bolted away.

"Hey, wait!" he called. "Kaori, get after her, quick! She's trying to run away without paying the fee!"

"U-um, I don't think I can stand..." I'd been scared senseless, and my legs were as shaky as a newborn fawn's.

"Jeez, fine!" Without warning, he picked me up.

"Thank y—"

"Whoa, you're kinda hea—"

"Don't you *dare* finish that sentence."

Kinme stepped out into the street and spread his wings. A sense of weightlessness came over me and suddenly we were flying through the air. Glimmerflies began to gather around and follow us, drawn in by my human aura.

We flew with a comet tail of glimmerflies behind us, searching for the runaway woman from above.

"Ah, right there!" I said, seeing the woman slip around a corner at a crossroad up ahead.

"Feel free to close your eyes if you get scared!" Kinme sped up, beelining for the crossroad. The wind roared against my ears, and I decided to take him up on his suggestion and shut my eyes. Then I heard him say "Huh?" He sounded deeply confused.

The shaking had stopped, so I figured we'd landed. When I opened my eyes, I saw nothing but a dark alleyway. I looked around, but the woman was nowhere to be found. "She got away?" I asked.

"Looks like it."

We shared a look and sighed. My fatigue hit me all at once and with nothing to show for it.

An unfamiliar yet familiar voice called out. "Oh? Is that Kinme I spy? What're you doing here?"

"Sensei!" Kinme said, face beaming. Kinme didn't open up to many people, so it was a surprise to see him like this.

A man approached, his leather shoes drumming as he walked. He had the appearance of a gentleman and wore a British-style suit, a fresh and unwrinkled shirt, and polished leather shoes without a speck of dirt on them. His hair was gray with streaks of white and combed to the side tidily. His eyes smiled softly and were a soft brown that reminded me of caramel. Smile lines were evident at the edges of his eyes. He seemed to be somewhere around his late forties but gave off the air of someone much younger. Toochika-san was around the same age, but he was more showy, like a rose, whereas the man before me now had a dignified elegance, more of a white magnolia blooming to a wintry sky.

The way the ends of his lips curled in a smile captured his mature charm well.

"Out searching for something this early in the morn? I see Nurarihyon's really putting you to work as well," the man said.

"Actually, we're not working for Nurarihyon today but chasing down someone who's trying to skip out on paying bookstore fees," Kinme replied.

"Oh, I see. I take it you've lost them?"

"Sadly, yes."

"Ha ha! Looks like you've got your work cut out for you."

Who's this? I've never seen this guy before.

I watched the pair talk briefly, and then Kinme introduced me. "This here is Seigen. He's an acquaintance of Sojobo."

"I'm just some insignificant fox spirit, a nobody compared to the Great Tengu of Kurama," Seigen-san laughed. By fox spirit, Kinme had to mean a Youko. Looking at the glimmerflies fluttering around me, Seigen-san said, "You must be the bookstore girl. I've heard quite a lot about you from Kinme."

"O-oh, um, right," I stammered. "I'm Kaori. Nice to meet you."

Seigen-san nodded warmly. "I think I might've spotted where that spirit you're looking for went."

"Really?!" I said.

"I believe so. Were they wearing a white yukata? If so, then I saw them pass through the gate to the Hell of the Black Rope in a hurry. It struck me as odd, since it's so early in the day."

"Th-that's them! But the Hell of the Black Rope...? Doesn't that lead to the Hokuriku region of Japan, Kinme?"

"I think so," he said. "If the tale of the candy-buying ghost is told there, maybe we can narrow down where the woman lives."

Seigen-san chimed in, "Oh, I happen to know that the tale originates from around Kanazawa in that area."

Kinme and I looked at one another and smiled. I surprised Seigen-san by firmly gripping his hand. Overjoyed, I said, "Please, tell us more!"

"O-oh, of course. Actually, why don't I go to Kanazawa with you two as your guide? There are many temples that claim to be the origin of the candy-buying ghost tale, so it'd probably be better if I came along rather than giving you directions. What do you say?"

"Oh... But we have our part-time job today," I said. I would've loved to take him up on his offer, but I couldn't skip work.

Kinme smiled. "You should go with him, Kaori. I'll tell Toochika what happened. You've been holed up in the house a lot lately; now's a good chance for you to get some sunshine."

"Are you sure? ...Suimei will definitely get mad."

Seigen-san raised an eyebrow and smiled softly. "Is that your boyfriend? He sounds like quite the protective one."

"U-um, well, no, he's not my boyfriend, per se..."

"Then what's the problem? You were planning on heading out in any case, correct? As long as Kinme-kun here keeps quiet, no one will find out."

"I don't know..." It felt kind of wrong, what with how worried Suimei was for me. But at the same time, I did kind of want to see what Kanazawa was like, especially the train station, since it had been recently refurbished as part of the Hokuriku Shinkansen development project. I glanced up at Seigen-san. He was waited patiently for my reply, his soft eyes—the color of caramelized sugar—smiling. *Kinme seems to trust him. I guess it should be okay.*

I made up my mind and accepted his offer. We decided to meet up after breakfast.

"Wonderful. I look forward to journeying with you," he said.

So that was how I ended up going to Kanazawa with Seigen-san.

I'll be honest: Any guilt I felt about the trip vanished the moment I arrived in Kanazawa.

"Whoooa! The Tsuzumi-mon gate is huuuuge!"

Styled after the drums used in Noh plays, Tsuzumi-mon gate loomed imposingly above the entrance to Kanazawa Station and acted as something of a grand entrance to the city. It was also so large that I grew dizzy just looking up at it.

"Don't get too worked up. You might get sick from excitement."

"I'll be fine! I'm an adult!" I replied enthusiastically.

"If you say so," Seigen-san said, with just a hint of exasperation. After we'd explored Kanazawa Station to my satisfaction, I said, "All right, let's go look for that temple the candy-buying ghost tale comes from... Huh? Is something wrong?"

Seigen-san turned on his heel, his look of exasperation transforming into a smile of total confidence. He put a hand on my shoulder. "Let's worry about that later. You've come all this way to Kanazawa, so you might as well take some time to enjoy it."

"Oh, I don't know... I lied to come here, so I'd like to return as soon as possible if I could."

"Ha ha ha, I thought you said you were an adult? Adults live by mixing lies with the truth all the time. It's nothing to worry about."

I frowned. "I'd rather not live like that."

"Oh? But you already lied to come here today, right?"

"Urk..."

He let out a throaty laugh, put an arm around my shoulder, and started walking.

"Wh-where are we going?" I asked.

Seigen-san's caramel-brown eyes sparkled like a little kid's. "To get something to eat. I'm thinking...sushi! Yes, sushi sounds nice. You can't visit Kanazawa without trying the sushi!"

"O-oh, sushi. I'm not sure I have enough money on me for that."

"What're you saying? It'll be my treat, of course."

"Huh?!"

Seigen-san laughed heartily. "I'm the one who's showing a youngster around town, it's only natural that I treat."

"Er, excuse me...?"

"Whew, it sure feels nice. Look at all the other middle-aged men looking at me green with envy! I bet they haven't spoken to someone under thirty in years."

"H-hey, I'm not some kind of showpiece! If you're an adult, shouldn't you at least know how to treat others with respect?!"

"Huh. Is that something adults do?"

"You can't feign ignorance whenever it suits you... Although that *also* sounds like something adults do."

I continued to complain, but Seigen-san didn't budge. In the end, the candy-buying ghost issue got sidelined, and I was dragged into Kanazawa City. We first went to a sushi restaurant like he wanted. It was my first time going to a sushi restaurant that wasn't the cheap conveyor-belt kind, and honestly, I don't think I can ever go back to the person I was before.

"My life will never be the same again... I've been ruined for all other pleasures," I said.

"Could you not phrase that in a way that invites misunderstandings?"

"How can you be so cold? Take some responsibility."

"Wh-what? ...How?"

"Ice cream!"

"Are you sure you want to sell your 'purity' for so cheap?!"

After ice cream, we went to Omicho Market, a place affectionately known as "the kitchen of Kanazawa." There were a variety of both fresh fish and fresh fruit stalls, as well as general goods stores, all closely packed together in a narrow street. Business seemed to be thriving, since scores of people were around.

"Whoa, it's as bustling as ever," I said.

"Oh? You've been here before?" Seigen-san asked.

"Yes, I came once with my father!" I picked a vegetable as I reminisced. "I was around six years old, I believe. We came because my father had something work-related in the area. Oh, and by father, I mean the spirit who adopted me, Shinonome-san. Anyway, I remember we heard from a local that there was a ninja temple nearby, so I pestered my father to take me there."

The ninja temple in question was Myoryuji Temple, a temple established by Maeda Toshitsune, the third lord of the then Kaga Domain. It had been built to act as a back-up castle, so it had devices like an offertory box that became a pitfall and floorboards that could be moved to reveal hidden stairs, hence earning it its nickname: "ninja temple."

"It's just the sort of thing a child would like, don't you think?" I said. "I was really looking forward to it, especially after waiting for Shinonome-san to finish his boring business discussions. But in the end, I didn't really enjoy it much..."

I recalled a certain man-child ruined the experience... *"Whoa, for real?! There were stairs under these?! So, if an enemy attacked, you could flee through here... Incredible. I need this in my own house!"*

"That fool got so into it, the tour guide had to ask him to calm down. I was so embarrassed..."

"L-Let's go home already, Shinonome-san!" I remembered insisting.

"No way. I'm not leaving until I learn everything there is to learn from this place!"

"What's the point of learning these weird things, you dum-dum?!"

Later on, he really had added a set of hidden stairs that was now in our bookstore.

"That man is honestly such a child," I muttered with a smile. "I was so grumpy with him on the way home, but now his childishness is nothing but a fond memory."

"Right..." Seigen-san said, sounding uninterested.

I looked over to see him pick up a vegetable roll and put it back down. Somewhat apathetically, he said, "You were adopted, right? Hard to imagine how you managed to become so close."

I blinked a few times, then smiled as I saw a bit of a pouty child inside the self-proclaimed adult. "Are you having troubles with your own children?" I asked.

"What's that got to do with you?"

"Nothing, I suppose..." I said. *Hmm... Would it be overstepping my bounds to push further?* As I took a brief pause to think, an interesting shop caught my eye. I returned the vegetable I was holding to an employee and said to Seigen-san, "Wait for me, I'll be right back!"

I sped to the shop—a butcher's—bought what I wanted, and sped back to my tour guide. He looked at what I'd bought and raised an eyebrow. "You just had ice cream and now you're eating again?"

"Aha ha ha! Well, there's always more room for junk food!" In my hands were two large croquettes. I cracked open the thin, deep-fried coating on one and grinned, over the moon to see plenty of minced meat goodness stuffed inside. An amber-brown hint of onion was also in the mix, adding sweetness to the mouthwatering smell. I hadn't felt hungry at all before, and yet I still couldn't help but gulp. "They're croquettes made with Noto beef. Did you know Kanazawa's also known for its beef?" I said, holding one of the croquettes out to him.

Seigen-san seemed momentarily bewildered, but he soon knit his brows. "What's this for?"

"I dunno, I thought we'd share!"

He looked at me funny.

"C'mon. Things are twice, maybe even three times as nice when shared with someone else."

Seigen-san didn't reply immediately. His eyes seemed somewhat emotional before he dropped his gaze. I took his hand and half forced the croquette onto him, staring intently, if a bit bashfully, into his caramel-brown eyes. "Certainly, Shinonome-san and I aren't related by blood… But I don't believe blood is what makes people a family in the first place. Forging memories, holding one another dear, sharing all sorts of things—that's what turns strangers into family. You should share something with your own children sometime."

"…Perhaps," he said. "Are you this kind to everyone?"

I swallowed the bite of croquette in my mouth and said, "Well, I'm no god, so I can't be kind to *everybody*! But I was taught to at least return the kindness given to me by others, and you were kind to me, so, y'know…" I paused. "Am I being too nosy? Heh heh, sorry." I got bashful again and distracted myself by taking a large bite of my croquette.

Seigen-san simply watched me, not speaking another word.

A light drizzle began to fall as evening neared, but we didn't bother with umbrellas. The clouds remained thin enough for the evening sun to shine through, hinting that the rain would soon pass.

We arrived at the most famous location featured in Kanazawa's version of the tale of the candy-buying ghost: Ameya Slope, which literally meant Candy Shop Slope. It was located next to one of Kanazawa's three clusters of temples and shrines near the Asano River and directly connected the Mount Utatsu-Sanroku Temple Complex with Koukaku Temple. In the past, the slope lived up to its name and was lined with candy shops, most of them branch stores of the well-known Ame-no-Tawaraya. Now, however, it was but a quiet residential area.

After walking up the slope some distance, Koukaku Temple was before us. The asphalt of the street, wet from the rain, looked glossy under the evening sunshine.

"Let's see, four temples claim the tale of the candy-buying ghost as their own, and this is one of them. There should be a Jizo statue dedicated to the ghost around here, right?" I asked, looking at the travel guide I got from Kanazawa Station.

"Yes. It should be in the temple's cemetery."

"All right, let's go!" With enthusiasm, I continued up the slope. If worse came to worst and I couldn't get payment for the missed book fees, at the very least I wanted to get the borrowed book back.

Ameya Slope was so steep, they said children used to pull people up it on carts for pocket change back in the Edo period.

Climbing it was a bit of a challenge for someone as out of shape as me. "Almost...there..."

With great effort, I managed to overcome the slope. I wiped the heavy sweat off my brow with a handkerchief and took a breather. Maybe it was time to start working out. Kinme *had* almost called me heavy just that morning.

"Are you all right?" Seigen-san asked.

"Hah... I'm winded," I managed to reply. "You seem fine, though."

"I don't skip leg day."

Youth and endurance don't necessarily go hand in hand, I thought. Just then, I saw a white figure in the distance and exclaimed, "Ah!"

The figure soon faded into the shadow of a building. I'd seen that they wore a white yukata with a hydrangea design and had long hair. It was definitely the spirit I was after.

"Seigen-san!"

"Coming, coming."

Seigen-san showed no sign of hurrying, so I left him behind and ran. *My legs feel all wobbly! Ah, jeez, what kind of lifestyle have I been leading?!* As I ran through the temple grounds, I swore to myself that I wouldn't just exercise but change my diet as well.

I couldn't see a single soul around, so I ran toward the last place I'd seen the woman go: the back of the temple. There, I found some stairs that led up to the cemetery. I despaired. *Oh no. Not another steep climb.*

The city of Kanazawa was situated on a river terrace, like one floodplain stacked on top of another, giving it many steep slopes. What was more, this temple was at the base of Mount Utatsu, so this particular slope was even steeper than most.

And I was trying to run up it.

"Haah, haah, haah…" My legs grew shakier by the second as I continued up the mossy steps, trees lining both sides of the path. Eventually, I reached the top, where I found the woman standing together with many Jizo statues. Three particularly grand Jizo statues stood at the base of a large tree. While mossy, the statues were clearly looked after. There were even flowers set out for them. The woman was gently stroking the red cloth bundle in her arms, whispering something indistinct.

The drizzle came to a halt. The clouds parted and sent a soft beam of light down, like a ladder up to heaven. It shone with a brilliant evening glow, filling my vision with rose-red light and elongating the shadows around me.

"Um, excuse me…" I said to get the woman's attention. She slowly turned to look at me. My heart jumped when I saw that she was weeping bitterly.

"How dare you…" she said.

"H-huh?"

"How dare you come here after what you've done!" Something was different about the woman. She didn't have that eerie, ghostly quality she always had at the bookstore but instead now had a forceful presence that only a living person could command.

What does she mean by "what I've done"?

The woman put her cheek to the red cloth bundle in her arms. "Did you not hear me? Do the wails of a mother pained to part with her child fall on deaf ears? Can you not understand? Does the resolve of a mother who does all she can to feed her child evade you? You, who abandoned your home, abandoned your parents, and wormed your way into the spirit realm..."

"...Huh? Are you trying to tell me something?" I said. My head heated up. Something about the woman's words irritated me. She talked as though she knew me, but she didn't know the first thing about me. The spirit realm *was* my home. I might have been born in the human world, but that didn't matter. I had been raised in the spirit realm, and I was proud of it. What right did she have to deny that? I'm sure my annoyance showed on my face.

She looked at me vacantly, still in tears. "Hah. Am I trying to tell you something, you say? There's so much I want to tell you. Yes...yes, perhaps you know nothing. Why don't I begin by showing you this?" With unsteady steps, she drew near. Her eyes were devoid of emotion. Her lips were a dark purple, nearly black, and her face was gaunt. Even bathed in the sunlight of the human world, she looked ghastlier than she ever had in the eternal darkness of the spirit realm. I took a step back out of fear. "I must have you know. Yes... Yes... Now, look. Look!" She came to a stop before me. Her face warped with grief as she undid the red cloth bundle in her arms. A fly buzzed out of its folds.

The moment I saw what was inside, I recoiled and fell backward onto the ground. Nausea assailed me, and I vomited. My vision wavered. The world spun from beneath me.

The woman was holding the corpse of a baby.

A great deal of time must have passed since it died. Its discolored body was sloughing apart in places, and it stank unbearably of rot.

I couldn't comprehend what was happening. My mind raced chaotically to work out why she would show me such a terrible thing. But the words she spoke next multiplied my confusion. "You might as well be the one who killed my child."

"Wh-what? I...?" I stammered. *Agh! Seigen-san! Hurry up and get here already!* I thought, desperate for the missing old fox. Hoping to put some distance between me and the woman, I inched backward.

The woman touched a finger to her baby's cheek. In a flat voice, she said, "This child was born this winter. I raised the child dearly, so, so dearly...yet one day a human took them from me. I searched all over the spirit realm for my child, to no avail. I was without hope, but then that man told me where my child's remains were."

She pointed behind me. Trembling, I slowly turned to look. I couldn't believe my eyes.

"Hey there!" It was Seigen-san, standing with the setting sun against his back. He smiled and waved.

"Seigen-san...?" I said, wide-eyed.

The woman spoke again. "That man there told me of your ties to human world exorcists. He told me how you deceived your way into the bookstore and tricked all the spirits there. You've been selling the body parts of spirits to exorcists for money, haven't you? Did you kidnap my child for money too?!"

"What are you talking about? I would never do anything like that!"

"Lies! I know you're harboring an exorcist in your bookstore! Is he the one you sell to?!"

"He's a *former* exorcist, and he would never do such things!" Blood rushed to my head.

The woman's pale face contorted into a scowl. "There's not an ounce of truth in your words. You had my child kidnapped, didn't you?! It's exactly as that man said… Everything, everything is your fault! Unforgivable. I would have killed you sooner if I could, but Nurarihyon would have known if I tried anything near the bookstore. But you came here yourself… Running headlong toward your own death! Oh, such joy. I'm more than happy to give you the death you seek!" she yelled, her black hair writhing wildly. She broke into a nightmarish grin, a crimson drop spilling from the skin on her lips as it split. "Don't worry. I'll make sure this is excruciating for you."

Without warning, her neck began to *float up away from her body*. She cackled as her head swayed in the air, her black hair fluttering behind her. "I'll gnaw your neck to pieces and scatter your innards all over this place!"

"Y-you're a Hitouban?!" I exclaimed. I ducked as she sped toward me, barely managing to dodge. I heard something tear and felt a sharp pain on the side of my head. Some of my hair had been torn out.

What in the world is going on?! I crawled away, confused and unable to summon strength into my legs. I looked up at

Seigen-san only to see him standing there with his arms crossed and a thin smile on his face. He had no intention of helping me.

...*I was tricked.* Tears welled in my eyes at the realization. After so many warnings from Suimei, I'd gone ahead and followed a stranger to the human world. How could I have been so stupid? I even understood now why I'd felt so much fear during all my prior encounters with the woman. Her eyes had held unfiltered malice and hatred for me, but I was too damn thick-headed to realize it.

The woman, who I now knew was a Hitouban spirit, roared. "Sit still and let me eat you!"

But I couldn't allow myself to simply roll over and die. I did my best to sidestep her attacks and sprinted away in the opposite direction of where Seigen-san was. My legs were still shaky from running up the slope; I thought I might tumble at any moment. The faces of everyone at the bookstore came to mind. *I lied to everyone. I have to return and apologize to them!*

I ran as fast as I could down the stairs and weaved through the headstones of the cemetery. But the sinister Hitouban followed me easily, cackling as it scraped pieces of flesh off my arms and legs. "Suffer, suffer, suffer! Suffer like my child did! Gya ha ha ha!"

I had never felt so much pain. Hot blood oozed from my wounds. I thought I could hear death's footsteps fast approaching from behind, so I ran as hard as I could—but my vision was starting to blur. "No... Somebody... Help me..."

I cursed my own powerlessness, more so than ever before. If only I had strength like Shinonome-san. If only I had medical knowledge like Noname. If only I had spirit magic like Nyaa-san.

If...if only I had *his* bravery and ability.

"Suimei! Help me!" I yelled. There was no way he could be here, and yet the only thing on my mind was him. I looked around, searching for him.

"Gya ha ha ha, gya h—" The maniacal cackling stopped abruptly.

"Huh? ...Ah, whoa!" Distracted, I tripped over my own foot and tumbled. I slammed into the ground hard and groaned in pain. I tried to get up right away, but my body wouldn't listen after all the strain. *No, I have to get up! Before I get eaten!*

As I envisioned the death awaiting me, a pair of bright red shoes entered my field of vision. They looked familiar. Just like the pair a certain awkward and unsociable boy used to wear.

"What...?" I looked up and saw Suimei looking down at me, a frantic look about him.

"What the *hell* are you doing here?!" he said. He propped me up, checked my wounds, and frowned.

"Ah... I..."

"Don't talk. You can explain later." He took some medicine from his pouch and began treating my wounds.

"Why are you here... In Kanazawa..."

"I said don't talk... Oh, whatever," he sighed. "A Hitouban child went missing, so Nurarihyon sent me here to investigate. I couldn't find them no matter where I looked, but then Kinme said he saw them around this way, and so I came to check the place out. I'd like to know what the heck *you're* doing here, though."

Kinme... Kinme, Kinme, Kinme! My heart felt like it was being wrenched from my chest. My mind was a mess. I didn't want to think about what my precious childhood friend might have done by sending me here.

I gripped Suimei's sweatshirt and quietly sobbed. Without saying a word, he put his arms around me and hugged me close.

Something dark leapt out the shadow of a headstone.

"Suimei! I stopped the spirit for now!"

I realized it was Kuro, with his adorable squat legs and long torso, and let out a sigh of relief. My relief was short lived, though, as his small body was knocked away by a dark figure that leapt out from the side.

"Aun!" Kuro whined.

"Kuro!" Suimei exclaimed.

A four-legged beast at least twice as large as Kuro had appeared. It had the same colors as Kuro, but its body was muscular like a wolf's. Suimei immediately reached for the talismans in his pouch but froze, wide-eyed, when he saw the person behind the beast—Seigen-san.

"F-Father?" Suimei said.

I heard a dull impact, and Suimei collapsed. Covered in injuries and exhausted to my limit, I fell down beside him, unable to support my own weight. From where I lay, I saw Suimei slowly closing his eyes, and Kinme behind him holding a bloodied rock.

"Kinme? Why?" I cried, but he averted his eyes. I shook my head and wept. "No... You couldn't have. You couldn't have!"

"Whew. I finally got this punk back, and I owe it all to you, Kinme," Seigen-san said cheerfully. He wore a warm smile, but then he went expressionless, like a switch had been flipped.

He reached a hand out to my neck. I was helpless to resist. "I suppose I should thank you as well, Kaori. I couldn't have done it without you either. Rest easy, now."

He clenched his hand around my carotid artery, and I felt my consciousness begin to fade.

Shinonome-san, I'm so sorry.

As tears streamed down my face, I apologized in my mind over and over to the father who raised me.

CHAPTER 4

False Memories Imparted on a Flowering Dogwood's Wish

My world was shapeless. Everything existed in a blurry haze of color and sound. I couldn't distinguish between self and other, and my consciousness threatened to fade the moment I let my mind wander.

I tried to think, but any thought I began soon scattered. The only things I understood were that I was lying in a Japanese-style room, in a white yukata, gravely injured, and that the room was teeming with the sickly sweet scent of incense. Everything else remained unclear.

A certain man was constantly by my side.

"How are you feeling today? Are you ready to change your bandages?"

He was always so kind. He tended to me with gentleness, as though handling something fragile. He stayed by my side day and night, nursing me through my fevers. Thanks to his efforts, my body began to recover. But apparently some scars would remain forever.

"Those mindless spirits are beyond redemption. How dare they hurt one of my own like this."

Every time he finished tending to my wounds, he would grieve. He would grieve how my scars would never fade, and he would apologize, over and over, incessantly. And every time he did so, I would trace a finger across his cheek and smile. In what voice I could manage, I would say, "It's...okay. Thank you. You're so kind."

He always made such a sad face when I told him that.

"Don't worry about me. Let's read. Can you continue from yesterday?" I asked. He would always read to me, as he knew I loved books.

I listened to his soft voice and closed my eyes. I tried to concentrate on the story, but my consciousness was too dim to follow. Every time I tried to focus on anything at all, the room's sweet smell entered my mind and hindered my thinking. Still, the soft tone of his voice was relaxing, so I didn't want him to stop. I let time pass by, listening to his voice as though it were melodious music.

I heard the sound of a book closing. He smiled, crow's feet appearing around the corners of his caramel-brown eyes. "Let's stop here for today," he said. "We'll pick up where we left off tomorrow. You must be tired, please rest." He brushed my hair to the side and kissed my forehead.

"Thank you. Seigen-san."

"Not at all, Midori. Anything for my beloved wife." He brushed my hair to the side one last time before leaving the room.

FALSE MEMORIES IMPARTED...

I watched his back leave my view as he slid the door shut, then took a deep breath. Shutting my eyes, I let myself drift off into shapelessness once more. My still-healing wounds throbbed with pain, but once I let the sweet smell of incense take over, the boundary between myself and the world melted away. I swayed in nothingness. I felt a tinge of fear at the haziness of it all, when suddenly a memory of who I was returned to me: My name was Shirai Midori, and I was the wife of Shirai Seigen, the man who had just left. I had been severely wounded the other day and was now recovering at our home.

After two weeks, my body had healed a great deal. I still lacked some feeling in my arms and legs, but I could move as long as I had some assistance. Seigen-san was delighted to see my condition improve.

"Thank goodness, you've gotten so much better! At this rate, you'll be back on your feet in no time. Do you think you can try some walking?"

"Yes, if you're with me, Seigen-san."

"Oh, dear... You say the sweetest things."

Starting the next day, Seigen-san began taking me outside for physical rehabilitation. On the first day, we simply sat on the veranda outside my room. The following day, we walked a little farther, and so on. My body was weak from being in bed for so long, but Seigen-san patiently supported me throughout.

Rehabilitation was difficult, but I could feel myself recovering day by day, and that made me happy. Still, one thing bothered me: "Seigen-san, when can I see Suimei? I haven't seen his face in so long."

"He's off somewhere far away for work right now. There's no need to worry about him. He's taken over the family trade. Your body isn't built for that kind of work; you should spend your days relaxing here."

"I see..."

I had a precious son...supposedly. My mind was too dull to recall him clearly. That frustrated me, but I told myself my memories would grow firmer in time, just like my consciousness had as my wounds healed. Telling myself that relieved me, although the fact that my mind still felt hindered by something while my body was nearing full recovery had unsettled me as of late. I frequently had a headache as well, but it wasn't so painful as to cause much worry. Although I had to wonder: Why did my mind feel so dull? My body was gravely wounded, but could that really affect my mind to such a degree? I tried asking Seigen-san about this, and he said it was the effect of the incense in my sickroom. As far as I could remember, the smell of incense had been present since I first lay injured. Sickly sweet like honey, one whiff made my head numb and clouded my consciousness.

Afraid that the smell was making me sleep against my own will, I asked him if we could stop using the incense. As if he were reasoning with a child, he replied, "That incense is to dull your pain. You wouldn't be able to sleep at all without it. It's here for your sake, so please bear with it."

So bear with it I did. Everything Seigen-san did for me was out of kindness. How could I refuse what was done for my own sake? Besides, it would only be until my injuries healed. Until that long-awaited day came, I would continue to spend my days peacefully with him.

One day, I awoke to find Seigen-san missing from my side.

Didn't he say he would stay by my side until I awoke? I found it a bit silly how doting my husband could be but felt a tinge of worry all the same. As far as I could remember, Seigen-san had never broken a promise to me. The embers of the incense burner were dim. He had been gone for quite some time.

I draped a haori over my shoulders and quietly walked out into the corridor. The soles of my feet still lacked some feeling. Taking care not to tumble, I moved carefully across the wooden floorboards and wandered my home in search of Seigen-san.

The Shirai family home was of magnificent make. It was standing proof of our family's lengthy and famous history as Inugami-using exorcists. The corridor before me appeared to stretch as long as our history, the rooms to the sides seemingly uncountable. The end of the corridor was too steeped in darkness to make out.

It was eerie.

With a slight shiver, I averted my eyes away from the end of the corridor. The instant I did, I noticed something shining at the edge of my vision and looked down the corridor once again. "A butterfly...?" What appeared to be a butterfly scattered light at the end of the gloomy corridor. I found myself entranced by its ephemeral beauty and crept toward it, silencing my footsteps.

"Anything new to report?" Suddenly, I heard Seigen-san's voice coming from inside the room I was passing. His tone was stiff, completely different from the one he used to talk to me. In my surprise, I froze.

A different voice replied. "Things are going well. Arrangements are mostly complete. The negative emotions are building by the day. We can expect the spell to be complete soon."

What could they be talking about? I wondered. Each word uttered by the second party stirred unease in me.

I heard Seigen-san speak again. "I couldn't care less about that. I'm talking about the bookstore."

Bookstore? My heart began to race the moment I heard that word. I didn't know what inside of me was reacting to the word, but it worried me just the same.

A third voice spoke. "Oh! That's my report to make, isn't it? Well, I'd say things are going as you'd expect. Everyone's all worried sick about their missing girl. I kinda feel sorry for them a little... Oh?"

The third voice abruptly went silent. I thought it odd they'd stop at such a strange point, when suddenly the sliding door slid open beside me.

"Sensei, were you expecting a guest?" A dark-haired youth with golden eyes was on the other side of the sliding door. He was dressed in the unusual attire of a mountain ascetic. He looked me over head to toe rudely and gave me a shallow smile. "Nice to meet you. You must be Sensei's wife."

I blinked a few times in surprise, then bowed my head. "U-um, yes. I'm Midori."

I spotted another person behind the youth. He had black hair with red highlights and a slender face that looked like a woman's. His clothes were trendy, combining a hooded sweatshirt with a hakama-less kimono. I recognized him as Seigen-san's Inugami familiar.

"I thought you would be asleep for a little while longer," the Inugami said. "Is something the matter?"

I replied, "Oh, n-no, I'm sorry... It's only that I was worried because Seigen-san wasn't around."

"Ah, so you came to look for him. There must not have been enough incense, although I could have sworn I put in the usual amount. Forgive me. ...Master, if you would."

"I know." Seigen-san appeared from the back of the room and took my hand. "You must have been awfully surprised to find me missing. This timing works out well though. Why don't we have some tea?" His tone had changed again, back to the gentle one I was used to hearing.

I breathed a sigh of relief and squeezed his hand back. "Yes, please."

"Some brown sugar manju might be a good pairing with the tea today."

"That sounds nice," I replied.

As we walked down the corridor, I felt a gaze from behind and turned to see the youth with golden eyes.

"Ha ha..." He furrowed his brows slightly and gave an awkward wave before returning with Akamadara to the room they'd been in. I remembered the luminescent butterfly from before and looked around, but I couldn't find it. Perhaps my eyes were playing tricks on me earlier?

"Is something the matter?"

"No, it's nothing."

It weighed on my mind a bit, but I soon returned my attention to my husband beside me.

"They're beautiful," I said.

"Indeed. They bloomed wonderfully this year," Seigen-san replied.

Some days later, I was with Seigen-san and Akamadara looking at flowers in our vast inner courtyard. The flowers were maintained by Akamadara in a way that gave one something to appreciate in each of the four seasons. A few flowering dogwood trees were in bloom right now, their many small yellow flowers each surrounded by four petal-like bracts. Flowering dogwood was actually native to North America, but Seigen-san went out of the way to plant some here as he loved novel things. The pure white of the bracts felt right at home with the Japanese aesthetics of the garden.

Seigen-san and I sat on a bamboo bench underneath one of the flowering dogwood trees and gazed at the flowers at the height of their bloom. The rays of the spring sun were gentle and seemed to grant vitality to my feeble body. Seigen-san was out of his usual fitted suit, instead he wore a relaxed hakama-less kimono. Worryingly, however, I noticed that there were dark shadows under his eyes. He even seemed a bit thinner on account of having less of an appetite for the past few days. I asked, "Have you been staying up late?"

"Not at all," he replied.

"Please, you don't need to hide it from me. I can tell you're tired. Has he been staying up late, Akamadara?"

Akamadara, standing behind us, held his fedora over his chest and bowed. "It is as you say. Master has reduced his sleeping hours as of late."

"Akamadara..." Seigen-san gave him a pointed look, but Akamadara was unfazed.

"It is the truth, Master."

"I knew it!" I exclaimed. I gently put my hands on Seigen-san's head and brought it to rest on my lap.

"Wh-whoa."

"Hm, maybe this bench is a little small." I giggled and began stroking his gray hair. He seemed a bit shaken by this and blushed. I asked, "Is something bothering you?"

He was quiet for a few moments. Eventually, he said, "How are you feeling?"

"Me? Much better, thanks to you. I should make a full recovery soon."

"I see." Seigen-san scratched his neck like there was more he wanted to say. His hand, usually hidden in a leather glove, was on full display before me. Curious, I touched it. It was sinewy and covered in scars. It was the hand of a man who had been through much. I slowly traced his scars with my finger. He grabbed my hand and lightly squeezed it. "I'm worried," he said.

"About what?" I asked.

He moved his fingers about as though enjoying the softness of my hands and said, "I'm…worried you might leave me once you recover."

I found his words odd. We were married. Why would I leave him?

"I'm not going anywhere; I'm your wife," I said. "If you mean you're worried I'll pass away, then wouldn't you be more likely to leave me, since you're older?"

"That's not what I mean. That's not what I mean…" he muttered bitterly, squeezing my hand hard. "Can I tell you about my past?"

I nodded, making him breathe a sigh of relief. He began telling me of his early life.

"All my life, the places where I've belonged have been taken from me."

Seigen-san had not been born to the Shirai family but as the eldest son of a different exorcist family with a long, distinguished history. Trained to be an exorcist from a young age, he remembered growing up jealous of the normal children who could play while he stayed home studying.

His ability as an exorcist was, as he described it, painfully average. As the future successor of a distinguished family line, a certain level of strength was expected from him. He and all the adults around him tried various methods to make him grow stronger. The countless scars on his hands were a testament to that time.

"It was around then that my younger brother was born, a child born from my father and his lover. I thought he was an adorable little child...until that one day."

The day his younger brother turned five, he was given an aptitude test and was discovered to be an exceptionally gifted exorcist.

"From the very next day, my family's treatment of us changed. Our rooms were swapped, and he sat at a higher seat of honor than me when we ate. Everything that was once meant for me went to my younger brother, and I only ever received his leftovers. The position of family heir was taken from me. From that moment forward, I was no longer anything but a spare for my brother."

"That's cruel..." I said.

"That's how those kinds of families are; lost in their foolish, vain pride as exorcists."

The days following the change were bitter for Seigen-san. He had put up with his unreasonable conditions and excessive training all because he considered himself duty-bound to do so as the heir. But in a single moment, all his years of suffering were rendered meaningless. Even so, he wasn't allowed to start living a normal life either. As his brother's "spare," he had to continue his harsh training on the off chance that something happened to his younger brother. He was trapped by the antiquated conventions of his home.

"I was in my own inescapable hell. I couldn't leave or run away, was constantly berated by my younger brother's supporters, and had no choice but to endure it all. 'This isn't fair,' I would think. 'My younger brother is the one who should be *my* spare.'"

"...Are you all right?" I asked, brushing his shoulder with my free hand. I couldn't see Seigen-san's face from my position, but I could feel him crying.

He brought my hand to his cheek and continued. "After some time, my younger brother had a child, one more gifted than me. At long last, my role as a spare came to an end. Instead, I became a pawn for a political marriage."

He was married off to the daughter of a family with an equally long history as exorcists.

"I was relieved at first to hear I was marrying into the Shirai family. I thought I was finally free from my own kin. I wouldn't have to be an heir or a spare anymore, and I could finally have a place I belonged." He laughed bitterly. "I was naive. I was so caught up in finally being able to leave the family that I forgot I was a pawn in a political marriage and that a place for me wasn't necessarily guaranteed."

The Shirai family bloodline was possessed by Inugami spirits. Powerful Inugami were passed down among the family, generation after generation. The woman Seigen-san married was of weak constitution and couldn't fulfill the role of family head. That was why Seigen-san, who was from a respectable family line, was chosen to be her husband. But waiting for him was the position of family head in name only.

"The only thing this family needed from me was my name. It didn't need *me* at all."

"W-wait, hold on," I interrupted. My mind was whirling. What was going on? This was the Shirai family, right? And Seigen-san's wife was me...right? My voice trembling, I asked, "Do you have a wife other than me?"

With a start, he turned his head to look at me. He turned his body around as well and touched my cheek. "I'm sorry, that was...a story about someone else. Please forget it. You don't need to look so sad."

"...If you say so." Something was out of place, but I swallowed my questions. Even more than I wanted the truth, I wanted to set the world-weary man before me at ease. "It's okay. I understand what you mean to say. You enjoy being with me, so you're afraid something might happen, and I'll disappear." I combed my hand through his hair. It was disheveled from him resting his head on my lap. His face was as sad as that of a lost child, and I giggled at the sight of it. "It's all right. I'll always be here to give you a place to belong." His eyes widened a bit in surprise. I brushed the hair covering his forehead to the side. "It must have been so hard to not have a place you felt you belonged. No place to hide, no place to go when you're hurt. It's hard for me to imagine a life like that."

Everyone needed somewhere they belonged, somewhere they could rest their weary heart. It didn't need to be a physical place. It could be a person or even an activity, a lover, a family member, a friend, or even a hobby. It didn't matter what it was, as long as it was a place you could relax and where you wanted to stay, a place that made you no longer afraid of tackling the coming day. It was a simple thing really, one we took for granted. But once lost, it was hard to rediscover.

"I won't go anywhere," I said. "You've treated me dearly, and I was taught to return the kindness shown to me by others."

Taught by who? My mind wandered. I felt another headache coming on. For a brief instant, the face of a man with an unkempt beard surfaced in my mind. *Who is that?*

I was confused but then saw Seigen-san looking up at me sadly. I smiled and said, "You don't need to fear losing the place you belong anymore."

He hugged my hips tightly, like a spoiled child might. In a raspy voice, he said, "Wouldn't that be nice."

My eyes widened slightly with surprise. I patted his back gently and thought, *What a clumsy yet adorable man.* I looked up and saw the darkening spring sky, as well as the dogwoods' flowers in full bloom. If my memory served me correctly, flowering dogwood meant "please accept my feelings" in the language of flowers. *I wish to do just that,* I thought. *As your wife, I wish to reciprocate your feelings of love.*

A flower on one of the trees moved despite the lack of wind. I looked closely and spotted the luminescent butterfly I'd seen the day before. Excited, I shook Seigen-san's shoulders. "Seigen-san, look! There's a strange butterfly right over there!"

But he didn't look up. He simply tightened his hug on me and mumbled, "There's no butterfly. There's no butterfly, Midori…"

Thinking it strange, I looked back at the butterfly and saw it fluttering around a flower. Unlike the day before, it hadn't disappeared. It was there, but Seigen-san said it wasn't. Maybe my eyes were playing tricks on me again?

Worried, I looked to Akamadara. His expression betrayed nothing, his pomegranate-colored eyes narrowed deep in thought.

I awoke suddenly during the night. The pale light of the moon shone into my room through the paper sliding door. The air was sultry, even though the rainy season was still far away. I loosened the collar of my nightwear and reached for the pitcher of water by my pillow, then froze stiff upon noticing a person at the edge of my vision.

"Oh, you're finally awake. I figured it was about time the incense ran out." It was Akamadara. He sat beside my bed, staring at me. "I seem to have surprised you. Forgive me."

"Why are you here?" I asked. "Where's Seigen-san?"

"He was exhausted, so he retired to his room. That works out well; it's better I'm alone today."

"Huh?"

"It's nothing. Just talking to myself." He plastered on an empty smile.

It was rude to intrude on a woman's room and avoid giving a reason. I was about to glare at him, but my head began to throb, so I stopped. The throbbing was worse than any time before.

It felt like my head was being pounded by a hammer. As I tried to withstand the pain, a cup of water was offered to me. Although my vision was blurry, I managed to look up and saw Akamadara there with an ambivalent smile on his face.

"Here."

"Th-thank you..." I took the cup and drank its contents in one go. The lukewarm water seemed to permeate every corner of my body, easing my pain a smidge. I sighed. "Ahh... Thank you. I've had so many headaches as of late."

Akamadara's crimson eyes narrowed thoughtfully. "It must be because the incense is losing its effect. Humans can grow accustomed to anything, after all."

"The incense...? Oh, the incense that dulls my pain."

"No, that's not its true function. While it does have a numbing effect, its main use is to dull your thinking and evoke false realities. It's a special incense we use to brainwash captured spirits."

Brainwash? My heart raced at that disturbing word.

Akamadara smiled thinly, as though enjoying my reaction. He said, "Your painful headaches are proof that the brainwashing is fading. Personally, I'd rather it faded all at once, but what can you do?"

Wh-what is he saying?

He began to ask me questions like a doctor might. "How frequent are your headaches?"

"Huh? Um, quite frequent."

"Have you felt like your thoughts were being hindered by something?"

"Um... Yes. Yes, I believe so." I answered his questions without thinking too deeply.

Akamadara nodded, satisfied, and then pointed to my pillow. "Search beneath that. You'll find something interesting."

"Huh...?" I did as he said and felt something inside the pillow. I pulled it out and found it was a handful of jet-black raven fathers. *They're the same color as the hair of that youth with golden eyes,* I thought. My headache became almost unbearable. I did my best to endure the throbbing pain.

Akamadara began to speak again. "It seems it's about time. This might make my master furious with me...but necessary it remains. This, and everything else, is for the sake of granting his wish." He smiled another superficial smile. "Now then, why don't we go for a walk?"

"At this time of night? I can't go without Seigen-san's permission..."

"It's fine, this walk is for his benefit."

"Huh?"

Akamadara's words were lost on me.

He snickered at my visible confusion but soon turned serious. "Actually, you have no right to refuse in the first place. You will come." He pulled out a matchbox from his breast pocket. "Hold one of those feathers in your hand. The rest you can store away in your breast pocket." He lit a match against the box. The air began to smell of smoke, and a single tiny flame lit the dim room. Our shadows grew long, dancing as the flame wavered. "I'm... also someone without a place I belong," he said, smiling weakly.

He stared into the match flame as he continued. "I overheard your conversation with Master earlier this afternoon. Your words resonated with me, so much so that it hurt. I only have Master in my life. But he doesn't find comfort in being by my side, so I'm left without a place to belong.

"But you're different," he continued. "You have somewhere you belong, a place you can return to. No, you *must* return. You cannot fulfill what my Master wishes, so instead I will have to wake you from your illusion." He blew on the match flame. It turned from red to blue and began to give off prismatic sparks. I was stunned by the mysterious sight and didn't notice when he brought the flame to the feather in my hand. A large spark jumped and set the feather ablaze at its tip.

"Ah!" I exclaimed, about to let go of the feather.

"You mustn't drop it. You need this to see the truth," he said, grabbing my hand. He gazed at the multicolored sparks, spellbound. "When this burns away, you will wake from your dream. Are you ready?"

I swallowed hard. "Before that, let me ask one thing. Did Seigen-san really lie to me?" I could feel myself near tears. I didn't want to believe it. Seigen-san was so kind. So caring. Could he really have brainwashed me? "If I'm not his true wife, then… why me?"

Akamadara didn't answer my question. Instead, he smiled knowingly and looked down his nose at me. "While I could tell you everything now, that wouldn't be for the best. I know very well how twisted I can be, and I doubt that I could give a truly objective explanation. It's best that you see the truth with your own eyes. Oh, but I will tell you one thing..." He paused for emphasis. "Simply having a child does not make one a parent."

His words were a mystery to me. I stood there confused, but he looked refreshed by the topic and went on. "These feathers come from a certain raven Tengu, one with a knack for deceiving others. His illusions are so advanced, his victims don't even realize what they're seeing is an illusion. Of course, his ability to wake someone from an illusion is just as superb."

At that instant, the feather began to emit a light too bright to look at directly. I instinctively shielded my eyes. I felt heat along my fingers until, suddenly, the feather was gone.

"Huh...?" Cautiously, I opened my eyes. To my shock, my surroundings had changed completely. The spotless walls of what should have been my room were now riddled with cracks. The ceiling was covered in spider webs strewn with dried insect carcasses. The paper of the sliding door was tinged yellow, and it had been torn. The tatami mats were bulging and misshapen because a plant was growing through the floor. Through the crumbling ceiling I could see an unfamiliar pale-pink night sky. It was like I had suddenly wandered into an entirely different world.

A glowing thing fluttered closer. It was the luminescent butterfly I had seen before. It danced about the air, coming close enough to brush past my face.

"Ngh...!" My greatest headache yet struck me. My head felt like it was splitting as a harsh fever took hold of me. I could feel my veins pulsing underneath my skin. Every time the butterfly flitted past my vision, a scrap of memory flickered to mind briefly. I had no recollection of any of the memories, and yet my heart raced as though they were precious to me. "I-I'm..." I fell to my knees and tried to bear the pain. Memories of my true self tore through my mind. There was a younger me. A world of darkness. Gathering butterflies. Endless fear. A stream of tears. And... people. Kind people who cared for me. The place I belonged was where they lived. It was a place filled with values different from those of humans, a place filled with frightening yet lovable spirits. The spirit realm.

"Everything's going to be all right, Kaori. I'm right here."

Shinonome-san... My eyes welled with hot tears. *I'm not Midori, am I? I'm...*

"Kaori. I'm Kaori. And...I live at the spirit realm's only bookstore."

Hearing me finally speak, Akamadara nodded. Quietly, he said, "Yes. You are Muramoto Kaori, and this is the spirit realm, a world of eternal night, only a thin paper's width removed from the human world. This is your true reality." He slid open the closet and took out a paper lantern. With a practiced hand, he put the nearby glimmerfly into the lantern and turned to face me. He smiled sadly. "Allow me to guide you. I will tell you what I can along the way."

Akamadara led me to another room in the residence. It was a dim room—the light from the corridor didn't reach that far in—and it appeared to be a dead end. But after removing the floorboards, he revealed a hidden set of stairs that led underground.

We slowly descended the stairs, relying on the light of the glimmerfly alone. The air was stagnant, and the smell of mold made my nose wrinkle.

At the bottom of the stairs, we were met by absolute darkness. I was reluctant to rely on the weak light of the glimmerfly lantern. I put a hand against the wall and found it was bare stone, damp to the touch.

Just as he had offered, Akamadara filled me in on things as we made our way along. According to him, I had been brought straight to the spirit realm after losing consciousness in Kanazawa. I was brainwashed with the incense to think I was Shirai Midori, Suimei's late mother, and lived as though I were Seigen-san's wife.

"Why though? What could he get out of doing that?" I asked. Even though the incense had worn off, I still had my memories from when I was Midori. I remembered the faces of my supposed parents, as well as things that happened in my youth. I even remembered the day I married Seigen-san. It was mind-numbing to think the incense was powerful enough to make all those fabrications feel so real. "What reason could he possibly have for going to such lengths?"

"In the beginning, you were meant to be our trump card to make Suimei obey Master," Akamadara answered. "But as time passed, it seems he had a change of heart... I don't know the exact details, though."

"I see. Still, exorcists are really something else. To think you guys could brainwash someone into thinking they were a different person..."

"To tell the truth, most exorcists don't know that incense exists. It's something of a family secret. Families with long histories like the Shirai all pass down some dark, secret art or another."

According to Akamadara's explanation, the incense was mixed with a piece of the original person whose memories I took on. I wasn't exactly keen to learn *what* piece exactly, but it seemed that the memories implanted in me were indeed those of the actual Shirai Midori. ...Then what of the feelings I felt for Seigen-san? Those warm, sweet, and sometimes excruciating feelings. Was that Midori-san's love for him?

As I sank deep into thought, Akamadara switched topics. "Have you figured it out yet? About the Shirai home?"

"Huh?"

He sighed with some exasperation. "I was so certain you, of all people, would remember. The spirit realm is where things lost to the human world are reborn. Such is especially the case with places bound by strong memories. Certainly you understand what it means for this residence to be in the spirit realm?"

"W-wait..." My plate was full enough from adjusting to my situation; I hadn't even begun to question *why* this place was in the spirit realm. I started putting the pieces together: Things gone from the human world came to the spirit realm. The Shirai residence was in the spirit realm. Which meant... "The Shirai residence is no longer in the human world?"

"Correct. As a result of the curse backlash caused by Suimei-sama severing his connection with his Inugami, that home no longer exists in the human world."

FALSE MEMORIES IMPARTED...

"Oh... Oh."

My face paled as I recalled Seigen-san's words: *"All my life, the places where I've belonged have been taken from me."* After all he had been through, the final place he belonged was taken from him by his own son.

The Midori inside me cried at the realization.

An iron grid door appeared before us from the darkness. Akamadara came to a stop. He undid the lock and gestured for me to enter. "The cause of this home's downfall is just ahead. I'm sure you've been dying to meet him."

I gasped and took the lantern he offered. I passed through the grid door and ran forward recklessly into the darkness. I didn't care if I tumbled. I didn't care if I collided with a wall. I wanted my legs to carry me to him fast, faster, even a second sooner.

The sound of my panting and my footsteps echoed off the walls. I heard a weak voice from somewhere.

"Please, let me out of here..."

It was the voice of a young boy. I sped up, my heart aching in my chest.

What Akamadara said about the spirit realm being where things lost in the human world went was true. But that didn't mean things reappeared here the same as they once were. Places were slowly consumed and claimed by the spirit realm, often becoming unrecognizable as their former selves. The sorry state of my room was such an example. But there was more than a mere physical change. Strong sentiments and emotions that imprinted on places during their time in the human world would replay like a broken record, over and over. Just like how a young boy's voice echoed here now.

"*Why? Why am I not allowed to smile?*"

"*I'm sorry. I'm sorry. I won't cry anymore. I won't smile. I'll suppress everything.*"

"*Mother... Mother... Why won't you come see me? Why, Mother?*"

The sound of sobbing. The sound of begging for forgiveness. The sound of cries for a mother. My heart felt like it would tear apart each time they reached my ears.

Eventually, I found a light in the darkness: a small, fixed paper lantern in front of a zashiki prison cell. Nearly tripping over my own feet, I ran toward it and yelled his name through the wooden lattice grid. "Suimei!"

I could vaguely make out a figure in the gloom, but it was too dark to be sure. Frantic, I released the glimmerfly in my paper lantern and let it fly through the wooden lattice grid. The yellowish light of the glimmerfly lit the corners of the cell, revealing Suimei with Kuro in his arms, draped in a discolored blanket.

"Suimei! Suimei! Are you all right?!" I called, but he didn't move a finger. He couldn't be dead, could he?

I heard a large sigh spill out behind me. "Please, calm yourself. Humans, I tell you..." Akamadara unlocked the door to the prison cell. "Go on ahead."

Without even pausing to thank him, I rushed in. Running up to Suimei's side, I noticed a sickly sweet smell hung in the air.

"Master used the incense on him as well," Akamadara said.

"Then he's being brainwashed with someone else's memories?"

"Indeed, although he is far more resistant to it than you were. He's not the next head of the family for nothing. It took a great deal of effort to lock him in here. Now I'd say it's time we wake him up, Kaori-san. Hand me the rest of the feathers you brought."

"Oh, right!" I pulled out the feathers I had stashed away in my breast pocket and handed them to Akamadara. He quickly set them alight, then thrust them before Suimei's eyes, sparks of all those prismatic colors flying off. After the feathers finally burned away, Suimei's eyelids began to flutter.

"Ugh... My head..." He scowled as though in pain and slowly opened his light-brown eyes.

He's alive. I reached out and touched his face, my heart racing. The wound on his head was treated, and his complexion wasn't too bad, all things considered. But his cheeks were wet with tears.

"Mother... It's dark. I'm scared..."

Hearing that voice from the distant past, Suimei quickly covered his ears.

Had he been stuck in this dark and gloomy place listening to these voices this whole time, forced to relive the days when he endured a hell so cruel his hair turned from black to white? I didn't want to imagine what it must have been like. *Horrible. How could anyone do such a thing...*

"Kaori...?" Suimei squinted, noticing my presence. "You're all right. Thank God. I was so worried that bastard had done something to you."

Overwhelmed with emotion, I threw my arms around Suimei's neck. "You should be worrying about yourself first! You're clearly worse off... I was so worried about you..."

He patted my back. With some relief, he said, "I'm not worth worrying about. I couldn't even protect *myself*, even after talking so big to Shinonome about protecting you."

"Oh, be quiet. I'm just glad you're safe. Really..." I began to sob.

"Hey, don't cry on me now. I'm not gonna kick the bucket that easy." Smiling wryly, Suimei stroked my back as if I were a child. His hands felt gentle and warm, their comfort only making me cry more.

"*Ahem*. I hate to break up this heartwarming reunion..." Akamadara looked ill at ease. "But you seem to be squishing Suimei-sama's Inugami, Kaori."

"...Ah!" I quickly separated from Suimei. Between us was a squished Kuro.

"Aun..." he whined.

"I-I'm so sorry, Kuro!"

"K-Kuro, are you all right?!"

We stroked Kuro's fur to comfort him.

"Now then, it seems we're ready," Akamadara said. "I would like to take you both to see my master now."

Suimei shot him a suspicious glare. "What are you planning? And what *are* you anyway? Kuro should be the last Inugami in the Shirai family, and Seigen isn't capable of making any new ones."

"Oh dear. You sure hold your own father to low standards."

"That bastard is the head of the family in name only. He lacks talent. The elders tried to have him make a new Inugami after mom died, but it was an utter failure. There's no way he'd be able to make an Inugami strong enough to take human form."

Akamadara let out a throaty laugh and spun around, turning his back to us. "It really isn't such a mystery. Master was…desperate. He was willing to rely on a total stranger to try and protect the only place he felt he belonged." He stepped through the wooden lattice grid prison and looked back at us. His expression was hidden by the darkness. "Suimei-sama… After you left, the backlash of your Inugami's curse brought ruin to the Shirai family. Master's birth family did nothing to help—they were more than happy to be rid of the Shirai. Driven to despair, Master was ready to take his own life. But then his savior appeared." The light of the glimmerfly wavered with each beat of its wings. Akamadara's eyes, the color of ripened pomegranate, reflected a profound, vivid darkness. "A hero who called themself the mermaid-meat seller."

"Mermaid meat? …No. It couldn't be." Suimei paled.

Akamadara smiled knowingly. "Mermaid meat is quite the rare item. It can grant any wish one desires, even eternal life, for example. My master wished for great power; power befitting the head of an exorcist family, power that was more than enough to command an Inugami. And so…I came to be." He sighed bitterly. "Why don't we bring an end to this charade? Allow me to show you the way."

Suimei and I shared a look, then stared back at Akamadara. He had a look of resignation on his face.

Akamadara led us up to the inner courtyard. It had been beautiful the last time I saw it, but now it was beyond recognition, claimed by the spirit realm. A pale-pink sky overlooked everything. The once meticulously arranged garden stones, hedges, koi pond, and all else were overrun by a grove of flowering dogwood. The courtyard was in a state of total ruin, and yet the pure-white bracts and the fluttering glimmerflies shone so beautifully against the night, it was otherworldly.

"Hey. I was beginning to worry when I couldn't find you in your bedroom. Where'd you go?" Waiting for us was Seigen-san in his fitted suit. He looked too well dressed for these surroundings, hands covered by leather gloves and a warm smile on his face. He looked between me and Suimei and let out a great sigh. "Now, now. It's still a bit too early to be releasing that one. It still needs more discipline. Can you return it for me, Midori?"

"I'm *not* Midori-san. And don't treat Suimei like an object!"

Seigen-san pulled a small bag out of his pocket. "Then I can make you Midori again. There's still more incense left, and I can't have you leaving me just yet." His tone was as gentle as before, the only difference was that I could now tell he wasn't looking at me at all, but at the figment of Midori-san inside of me. He turned his gaze to Akamadara. In a chilling voice, he said, "I didn't think you would betray me."

"I do not believe I have, Master. My only goal is to save you and grant your wish. Nothing more and nothing less. I did what was necessary."

"What drivel. I should've known better than to trust a non-human. Hmph... Your very appearance is an eyesore. A beast should look the part." Seigen-san swung his hand. Immediately, Akamadara fell to the ground, grimacing and hugging himself. "Return to your base form, Akamadara."

Akamadara groaned in pain as black hair began to sprout from his entire body. He quickly transformed into his Inugami form, with musculature like a wolf's. He remained lying slack on the ground, whining painfully after the forced transformation.

"Hmph. Grovel on the ground like the beast you are. Don't move until I say you may," Seigen-san ordered. It seemed Akamadara was unable to disobey. He looked at his master with crimson eyes filled with sorrow.

"Suimei?!" I yelled, surprised to see him run forward with no hesitation. By his side was Kuro, who had only just woken up.

"Sorry, Kuro. I know you're not in top form, but do you mind backing me up?"

"Not at all! You and I are partners!"

They charged at Seigen-san. Suimei deftly drew symbols with his hands and mumbled something, and Kuro's body began to faintly glow and speed up. But they were no match for Seigen-san.

Kuro whipped his tail at him, but Seigen-san caught it effortlessly and slammed Kuro into the ground.

"Aun!" Kuro whined.

"Kuro!" Suimei, who had been keeping his distance from Seigen-san, ran forward in a panic. He lunged in and struck with the heel of his palm—only for his hand to be caught.

"What sense is there in an Inugami exorcist closing in on his opponent? You lack composure, my son." Seigen-san twisted Suimei's hand, and Suimei dropped to the ground. "Hmph. You can't even manage a single blow against me. You lack training as well." He snickered, his caramel-brown eyes narrowing in a smile. The kind husband was gone, replaced by a sadistic man. He watched Suimei groan in pain. "Foolish boy. Did you think you could neglect your training just because you quit being an exorcist? Look at yourself. You lack the strength to protect what's important to you."

"Damn you...!" Suimei groaned.

"You should obey me without complaint. You are my puppet. A fool that will move as I like. Be good, and I'll even give you a proper reward from time to time."

"Wait!" I yelled, unable to bear seeing any more.

Seigen-san looked up and smiled happily. "What is it, Midori?"

"What you're doing is no different than what was done to you! How can you be so cruel after all you suffered?!"

He raised a brow at me slightly, then burst into laughter. He pulled a hip flask out his breast pocket and drank from it. "Now,

now, Midori... I simply have my sights set much further ahead." He stashed away his flask. With a flush in his cheeks, he explained, "This country used to be rampant with spirits. They flooded in from the spirit realm to eat the people of the human world as they pleased, sowing fear wherever they went. The people begged the exorcists for help, so our ancestors used our painstakingly created techniques to challenge the spirits. At its height, our influence even reached into the halls of government. Incredible, is it not? There truly has been no greater paradise."

His eyes seemed lost in a trance for a moment before his whole expression clouded over. "But what of now? The spirits have secluded themselves in the spirit realm, and we exorcists struggle just to get by. The human world calls us unscientific swindlers, even though we gave them power greater than any of them could imagine! I'm fed up with this world. And I'm fed up with my own powerlessness as well."

Seigen-san's gaze softened. He balled his hand into a fist. "But I have power now. I ate the flesh of a mermaid! Now I can do nearly anything. I can change this world! I'll send it back to the era when humans lived in fear of the darkness and exorcists wielded their power freely! I've spent quite some time preparing for this. I couldn't keep the spirit realm in perpetual winter as I wanted, but otherwise things are perfect."

He continued, "I've gathered negative emotion by kidnapping the children of spirits and killing them, then spread rumors that it was the work of humans. With that accumulated negative emotion, I'll form a powerful curse and cast away the boundary between the spirit realm and the human world. Surely you know what'll happen after that?"

I remembered the Hitouban who attacked me without even hearing me out. With the powerful resentment now built up by the kidnappings and killings, it wasn't unimaginable that we would see spirits attacking humans en masse.

"Soon, we exorcists will have our paradise back!" he continued. "So sit tight and leave everything to me, Suimei. You don't have to worry about a thing," he said softly.

Suimei scoffed. "I don't have to worry about a thing? How stupid. You don't actually care about me at all, do you, Father? Tell me..." He stopped to take a breath and scowled. "Why did you put your own memories in the incense you used on me?"

Seigen-san's expression went blank. He looked down at Suimei and let go of his hand. Not one to let the opportunity slip, Suimei immediately tried to get some distance, but Seigen-san grabbed his shoulder and twisted it hard. There was a dull cracking sound, and Suimei writhed backward in pain.

"Gaaaaaaah!"

"Suimei!" I yelled.

"I'm sorry. I really didn't want to hurt you if I could help it."

A chill ran down my spine. Seigen-san's voice was ice-cold even after hurting his own son.

"I wanted to keep Midori's impression of me as positive as possible," he said. "But you forced my hand. I'll be direct: Suimei, you are to be my new container."

"Wh-what?" I said. "Seigen-san, what are you talking about?!"

"I'm sorry for hiding it from you, Midori, but I don't have much time left." He slowly began to undo his shirt buttons. I gasped as he pulled up his shirt and revealed a blackened abdomen. "It seems my wish was not a good fit for the mermaid meat. Its effect is undeniably powerful; it gave me the power I sought by turning me into something inhuman, but my body is too weak for it. My organs have already started to rot. I can't move at all without drinking this analgesic." He took out his hip flask again and drank it dry, then tossed it aside. It clanged against a garden stone before disappearing into the undergrowth. "That's why I need a new body. As luck would have it, I have a child. Transferring my soul to him, a secret art passed down by the family, will be an easy task. I have nothing but appreciation for my ancestors." He smiled thinly and grabbed Suimei by the hair. He growled into his ear. "This is what you deserve for all you've taken from me."

Through his pain, Suimei managed to mutter, "Wh-what? What the hell are you talking about?"

"Don't play dumb with me. You know what you did!" Seigen-san yelled indignantly, anger in his eyes. "The Shirai family fell to ruin because you left!"

"You're the reason Kuro wanted to release me from the family in the first place. Who knows how much longer I could have borne suppressing my emotions in that house. You dug your own grave!"

"It's your own fault for not having better self-control. But that's not the only sin you've committed. Midori died because she gave birth to you." The color drained from Suimei's face. But the flames of hatred in Seigen-san's eyes didn't ebb. He pulled harder on Suimei's hair and yelled in his ear. "If only you hadn't been born. You... You took Midori from me!"

Unable to bear it any longer, I ran forward.

"Stop it!"

I pushed Seigen-san away as hard as I could and hugged Suimei. Even though he could have easily avoided me, Seigen-san fell to the ground with a look of shock on his face.

"Suimei isn't your puppet, and he isn't your container either!" I glared at him.

He blinked a few times before wrinkling his face into a frown, like a child whose toy was taken away. He lashed out at me, not even trying to hide his displeasure. "Why? Why?! What reason do you have to protect that *thing*?! You're supposed to be on *my* side. While they all mocked me, you promised you would give me a place to belong. Don't you remember? Come to me. We don't need that thing!"

He held a hand out to me. I knew his relationship with Midori-san was strong; I could feel it in her memories. He was scorned by the others for being an outsider to the family. But not by Midori-san. She genuinely tried to be his family, and he found his place by her side.

But that was precisely why he cursed his son's birth so terribly, for cutting short his dear wife's life.

It was finally clear to me. Seigen-san wasn't Suimei's father, at least not in the truest sense. They might have been connected by blood, but Seigen-san had never once seen himself as Suimei's

FALSE MEMORIES IMPARTED...

parent. I could feel the Midori-san inside me grieving. She truly loved Seigen-san and had wanted eternal proof of their love. It was she who'd wanted a child. But Seigen-san didn't understand that feeling. No, perhaps it was better to say he didn't even try to understand. He couldn't bring himself to feel anything for his child.

I'm sorry, Midori-san. But I can't choose Seigen-san. I apologized to the woman inside me. It was as Akamadara said: I couldn't fulfill Seigen-san's wish. I couldn't love him like his wife had.

I took a deep breath and gently brushed Seigen-san's outreached hand away. "Like I said, I'm not Midori-san." My heart ached, but I pressed on regardless, looking him straight in the eyes. "I can't replace her, no matter how much incense you use. The one I want to support...isn't you."

I hugged Suimei tightly, afraid. Seigen-san could kill me for this. But I had to say it. I had to show him I wasn't the Midori he wanted me to be. "I'm sorry, but the one I want to be with is Suimei. He's the one I love, so please, don't hurt him anymore." A single tear fell from my eye. More followed soon after, with no sign of stopping. My own feelings and Midori-san's memories were a dizzy mix. I wanted to show Seigen-san kindness. I wanted to heal him. But the one who had my heart was Suimei.

"Kaori..." Suimei hugged me back. "Ngh...gh..."

"Suimei?!"

His face contorted in pain, and he was breaking out in a cold sweat. I thought for a moment that it was the shoulder Seigen-san had injured but realized otherwise when he clutched at his chest. Strange things began to happen around us. The branches of the flowering dogwood trees waved without wind, their leaves and flowers rustling. Some rocks on the ground began to defy gravity and float. The earth rumbled and cracked.

"Master! Please, you must steady yourself!" Akamadara raised his voice, betraying panic for the first time. His voice went hoarse. "You mustn't feel jealousy! You'll kill Suimei-sama!"

Finally understanding what was happening, I looked up at Seigen-san. Inugami exorcists sometimes hurt others when they felt jealousy. That was why they suppressed their emotions, like Suimei had to for most of his life.

"Ha ha... Ha ha ha ha ha!" Seigen-san slowly heaved himself up, swaying like the leaves of a willow tree. In a strained voice, he said, "Jealousy? Impossible. Unlike that failure, I have perfect control over my emotions. I even have power now. Power greater than that brat's! With this power, nobody can take anything from me again, and anything I want will be mine! Yet you say I'm jealous? That's impossible. That's impossible..." He spread his arms wide and sighed. He sounded so tired. "What does it all matter?"

A white fox mask appeared in his hand. He put it over his face, and pale strands of glowing light started to flow from the mask. The strands formed complex patterns in the air, similar to the ones I'd seen on Suimei's talismans.

"More than enough negative emotion has gathered," he said. "I'd hoped to wait until I had Suimei's body, but you leave me no choice. I'll open a hole between the two worlds now, so that spirits can flood the other side and exorcists will be needed once again. When that comes to pass...surely you will need me too, Midori!"

"Stop...it, you...dumbass!" Suimei groaned.

"Don't!" I yelled.

He ignored us both and traced symbols in front of his mask with his hands, and a harsh gust of wind blew through the courtyard. "It's time now, let us return to the world of the past, where the place I belong surely lies!"

At that instant, there was a thundering roar accompanied by a blinding flash of light. I shut my eyes, my skin trembling from impact for a moment until—silence.

"Wh-what was that?" I fearfully opened my eyes and went speechless.

The fox mask was shattered into pieces. White smoke rose from Seigen-san, who was covered in black soot and kneeling on the ground.

"M-Master!" Akamadara wailed, but he couldn't move because of his master's order; he could only watch with worry.

"Uwa ha ha ha! It went perfectly, Kinme!"

"Phew, I was worried for a second there. Thank goodness, right, Ginme?"

Hearing two cheerful voices, I looked up and saw a crowd of people perched on the roof.

"Kaori, Suimei, Kuro, are you all right?!"

"Goodness... Do you realize how worried we were about you darlings?"

"How much longer are you going to stay down, mutt? Get up!"

It was Shinonome-san, Noname, Nyaa-san, and the raven Tengu twins. Behind them were Tsuchigumo, Oni, Koppa Tengu, and many more spirits I didn't personally know.

"Oho ho ho. I'd say that went rather well. Rather well, indeed!" A single spirit came down from the roof. He floated down with a giant jellyfish accompanying him and strolled over to me and Suimei. He bent down and showed us a handsome, smiling face. "I'm sorry we troubled you all so. You must've been quite scared."

I recognized the spirit. "N-Nurarihyon!"

"What's the meaning of this?!" Seigen-san yelled. Even in his sorry state, he staggered to his feet.

The great leader of the spirits, Nurarihyon, turned a cruel smile on Seigen-san. "You haven't figured it out yet? You've been dancing in the palm of my hand from the very beginning. There's no grudge between the spirits and the humans for you to use."

Nurarihyon began to explain. Early on, he had suspected an exorcist was planning to use the negative emotion growing in the spirit realm. The Tsuchigumo incident deepened his suspicions, so he and the others set about controlling those emotions.

"It was clear someone was trying to make the spirits hold a grudge against the humans of the human world, so we went to all the places where an incident had occurred and cleared up the misunderstanding. We explained the culprit wasn't a human from the human world but a has-been exorcist who moved to the spirit realm. You were correct in thinking negative emotion had been building up in the spirit realm, but all that ill will is directed squarely at you. Of course, you didn't know that. And so you cast your spell, and the rest is as you can see. The power of the negative emotion ran its course and struck its intended target."

"...How did you know it was me, though?"

"Oh ho ho! Let's just say we had a reliable collaborator." Nurarihyon glanced at Akamadara.

Akamadara's ears drooped, and he let out a weak whine.

"You!" Seigen-san seethed.

"It's not what you think!" Akamadara said. "I...I told them because I can't see how fulfilling your plan would ever make you happy. Do you really think you would be happy transferring your soul into your own son's body and implanting your late wife's memories in that girl? Would such twisted means really give you the sense of belonging you've sought? There's no way it could, Master..."

"Th-that's..." Seigen-san was at a loss for words.

Nurarihyon grinned and quietly picked up where Akamadara left off. "You have a caring familiar, one willing to put his life on the line to stop his master from treading down the wrong path. Perhaps you're not as alone as you think?"

"I..." Seigen-san's voice faded.

"Okaaay! Don't forget about me now!" The next to speak was Kinme, who grinned broadly. He was covered all over in painful-looking bruises. Seeing my face stiffen, he let out a belly laugh. "Oh, don't worry. This is all from Shinonome. He didn't know about the plan until right near the end, so when I told him I handed you over to Suimei's dad there, he blew a gasket! Phew, that was scary!"

"Hey, you didn't have to tell her!" Shinonome-san groaned. "Ugh. I suppose I went a little too far."

"No, no, not at all. I didn't account for the Hitouban hurting Kaori. I deserved what I got for not being more careful. Sorry, Kaori." Kinme bowed apologetically.

Seigen-san shot him an angry look. "You... How dare you betray me as well!"

"Ha ha. What was it you said again? Something like, 'Do as I say, or I'll kill Ginme'? Sure was an effective threat, I guess. But you didn't account for the fact that people other than Ginme are dear to me." Kinme grinned, his expression as boundlessly cheerful as Ginme's. "Obviously, Kaori's one of them. How could she not be? I owe her my life, and she's my childhood friend. But I've recently been talking to my brother about expanding my world, so now Suimei is included on the list of people dear to me too. Now clearly, I'm not going to let you walk away with *two* people on my short list. So instead, I went straight to Nurarihyon and spilled the beans. Akamadara showed up around then, together we did a ton of planning, and *ta-da*! Spy Kinme is born! Man, being a spy was a lot of work. You should all be thanking me, seriously."

He pulled something out of his breast pocket: the small jellyfish I'd received from Nurarihyon a while back. "You all have me to thank for hiding this too! This li'l jellyfish here is one of Nurarihyon's 'eyes.' It's been following Kaori around for a while now. Even listened in on all of your plans, Sensei. All that care you've been showing Kaori bought us more than ample time to get ready. So thanks, I guess!"

FALSE MEMORIES IMPARTED...

"Don't you dare mock me, you lowly creature!" Seigen-san snarled.

"Aha ha. Big talk coming from someone who got tricked by a 'lowly creature.' You do realize you're not exactly human yourself anymore, right?" Kinme's gaze turned cold, his voice flat. "It's over. The spell you've been preparing has backfired and destroyed itself. Surrender, and let yourself be devoured."

The air around the gathered spirits changed. Their eyes gleamed, and their bodies exuded bloodlust. They were no doubt the parents of the spirit children Seigen-san had kidnapped.

"Damn it! Damn it, damn it, damn it!" Seigen-san pounded his fist against the ground.

I looked to Suimei by my side, curious how he felt about all this. Noticing my gaze, he hissed, "He reaped what he sowed. The spirit realm is different from the human world. He has to pay for his crimes with his life."

"I know..." I began. "I know, but..." *Is that really all right?* I squeezed Suimei's hand anxiously. He looked up at me and squeezed back.

"Master! Please run away!" Akamadara bellowed. He tried his hardest to move despite the order binding him. "Kinme! Nurarihyon! This isn't what we agreed to!"

Kinme tilted his head to the side curiously. "What do you mean? I said his punishment would be decided the spirit realm way, didn't I? I kept my word."

"But I never would have agreed if I'd known it would end like this!"

"Oh. Well, that's not my problem," Kinme said.

Akamadara seethed. "Master, grant me power! I'll get rid of all these guys for you!"

"B-but..." Seigen-san hesitated.

"You can trust me. I'm on your side. Always have been, and always will be!"

Won over by Akamadara, Seigen-san sketched a few symbols in the air with his battered hands. He grimaced, the damage he'd endured taking its toll on him. His arms began to bleed, his body unable to withstand the power he was using. "Ngh...!"

"H-hey, what's going on with that guy?!" The spirits watched in shock as Akamadara growled, foaming at the mouth.

"Grrrowl!"

Something was terribly wrong. Akamadara's crimson eyes had lost all remnant of sanity. Even Seigen-san looked panicked, not at all expecting such a change.

Akamadara abruptly leapt to his feet and glared at his surroundings. Crouching low, he stalked forward, continuing to glare everywhere—like how a wild beast might size up their prey.

"Kaori, Suimei! Get away from there!" Shinonome yelled from atop the roof.

Just then, Akamadara dashed toward me and Suimei.

"Shoot. Everyone, protect those two!" Nurarihyon ordered, but Akamadara was already upon us. Suimei and I didn't even have time to move.

"Aaah!" I screamed.

"Kaori!" Suimei pushed me down and shielded me with his body, realizing it was too late to run. I could do nothing but watch in horror as Akamadara fast approached, drool dripping from his mouth. But my vision was soon obstructed by the broad back of somebody else. They took off their battered suit and tossed it aside, then spread their bloodied arms wide. Without a sound, they stood there and allowed Akamadara's sharp fangs to plunge into their neck.

"Seigen-san!" I yelled.

Seigen-san fell to his knees. He hugged Akamadara's body gently and whispered, "Calm down, Akamadara. Everything will be all right…"

Sanity seeped back into Akamadara's crimson eyes. He slowly opened his mouth and stared in a daze at his bloodied master.

Seigen-san spoke through his exhaustion. "Good grief. Both my children can be such a handful."

It won't stop. It won't stop. It won't stop!

I tried as hard as I could to dam the fountain of blood with a cloth. Seigen-san was sprawled on the ground, panting heavily and staring blankly up at the sky. His face, covered in fierce burns from the spell's backlash, grew paler by the second.

"Why, Master?!" Back in his human form, Akamadara wailed at Seigen-san's side, his usual composure nowhere to be found. He held his master's hand and wept like a child might for their parent. Suimei, though, stood at a distance, looking down at his collapsed father. His face was pale but betrayed no emotion at all.

"Wh-what do we do?" I said. Nothing I tried was working. I could feel Seigen-san's life slipping through my fingers and began to cry at my own powerlessness.

This was beyond my means.

"Suimei..." I looked to Suimei, who worked at the apothecary and was well versed in medicine. He made no move to help, but I couldn't blame him for that. Not after all Seigen-san had done. I wiped the tears from my eyes and pushed my mind to its limit. *How can I save him? Think. There has to be a way.*

"How absurd," a voice said. A bloodied hand reached out to me. It was sinewy and covered in scars, proof of many years of hardship. A pair of caramel-brown eyes curved into a smile. With some exasperation, the voice said, "How can you be so kind after all I've done to you?"

I blinked a few times, then wiped the mess of snot and tears off my face. "Somebody else asked me that exact same question once. They had that same glum look on their face too."

"And yet you haven't changed?"

"That's just how I am."

"I see." He let out a long sigh and mumbled, "You're just like Midori in that regard."

I shook my head. "I'm not Midori-san."

"Hah. I know. I was at both her deathbed and her burial."

"Then why are you so insistent on calling me by her name?"

Seigen-san grinned wryly, a faraway look in his eyes. "Do you remember when you said you wanted to share with me in Kanazawa? That sounded like something Midori would say. She loved to share. She told me she wanted us to be a couple that would share everything: the good, the bad...all of it. You really do resemble her. I'm sure if it weren't for the Inugami's curse, she'd be able to smile happily like you."

He sighed again and gazed at me. "I'm sorry I got you involved in all this. I only intended to use you to threaten Suimei into obedience, but it felt so much like I was with her again when I had you by my side. It was as though I had won back everything I'd lost: the place I belonged, her warmth... I was...in a dream."

"I see." I stared at his blood-stained hand, the very hand I had brushed aside earlier. I met it with my own hand this time and squeezed gently.

His eyes widened a little, and he smiled peacefully.

"Hey. So, you're Suimei's father then?" a disgruntled voice above me said. I looked up to see Shinonome-san, who made no effort to hide his anger. "Kaori, move aside for a bit."

"Huh—whoa?!"

Shinonome-san manhandled me aside and squatted next to Seigen-san. His lips were pursed, a habit of his when he was in a foul mood. I trembled in fear of what he might do to Seigen-san, who was already on death's door, when he quietly asked, "Why did you defend these two?"

Seigen-san gave Shinonome-san a tired look. He looked at me, Akamadara, and Suimei, one after another. In a faltering voice, he said, "I wonder why. I don't really understand it myself. I found myself standing there before I knew it." His eyes began to moisten. A tear formed, mixed with his blood, and ran down his cheek, leaving behind a red trail. "But I feel relieved knowing those two and Akamadara are safe. Relieved and...satisfied. Like I've accomplished something meaningful in my last moments. I regret nothing."

"Master!" Akamadara clung to Seigen-san's side. Seigen-san stroked his familiar's back, grimacing in pain all the while.

Shinonome-san sighed. "What the hell. You're just a regular old father."

"Hm?"

Leaving a confused Seigen-san behind, Shinonome-san stood up, cracked his neck casually, and began barking orders. "Tend to him, Noname. You better not let him die, you hear?"

"Wouldn't dream of it."

"Twins, quit daydreaming and cart Akamadara off somewhere he won't get in the way. And don't go starting any trouble!"

"Aye aye, sir!" the twins replied.

"Nyaa, go fetch Kuro! It's not like you're doing anything but lazing around."

"Fine, but don't expect me to be gentle."

Everyone set about following Shinonome-san's orders. The rest of the spirits watched everything unfold in blank amazement. One of them, a spirit with eight eyes—likely a Tsuchigumo—approached Shinonome-san.

"What's the meaning of this?" he hissed. "Hurry up and hand that man over."

Shinonome-san gave him a weary look and scratched his head, then glared and said, "No."

FALSE MEMORIES IMPARTED...

"What?" The Tsuchigumo's mouth dropped open in shock. Drooling, literally spitting mad, he yelled. "That man killed my child! You promised you would hand him over after everything was finished!"

Shinonome-san clicked his tongue and said, "Right... Well, I changed my mind."

"What in the world—" The Tsuchigumo was interrupted by Kinme and Ginme forcing their way between them and Shinonome-san. The twins' eyes gleamed with joy as they began to mock the Tsuchigumo.

"Whaaaat? Do you really not get it, old man? Are you new to the spirit realm or something?" Ginme said.

"Shinonome doesn't have a reason to hand Sensei over to you anymore, capisce?" Kinme said.

"What?!" The Tsuchigumo was furious. The twins put on vicious smiles and continued.

"I mean," Ginme began, "the only reason we were angry at all was because Kaori and Suimei were kidnapped."

Kinme continued, "But they're back now, and we can basically call things even since Sensei protected those two from Akamadara."

"And how careless do you have to be to let your own kids get kidnapped anyway?" Ginme said. "It's not like Seigen was your only enemy. Weren't you guys fighting with the Nue just last year?"

"Poor kids. But it is kinda your own fault. This is the spirit realm; it's survival of the fittest. Whatever happens to you is your own problem, promises don't mean jack, and most of all—we couldn't care less about your revenge!"

Together, they concluded, "Anyway, we've changed our minds about killing him. Spirits are fickle like that!" They looked at one another and laughed from deep in their guts.

The Tsuchigumo's eyes turned dangerous. A number of giant spider legs sprouted from his back. With a yell, he attacked the twins. "If you won't hand him over, then it's war!"

A wave of worry took over me, but the twins simply laughed and dodged the Tsuchigumo's attack as they grabbed Akamadara, who was nearby, by the arms.

"All right, bring it on!" Ginme said. "If you want to get to Seigen, you'll have to go through us!"

"Ha ha, Ginme, you sound like some villain's henchman," Kinme chuckled. "Not that I see us losing this. Hey, all you other spirits! Come join the fray if you still want Sensei!"

"H-hey, what're you guys grabbing me for?" Akamadara said, who had yet to fully grasp what was going on.

"You're fighting along with us, of course!" the twins said in unison. With Akamadara in tow, the twins moved to meet the attacking spirits. I watched as a powerful gust of wind blew a great number of the spirits away.

"No fair, I'm coming too! I haven't had a chance to let loose in a while." Nyaa-san joined in the fracas as well, with Kuro still dangling from her mouth. Kuro woke up midway through, his confused cries for help echoing loudly.

"I guess I should get in there too." The last to move was Shinonome-san. He stretched and began to leisurely walk toward the fight.

"What's the meaning of this?" Seigen-san muttered.

Shinonome-san stopped and smiled over his shoulder. "Didn't you hear the twins? We spirits are fickle; we change our minds at the drop of a hat. Besides, I heard you took good care of my daughter. I taught her that kindness needs to be repaid with kindness, and I'm just living up to that." With that, he waved and broke into a run. Halfway to the scene of the fight, he transformed into a dragon and entered the fray by fending off spirits with lightning.

"What's with you all?" Seigen-san muttered. Noname and I snickered; Suimei muttered almost the exact same thing whenever he was bewildered by our actions.

Suimei walked up then, coming to his father's side, and stared down at him. Seigen-san averted his gaze, so Suimei sighed and squatted down. He said, "They're utterly incomprehensible, right? That's how I felt when I first came to this world."

"Suimei..." Seigen-san muttered.

"Hey, um..." Suimei seemed to hesitate about what to say next. His father still wouldn't meet his gaze. "I won't apologize for letting the family fall to ruin. I don't feel any regret whatsoever about being freed from that house. But I do feel bad for causing you trouble. Sorry."

Seigen-san's expression darkened.

"I know what it feels like to want a place you belong. I've spent most of my life wishing for one." Suimei's light-brown eyes softened as he looked at me. "But I don't have to wish anymore. I found it, right here in the spirit realm. Here, I can express myself freely. I can do what I want, be with who I like. So maybe you can find your place here too." He slowly stood up and turned around. "Forget about changing the human world and try finding the place you belong here in this strange, impossible world."

Seigen-san watched his son walk away. He slowly turned to look at me. A single tear ran down his face. "Can I really find a place I belong here in this world?"

I smiled and brushed his tear away with a finger. "Yes. I'm sure there's a place for you here."

"Ah…" Seigen-san hid his face with his bloodied, scarred hands and quietly began to cry.

EPILOGUE

A Place for You Alone

I HEARD THE SOUND of fighting in the distance, but things seemed to be winding down. Our side was full of nothing but strong fighters, so much so that it honestly felt a little unfair. Like, c'mon guys, you could show a little mercy, you know?

Suimei and I had moved to the stand of flowering dogwood trees to avoid getting caught up in the fighting. Noname appeared to have a handle on Seigen-san's condition, so there was no need to stick around. We sat with our backs against a trunk, exhausted. I looked up at the brilliant night sky. Its pale-pink color was slowly taking on some azure here and there. It wouldn't be long until it turned the color of melon soda, and summer would be here. I reached a playful finger out to the gathered glimmerflies and peeked at Suimei, sizing up his mood. He seemed tired; his eyes were shut tight. "Does it still hurt?" I asked.

He opened a single listless eye and looked my way. After a deep breath, he closed his eye. "Not too bad."

"I see."

He sank into silence again. I reached a hand out to run my fingers through his hair, turned white long ago. It reflected all the suffering he'd endured as a young boy, imprisoned in darkness underground and forced to suppress his emotions. His hair was soft to the touch.

He seemed to find my hand ticklish and smiled. A bit exasperated, he said, "What?"

He looked at me, and I saw myself reflected in his light-brown eyes. I realized then that I was the type of person who wore their heart on their sleeve. My face reflected everything I was feeling, clear as glass. "It's okay," I said, near tears. "You did what was right."

Suimei made a pained face, frowning and furrowing his brows. He hugged his knees. "Honestly, I'm surprised I didn't finish him off myself. Since I came to the spirit realm, I've had so many dreams about killing him. In them, I'd get him back for all he did to me and watch him slowly die without a shred of remorse." He shut his eyes and grit his teeth. "I can't forgive him. Not now, not ever. He's selfish. He doesn't care about anyone but himself. I was never anything but a tool to him! But…I can't hate him anymore." He clenched a hand in his hair. "Because of that damned incense, I know everything he's been through. I know his turmoil, his suffering, his loneliness, his despair, his pain from having every place he belonged to taken from him one after another, all of it growing into his unbearable longing for a new place to belong! I didn't want to know all this. I was happier when I was ignorant and could hate him as much as I wanted! I…I wish I'd never learned."

Suimei buried his face in his knees. His expression was anguished, but his eyes were dry.

Having *been* Midori-san myself, I knew how the memories the incense imparted felt even more vivid than one's own. The emotions in the memories resonated deeply and overwrote your own, as though they had been yours from the start. Of course it was that strong, that's why the incense was used for brainwashing.

Suimei might not have given in to the incense entirely, but the potency of his father's memories dulled his anger.

"If it wasn't for me, he still might have had the last place he belonged," Suimei said. Finally, moisture gathered in his eyes. "I took it from him. I made him suffer. He has every right to hate me." A single tear fell. I had never seen him look so vulnerable. "I should never have been born."

I immediately grabbed his arm and shook him. "Don't say that!"

Suimei trembled ever so slightly. Perhaps it was his fault his mother had died, and perhaps it was his fault his father had lost so much that was precious to him. No matter what I did or said, I couldn't refute the fact that his birth might have played a part in all that. But that didn't mean he had to shoulder all the guilt. In the end, he could never know what might have happened if things had been otherwise.

I said, "Midori-san was frail to begin with; there's no knowing if she would've lived a long life even if she hadn't given birth to you! So don't blame yourself. There's no point in entertaining 'what-ifs'; it won't help anyone."

"But if I'd—"

"I said, *stop*!" I cut him off, tears welling in my own eyes. Suimei was the one suffering, yet I couldn't hold back my own feelings. I loved Suimei. I loved him more than anything and anyone. I couldn't bear to hear him say he wished he'd never been born. "I can't imagine life without you. You've saved me countless times. You've stayed with me through my hardest moments."

Suimei slowly lifted his head. His face was flushed, and he looked like a child on the verge of tears.

I didn't know love could hurt so much, I thought, my heart aching. I wanted to do something for him, but I didn't know what I could say that would reach him. It distressed me. He was the first person I had ever loved. I wanted to be his strength, so he wouldn't have to make such a pained face ever again. Why was I so powerless? Why couldn't I help him after all he had done to help me? Where were the magic words I could say to set him at ease? I searched my heart for those words, but they weren't there. Left with no other choice, I fumbled around for what words I did have and wove them into a tapestry with an invisible thread.

"I need you, I really do. And don't you ever forget it." I moved closer to him and put my hand against his back. I could feel his body trembling, so I began to rub my hand up and down, hoping I could ease the pain in his heart and end his shuddering as soon as possible. "Even if someone says you shouldn't exist, they'd be wrong. Because I, at the very least, know from the bottom of my heart that I need you. I'm thankful I met you, and I'm thankful you were born; I won't let anyone say it'd be better if you didn't exist, no matter who they are." I wasn't sure if my words would reach him, but I meant it all. I prayed the hopeful, warm feelings in my heart would seep through to him. "I wouldn't be here today if it weren't for you. You're irreplaceable to me. Thank you, for all the happiness you've given me."

Suddenly, Suimei was hugging me. He buried his face in my neck and quietly wept. I hugged him back tightly and whispered, "It's okay. Everything's going to be okay. I'm right here."

You'll always have a place to belong with me.

Just as Shinonome-san had when I cried as a child, I soothed Suimei by repeating the same words of comfort over and over. He continued to cry, trying his hardest to keep quiet. I felt warm tears wet my back and closed my eyes, rocking him like I would a young child.

"Are you feeling better?" I asked after his tears subsided.
"Jeez. I keep crying in front of you."
"Nothing wrong with that."
"It's lame." Suimei inched his body away from me. With a grin, I offered him a handkerchief, which he reluctantly accepted. He wiped his flushed face. "Oh, right. There's something I've been meaning to ask about."
"Yeah?"
"Earlier, uh... You said you love me, right?"
"...Whuh?" A super dumb voice spilled out of me, and I clapped my hands over my mouth. *Huh?! When did I let that*

slip?!* "Um, wha, I, uhh..." I hurriedly searched my panicked mind. A memory from only a short while ago cropped up:

"I'm sorry, but the one I want to be with is Suimei. He's the one I love, so please, don't hurt him anymore."

Aaaaaaah! The blood drained from my face. Like a rusty wind-up toy, my head moved jerkily to face Suimei. He looked dead serious. I swiftly turned my head away. I had no idea what to do. My heart was too aflutter with emotion, and I had no experience with romance whatsoever. I didn't even have any idea how I could explain away my little slip of the tongue. So, I started crawling away on all fours.

"Don't run away, you dolt."

"Eek!"

Suimei grabbed the hem of my yukata. Mission failed. Teary eyed, I looked back around at him and began to plead for my life like a peasant to a samurai. "Please! Find it in your heart to spare me! I said that in the heat of the moment!"

"Oh? You dared to lie in that situation?"

"It wasn't a lie! I meant what I said!" I said it with conviction, then realized what I'd done. Oh, heck. Well, in for a penny, in for a pound. I straightened my back and continued, "I-I..." I balled my hands into fists. They were slippery with sweat. My body trembled from me tensing every muscle. "L-Love..." My voice cracked. It was a struggle to breathe. My heart was ready to burst. I swallowed and took the final plunge. "You! ...I love you!"

I said it! I really said it! Out of my mind with embarrassment, I thrust my head between my knees and balled up. I couldn't stop trembling. My hands and legs felt cold, and I was a little dizzy. I was so worried about how Suimei would reply, but the moments dragged by, and he didn't say anything.

Huh? Wait, does this mean I'm rejected? Right, of course. What kinda absolute idiot would confess in this situation?! Farewell, my first love! I shed a lone tear for my all-too-fleeting first crush. But I didn't bawl my eyes out. Anything but that. I didn't want to be pitied; I was the older one here. Yes, a proper adult accepts heartbreak with composure... *Like hell! How's a girl with no romantic experience like me supposed to process this?! Gaaaah!*

My anguished mind raced to—in many senses of the word—sad conclusions. I held in my tears as hard as I could, then realized Suimei *still* wasn't saying anything.

"Hm?" Timidly, I raised my head. My racing thoughts ground to a halt the moment I saw his face. He was as red as a lobster. Sweat ran down his forehead. His hand covered his mouth. His gaze wandered restlessly. All things considered, it didn't seem like I was being rejected. In fact... "Huh? Wait, really?"

"Heeey! Suimei, Kaori! We're all done here!" Ginme barged on over, a big grin on his face. He threw his arms around both our shoulders and laughed. "Man, I'm starving! Let's head back. Noname says she'll cook us something!"

"Oh. Y-yeah. Let's do that," I managed.

"R-right. Let's go," Suimei stammered.

We stood. For a brief moment, we made direct eye contact. We immediately spun our heads away, both of us blushing furiously. Things were moving along, but I still hadn't heard his answer. I sneaked a furtive glance back at Suimei. He was covering his mouth with his sleeve and had his eyes glued to the ground.

Urk. This is super, super awkward.

"Something up with you two?" Ginme asked, giving us a funny look.

"W-we're a bit tired," I stammered. "We'll be fine. Let's go home!"

"Ah, gotcha. Yeah, let's hurry back. I'm dying to hop in the bath," he said. His laid-back attitude was so enviable right now.

Feeling bitter tears creeping up on me, I looked up to the sky. Hints of summer had just begun to sparkle there. Soon, it would be a full year since Suimei had arrived.

What do I do? I can't believe I confessed! I bit my lip anxiously. I—Muramoto Kaori—was in the greatest predicament of my life. *Dear God, Buddha, Mother and Father in heaven, what in the world am I supposed to do?!*

Sadly, my cry for help went without reply. Still lost at sea, I forced my aching body to walk home.

EXTRA STORY

Man's Best Friends

"AHA HA HA! Everyone's so strong, I can't keep up!"

It was right around the time Suimei and Kaori began talking while everyone else was making clean work of the spirits. Kuro the Inugami walked under a large flowering dogwood tree and sat down. His body ached all over. The damage Seigen had dealt him was greater than he'd first thought, so he'd decided to break away from the fight. Not many enemies were left, so he figured it would be all right if he sat this one out and left everything in everyone else's capable hands. If anything, he was a little worried that with so few enemies left to beat, he might accidentally poach the black cat's prey and earn her wrath.

He began grooming himself a bit, thinking no thoughts, his head empty. A thorny gaze coming from somewhere to his left directed itself at him, but he pretended not to notice, as he lacked both the condition and will to fight. The gaze quickly became unbearable, however, so he timidly looked at the source. "Um, hi? Is something the matter?" he asked.

"...No."

If Kuro's memory served, this was the Inugami named Akamadara. He was the familiar of Suimei's father and could wear a human form, unlike Kuro himself. His human form was also quite the looker. Kuro could imagine Akamadara appearing on TV and becoming a fan favorite of ladies worldwide.

"Then what's with the glare? Aren't you here to rest too?" Kuro said. He gave his paw a lick. A piece of spirit flesh was stuck there, and when he licked it, the foul taste spread in his mouth. It was pretty sickening. "Uuugh... Peh! Peh! Ah, jeez! I wanna go home already!" Kuro wasn't a fan of raw meat, much less spirit meat. He slumped flat on the ground, greatly missing the yummy food Suimei made for him.

That was when Akamadara said, "If anything, I should be the one asking you questions: What do you want? You wouldn't have sat here if you didn't want something from me."

Kuro tilted his head curiously. His only motive for coming to this tree was that it was a good tree. It just so happened to be the tree Akamadara was sitting under too. To him, it was an utter mystery why Akamadara was giving him such a nasty look. He answered, "Um, nothing?"

"Don't lie to me, you want something from me, don't you?!" Akamadara barked back without missing a beat.

"Whaaat?" Kuro was put off by Akamadara's intense, immediate response. He glanced over and saw bloodshot eyes glaring at him. Unintentionally, he let his true feelings slip. "You're kind of a pain in the butt, huh?"

Akamadara went red in the face. He began to tremble, tears welling in his eyes.

"Uh...?" Kuro was in mute surprise at this sudden shift, his mouth left half-open.

Akamadara sniffled slightly as he said, "Y-you're mocking me, I know you are! You think I'm not worth your time because you're the oldest Inugami in the Shirai family while I'm some fool who betrayed and attacked his own master, even if I was trying to help him!"

"C-calm down. There's no need to cry."

"I'm not crying!"

"Then what's that wet stuff on your face?"

"It's sweat, obviously!"

"You really are a pain..." Kuro sighed. Akamadara's face grew even redder, more and more tears forming on his shapely face, which scrunched up in frustration.

Kuro wagged his tail once and hesitantly said, "Well... I don't really think you did anything particularly wrong."

Akamadara blinked. He hadn't expected that.

Kuro rested his head on his front paws and gazed at Suimei sitting with Kaori some distance away. "We Inugami are tools created from curses. We're meant to be used as weapons by our exorcist masters to take on spirits way larger than us. If either the master or the Inugami slip up, somebody dies. I've seen tons of Inugami go out that way during the course of my long life."

The Shirai family once had many Inugami, and Kuro was always the one who led them into battle. He didn't think of himself as particularly gifted in any way. In fact, he'd known many Inugami who were far stronger than him, but they all died like the others. There was one thing, however, that separated him from the rest.

"You see, all the ones that died could never become anything *more* than a tool. They only did what they were told and never really opened their hearts to their master. And a tool that can't communicate breaks down. That's why they all died."

Akamadara sniffed. His tears had stopped falling.

He's like a little kid, Kuro chuckled to himself, forgetting the fact that he was treated like a child most of the time himself. "That's why I can't disparage you for trying your best to help your master. In fact, I think what you did was pretty cool. You might've messed up along the way, but your heart was in the right place. I can tell you love Seigen, just like I love Suimei. And those who are willing to go the distance for those they love are destined to live long lives. I guarantee it."

That being said, life's not all sunshine and rainbows. Love can sometimes backfire, he thought. A bitter taste, one other than spirit meat, spread in Kuro's mouth as he recalled the time he was struck down by Seigen, and Suimei had to rush in to help. That hadn't been a rational move. If Suimei had died because of that, Kuro would never have forgiven himself.

"Hmm... Maybe I need training. Yeah. I've been getting kinda weak lately," Kuro mused to himself. He felt that odd gaze again, glanced up, and was taken aback by the look on Akamadara's face.

"...Incredible..." For some inexplicable reason, Akamadara was staring at him with sparkles in his eyes.

"Wh-wh-what's with you?! You're seriously freaking me out here!" Kuro said, jumping to his feet.

Akamadara reached out with his long arms and caught Kuro, lifting him by the armpits.

"Wh-what're you doing?!" Kuro yelled.

Akamadara brought his nose right up to Kuro's and, with great excitement, said, "I can't believe it. To think I'd find somebody here who understood me so well."

"Wh-what are you talking about?!"

"Please, you needn't joke with me. You spoke as though you'd seen right through me, and so passionately too! I could feel the love shining through your words!"

"What? Love? Seriously, what *are* you talking about?!" Kuro said, but Akamadara was lost in his own little world.

"I'd lost my raison d'etre after my earlier blunder. I even contemplated death! But you've given me purpose! I thank you, from the very depths of my heart! Please, allow me the honor of calling you 'Master Kuro'!"

"Whaaaaat?!" Kuro yelled.

Akamadara smiled ecstatically, as though Kuro's confused voice was but the finest of symphonies to his ear. His eyes were locked on to Kuro's in a trance as he brought his nose closer and closer until...*boop*. Their noses smooshed together. "I respect you wholeheartedly. Please continue to show me the right path, Master Kuro!"

The blood drained from Kuro's face. "B-but you're stronger than me, remember?!"

"Ha ha ha, you jest! I know you were only feigning weakness to test me!"

"Why in the world would I do that?! Oh no, words are meaningless to this dingbat..." Kuro tried to run away, but his stumpy legs simply batted at the air. He yelled, genuinely terrified. "Suimei! Save meeeee! Some weirdo's become my discipleeeee!"

Afterword

Hello. Shinobumaru here. Thank you for purchasing and reading Volume 4 of *The Haunted Bookstore*. We've made it to number four already. Can you believe it? I'm feeling a bit emotional myself.

I'm going to avoid talking about spoilers here just in case somebody haphazardly reads the afterword before the story, but this volume cleanly resolved a lot of the foreshadowing scattered here and there starting all the way from Volume 1. Man, it feels like just yesterday I told my editor that *that* one character wouldn't appear yet, and in the end, well, they did. I lied I guess, ha ha. ...Sorry.

Let's talk about writing. When I write, I try to pay a lot of attention to keeping characters active and talking. Authors have these stories in their heads that we want to write out, but we often forget the characters are a living part of the story that need to spontaneously react to it as it develops. Characters can't be stage actors reading lines from the author's script, they have to ad lib everything. That's how you get realistic and unexpected dialogue, inflate your word count (heh), and add depth to your story.

I'd like to think Kaori and Kinme demonstrated such in this volume. Throughout the book, those two unwittingly used many of the words and actions of two other characters. In Kaori's case, it was Shinonome's words and actions; and in Kinme's case, it was Noname's. The care, affection, and kindness they received from others continues along to yet another. That was one of the themes I wanted in this book. If you have time, you might find it worthwhile to reread the book with those points in mind.

Now then, I'd like to end with some thank yous. To Sato, my editor at Kotonoha Bunko, thank you for your constant help. It couldn't have been easy to get this book through smack-dab in the middle of the COVID-19 crisis. As always, thank you for your praise as well. Keep it coming, if you don't mind.

Munashichi, thank you for yet another spectacular book cover! I'm from Aomori myself, so seeing my own hometown being used as a motif for the cover brings me joy. I want to stare at it forever. Thank you so much!

The Haunted Bookstore also has a manga adaptation coming out this month, drawn by Medayaki-sensei! The first manga volume covers up to the cicada story, so go buy it and bawl your eyes out! Everyone looks super cool and cute! My favorite is Nurarihyon.

AFTERWORD

That's all from me. I pray we meet again. Please do look forward to seeing where Kaori's confession takes her.

Written in the season the osmanthus
is its most aromatic,
Shinobumaru